IT WAS A NEW LAND—
A LAND OF BEAUTY, CRUELTY,
HARDSHIP AND LEGEND . . .

Once more the rising mist on the river, the sun coming over the limestone bluffs, the green meadow and the bunched buffalo grass on the slopes so entranced Parkman that he paid little attention to physical discomfort or danger. He could see the four braves, riding along the perimeter of the band, looking toward the hills and exchanging anxious glances. He could watch the women, on foot or on the mules pulling the travois, whispering nervously to one another and telling the children sternly to be quiet. But the day was too glorious for worry. . . .

Suddenly they heard Bull Bear call. The guide, Chatillon, yanked up his horse's head and he turned and galloped back. The whole band was gathered around the now stationary travois of Blue Eagle Speaks. Chatillon leapt from his horse, pushed through the group and knelt at her side. Parkman and Shaw followed and also dismounted. As they approached the stricken woman, they heard the death rattle in her throat.

There was silence for a long moment. Then a wail arose, heart-stopping lamentation, started by the women and taken up by the children and men. And as he listened to the cries, Parkman remembered the legend . . . that the Indians were descended from the ten lost tribes of Israel. . . .

ing something about the robbery, and Parkman ...
...ned.

THE AMERICAN EXPLORERS SERIES

FRANCIS PARKMAN

DAKOTA LEGEND

FRANCIS PARKMAN

DAKOTA LEGEND

William Krasner

A Dell/Banbury Book

Published by
Banbury Books, Inc.
37 West Avenue
Wayne, Pennsylvania 19087

Dell ® TM 681510, Dell Publishing Co., Inc.

ISBN: 0-440-02752-7

Printed in the United States of America
First printing—November 1982

"Well, then . . . I suppose it's settled?" Parkute said.

Chapter 1

The country was moving West. And Francis Parkman wanted to be part of it, wanted to see it with his own eyes, wanted to be among the wild and uprooted people of this great migration that would transform a nation no longer content to huddle in the security of its Eastern civilization. He would live among those people, sharing their exotic adventures; so too would he live with the natives of this vast, unknown land, the Indians whose lives were being disrupted by this westward sweep of the white man. He would share the lives of the invaders and the invaded, their hopes, their fears, their pain and triumphs in the wilderness. And then he would write it all down for posterity to contemplate and judge.

It was in the spring of 1846 that Francis Parkman, A.B., LL.B., Harvard, poet and writer of romances, a Boston Brahman, a mere twenty-two years old, went to the frontier for the opening of America's great adventure. He intended, as he later wrote, to strike out along the Oregon Trail, to see the West, and to "live in the midst of Indians, and become, as it were, one of them." He was accompanied by his

1

stolid and less talkative cousin, Quincy Adams Shaw, whose background and interests were similar to his.

Their fellow passengers on the *Radnor,* bound up the Missouri River from St. Louis to the great rendezvous area around Independence, Missouri, were not much like the polite folk they had encountered on the trains and overland stages that had taken them to St. Louis. These people were of a rougher sort as befits men who would live off the land and venture beyond the frontier where toughness, strength and cunning counted more in mastering their destinies than did the arts of civilized behavior. In the deck cabins were Santa Fe traders, gamblers, speculators and adventurers of all sorts, and in steerage, grizzled mountain men back from trading in St. Louis, blacks and even a party of wretched Kansas Indians who had wanted to see what a white man's city was like.

Along the banks approaching Independence, they could see the encampments of Mexican traders who worked for the Santa Fe Company, small groups of impoverished looking Indians over smoky fires, and always, long lines of wagons and mounted men moving west or wagons gathered in circles to keep livestock from straying, smoke from campfires tended by the women hanging in the air. Occasionally French trappers could be seen standing along the muddy banks, staring at the boat and the people as though, even after all these years, they couldn't believe it all.

In such company, Parkman and Shaw did not think they looked very remarkable with their Eastern clothes and their Eastern manners. Certainly no more remarkable than any of the other passengers. Parkman reminded his pipe-smoking cousin that they actually had more experience in dealing with the wild than did most of these people. They had gone on hiking and exploring trips all through New England and south-eastern Canada. Parkman had tramped through Europe. And he was good at languages. He felt he would be able to pick up the speech and dialects of the people they met, however uncivilized. In fact, Parkman and Shaw had been so confident of their abilities that they had decided to wait until they were in Kansas to get their guide and buy their horses and cart.

They got off the boat at Westport, just outside Independence, wrested their baggage away from some dockside roustabouts who looked as though they were going to steal it and started down the main street toward the tavern.

Westport was full of Indians. Their little shaggy ponies, so different from the English thoroughbreds of the East, were tied by the dozens along the houses and fences. From illustrations of Indian tribes that he had seen, Parkman recognized the Sac and Fox by their shaved heads and painted faces. There were Shawnee and Delaware wearing turbans and a number of them, strangely enough, were in fluttering calico dresses. The Wyandot were already dressed like white men, as though they had cast their lot shrewdly with the future. They moved in and out of the shops and lounged on the curbs and stoops. Around them, moving slowly and apologetically, were the miserable Kansas Indians, wrapped in tattered blankets. They were the dispossessed.

But none of these colorful sights quite prepared them for the aspect of the two men who approached them on the busy street. The one on the left wore a tam-o'-shanter of the kind that Francis Parkman had not seen since a visit to Scotland. The face was red from sun and wind and liquor and was matched in that color by his bristly beard and mustache. His coat was of Scotch plaid with fringes dangling, but he also wore plain homespun pants and hobnailed boots. Parkman recognized Captain Collins of the British army who was in America to do some hunting. They had met in the East and seen each other again in St. Louis. But, though he knew the captain drank, he was surprised to see him so drunk.

With the Englishman was a man apparently part Indian, wearing feathers in his hair and a buckskin shirt with trousers of homespun. On his feet were worn and tattered moccasins. As he lurched along with Collins, who was just as drunk or pretending to be, the buckskin fringes moved up over his belt, revealing a bowie knife on one side and a pistol on the other. Parkman decided he must be a mountain man, one of the legendary trappers who lived along the frontier like Indians, sometimes with Indians, but were superior to the red man in bragging and lying.

Shaw quit puffing his pipe at the sight of the odd couple. Collins greeted them effusively and introduced his companion. "This here gentleman is my friend. He's a chief, a real chief. Chief Medicine Calf. He's going to be my guide."

Clinging to each other for support, the captain and his guide staggered into the tavern. Parkman and Shaw followed.

A number of bearded men in homespun and buckskin stood up at the roughhewn bar. Several others sat at two tables on the dirt floor. Some of them glanced up and greeted Medicine Calf, but that was not the name they greeted him with. Parkman asked one of the men what name they had used.

The man stroked his tangled beard. "Well now, who did he say he was?"

"Chief. . . ." Parkman hesitated. He found that he couldn't say the Indian name without its sounding ridiculous to his Boston ears.

"Chief? Well, I guess so. Spends enough time with the squaws to be a couple of chiefs."

Another bearded man, wearing a fur hat despite the weather and the stifling heat in the tavern, began to laugh.

The man who called himself Medicine Calf smiled too, but his eyes were watchful. He had urged Parkman and Shaw to drink, but they hadn't tasted their liquor yet.

"I live with the Crow six months a year," he said. "I am . . . they make me a chief. I'm a trapper and guide." He thrust out his chest. "The best. Crow Indians know that better than anybody."

The man with the fur hat hooted. "Well," said the other bearded trapper, "I know what you're best at, Jim—when you ain't with the squaws."

"Jim?" Parkman asked.

"I'm Jim Beckwith," the man said. "The best guide, the best trapper, the best companion. For hire." His voice was deep and gravelly. He touched his hand to his feathers as though gallantly raising a hat and bowed deeply. "Since I am also a chief, I know how to avoid trouble with Indians more than anybody."

"Well there's some Indian in him somewhere," the hatted trapper grumbled. "Along with a lot of other things not worth much."

"Is he a good guide?" Parkman asked the trapper.

"Oh, he knows his way around up by the Platte and through Crow villages. No question."

"Well, I think Captain Collins might need a good guide," Parkman said. He looked dubiously at the red-bearded man whose head was resting on his out-stretched arm on the bar.

The fur-hatted man was once more convulsed. Parkman leaned over Collins and said, "Captain? Sir? Are you all right?"

Captain Collins opened his eyes, looked about him vaguely, then nodded. Shaw took his pipe out of his mouth for a moment. "I think we had better help him, Frank."

But Beckwith picked up the heavy military man and put him on his shoulder as easily as if he were a sack of sugar. "Oh, he's all right. Right, Cap'n?"

"We'd better come along," Parkman said. "If you don't mind."

"Welcome, gents. Welcome."

Parkman had thought, when he'd first met the captain, that he might ask him to accompany them. He'd seemed like a good companion, a man good with a rifle eager to travel West. Parkman and Shaw had ruled out traveling with any of the emigrant trains. He thought that the trains would slow them down and put other burdens on them. And, though he didn't want to seem snobbish about it, neither he nor Shaw found the emigrants congenial. Most were rough and unlettered. There were a few Daniel Boone types among them, and they were mostly admirable; there were many families, going West to try to make a new start, and they were respectable enough, but some of the travelers were religious fanatics, especially the Mormons, and others were, as Parkman wrote in his diary, "some of the vilest outcasts in the country." He and Shaw wanted to hunt, to observe and live with the Indians, to have experiences and discover new things that they could later write about at their leisure. Captain Collins understood these gentlemanly pursuits and he might have made a good and useful companion, at least until they got to Fort Laramie.

But did they want this semicomatose man being carried like a sack on the back of his friend the frontiersman as a companion on the trail?

They followed Beckwith into the street. A man in a fur hat standing next to a mule with loaded saddlebags seemed to find Parkman and Shaw vastly entertaining. He began to laugh, pushing his thumb up against his nose, a gesture which Parkman did not understand—and did not want to.

They entered another tavern and took the stairway to a balcony off of which were rooms. Beckwith did not pause in his stride. He opened a door, carried Captain Collins inside and dumped him onto a cot. He was not breathing hard. "Lucky man," he smiled wryly. "Got his own room."

"How did he get in this condition?" Parkman asked.

"Englishman. Not used to liquor."

"He certainly impressed me as a man who knows how to drink and hold his liquor decently."

"Not used to this kind of liquor. Got to get used to Taos lightning." Since he was speaking to greenhorns, Beckwith seemed to find it necessary to explain. "Not always from Taos. Some of those fellas around here make it, too." He shook his head.

"What are you going to do with him?" Parkman pointed to Collins, now fully asleep.

"He'll sleep. Tomorrow, maybe afternoon, he wakes up. Terrible headache. But ready to go. Next time, maybe, he'll be better used to this liquor."

"Well, weren't you supposed to start out soon? You were going to guide him?"

Beckwith smiled. Rimmed by black beard and

mustache, the gaps in his teeth and the one front tooth capped with silver were very evident. "He'll be ready in a day or two. Got a horse, maybe get another. This child will take him." Collins' leg had fallen off the cot. Beckwith kicked it back up onto the cot with his moccasin. The smile grew broader. "Now, sirs. Maybe I guide you instead. Or maybe you want to go with Captain Collins? Two sirs need a guide more than one Englishman."

"Perhaps. If we go with Captain Collins." Parkman signaled to Shaw and they left the room. Beckwith followed them downstairs, past the people eating and drinking in the tavern outside.

"Place to stay?" Beckwith asked. "I can talk to the landlord. I know him well."

"No, thank you, we have a place," Parkman said. They intended to camp close to their luggage, to go to the market early the next day to buy their horses and supplies, but they did not want to tell Beckwith that.

Beckwith followed them along the street, telling them repeatedly of his skill as guide, trapper, chief, friend of Indians, friend of whites, judge of mules, hunter and navigator, both by stars and by trails invisible to other eyes. They went back to the other tavern and engaged a room. Beckwith finally left them, touching his hand to his feathers, and bringing it down as he had done before, as though he were doffing some elegant hat.

"I see you tomorrow, sirs. Then we plan the trip." He waved his hand. "Think nothing of your friend. He is in safe hands."

Long after the moon was up and the noises of the street had almost stopped and they could see, through their window, a sky so clear of dust and heat that the stars seemed to press right against their streaked pane, they could still hear shouting and laughter downstairs. Parkman thought he could hear Beckwith's voice raised in song. Exhausted, they finally fell asleep, but were jolted awake later by shouts beneath their window, followed by howling and shots. Shaw rushed to the window, but he told Parkman he could see nothing. He did see light in the sky to the east, and knew that the night was almost gone.

Still they were up early, eager to buy horses and supplies, eager to be on their way. Some of the Indians they had seen the day before were still in the street, as though they had never slept. They moved their heads to regard Parkman and Shaw. Men slept against hitching posts or on the wooden platforms that served as sidewalks. They found some emigrant wagons, the canvas stained and battered, along the edge of town. Two men were tending the horses and a woman was stirring a pot on a tripod over a fire. Three solemn children, the oldest, a girl about ten, walked to the end of the street to see the two Bostonians come out of the tavern wearing red flannel shirts, faces still glistening from the washbasin, their beards combed. Perhaps, coming from some Missouri or Illinois farm, the children found the two Bostonians to be the most exotic things they had yet seen.

As the men passed, the youngest child, a boy of perhaps four, caught Shaw's right hand. Surprised, Shaw stopped. The boy had a surprisingly strong grip. "Hallo," Shaw said.

"Seem to have made a conquest, Quincy," Parkman said. "Sure you were never here before?"

"Come now, Frank." Shaw looked down into the boy's face. "Do something for you, sir?" he asked the boy.

The boy looked steadily into Shaw's eyes, but said nothing. Shaw started to take a step, assuming that the boy would let go, but the child stepped with him. The middle child, a girl of about eight, plucked at the boy's sleeve, but he ignored her. His eyes did not leave Shaw's face.

"I say there, young fellow." Shaw started, gently, to try to remove the hand. He found that gentle force was not enough.

A pretty girl, about seventeen, ran up to them. "Jeremiah! Jeremiah! Botherin' that gentleman!" She had a flat Missouri drawl and wore a gingham dress. She took the boy's other hand and tugged on it. "Now you let go, you hear? Now I mean it!"

The boy held on a moment longer, then reluctantly let go. "Beg your pardon, mister," the girl said. "He never acted this bad before."

"Not at all," Shaw said. "Compliment, I think."

"I'd wale him," the girl said.

"Oh, don't do that," Parkman said.

"Well, I said I would, most times." She paused. "Or Paw would." The boy's face began to cloud. He turned away. Her own face softened. "I reckon he's not feelin' so well. Our paw's sickly."

Parkman glanced at Shaw. Quincy had had some medical training. He had a kit with homeopathic medicines in his luggage, back at the dock. He had expected to secure favor with the Indians by simple treatments when they got farther West. "Do you have any help?" Parkman asked.

"There's a fella been to see him says he's some kind of doctor," the girl said. She looked down at the boy, who now held her hand. "Says he's goin' to git better when we git out where air 'n' water's better. Won't be needin' any help when we git out there.

Says it's awful purty and good for you, and there's lambs and things." She was talking to the boy. He raised his eyes to her.

"Lots of space to run," Shaw said.

A woman's voice called. "Yes, Maw," the girl said. "Comin'." To the men she said, "Now I'm sorry you was bothered."

"Not at all."

"Well, thank you." She bobbed in a kind of curtsy to the two men with the strange, Eastern accent. Parkman started to give the boy a coin, but she stopped him. "We sold our farm, thank ye. We ain't poor. . . . Now you sprats, you git on back!" They moved away. The girl did not look back at them, though the boy did, once.

Parkman said, "Those children—a sick father— they're going out to California?" All along the trip, as he had looked at the wagons and the whole movement of farmers, speculators and settlers, Parkman had been struck with a sense of mass hysteria in the teeming Westward movement.

They went to Captain Collins' room in the other tavern. Collins, dressed as they had left him, was dead out on his back, snoring away. Shaw shook him. Collins muttered, whispered a girl's name, but did not awaken. They let him sleep. "If we leave today, tomorrow at the latest, I don't think we can take him," Parkman said. Shaw nodded, puffing on his pipe.

They stopped at the log stable to see what was for sale or could be rented. The owner was not there. His hostler, a gangling boy with a cowlick in his hair and manure on his boots, said they seldom had horses to sell because everybody went to a kind of fairgrounds outside town where livestock was swapped and sold. And, he hinted darkly, this was the place to find any livestock the Indians had stolen. In fact, that was where the owner was now, to see what he could buy and to see if two of his own missing horses turned up.

The livestock exchange was simply a muddy open area on the outskirts of town. A few blanketed Indians were there with two good horses and a mule they were selling. Some of the emigrants were there to see what they could buy or trade. Two old fellows carrying long whips were arguing with each other about religion. They broke off their tirade from time to time to look into the mouths of horses and mules, making remarks about what they found. Parkman and Shaw went up to the Indians to look at the horses. They could not see brands or signs of cavalry saddles or bits. If these horses were indeed stolen, they had been stolen from other Indians.

A horse neighed at their backs and a familiar voice called out, "Ah! My employers, *mes bourgeois!* You have come to buy horses for our trip?"

It was Beckwith. The wide open smile, the familiar gap next to the canine, the silver tooth now reflecting the morning sun—no sign of fatigue or dissipation, of the drinking and fighting of last night. The beard was perhaps a little more ragged than they remembered, and the face had not been washed, or was it that they had not seen him in bright sunshine before?

Shaw had already asked the prices of the Indians' horses after a careful examination of teeth, coat and fetlocks. He was trying to decipher what the Indians were telling him through the common language of counting fingers and gestures.

"Those aren't bad horses," Beckwith said. "You be careful you aren't cheated. These are Kansas Indians, not Crow!" He turned to the Indians. "These are gentlemen, *mes bourgeois,* you hear?" He uttered what might have been an obscenity, though not in English. "How much? Don't lie!"

The Indian in charge answered with what he had told Shaw. Beckwith clapped his hands to his head in mock amazement and broke loose with a long denunciation, full of clicks and gutterals. It was Indian speech, but it may not have been the speech of Kansas Indians. They looked at each other, then shrugged and said something that indicated they either did not understand, or were not impressed.

Beckwith's face contorted. He jumped off his horse and went up to the Indians, shouting and waving his hands. Finally the Indians nodded. Beckwith's face immediately cleared. Smiling once more, he turned to Shaw and Parkman. "You have the horses. For less than you would have paid. Oh, much, much less."

Shaw examined the horses, a bay and a grey, once more. "Are they all right?"

"Oh, excellent. They came from a good place."

"How did you get them to come down?"

Beckwith grinned again. "I know Indians. I said I would report them at Fort Leavenworth."

"Report them for what?" Parkman asked. "Are these stolen horses?"

"They are good horses. You are not going to find better for sale here. Take them."

"But we won't take stolen horses!"

"Well . . . did I say they were stolen?"

"You certainly implied it!"

Again the shrug. "Well, some people, they like

stolen horses. You know? They think better for the same money. You know? So Indians go around saying they stole to get more customers. Good horses!"

"But see here, if there's any doubt about these horses being stolen. . . . Then why would they be afraid of Fort Leavenworth?"

"With Indians? Indians raid each other all the time. A great brave—they might name him Stealer of Horses. Great honor, oh yes. Crow steal from Blackfoot, Dakota steal from Crow. They sing songs, brag all the time, big warriors. Who knows whose horses they used to be? But they know white colonel in Leavenworth is crazy. He can make trouble, he is not proud of horse stealer. So you get them cheap."

"Well . . . you sure these were never stolen from the army? From white men?"

Beckwith appeared thoroughly exasperated. "Who knows who took from who, a long time ago? These Indians did not steal. They did not steal from whites —not horses, they didn't. Some Indians maybe stole from Indians, maybe not. . . . You don't want these horses, I don't ride and lead you."

He leapt from the ground directly onto his horse, galloped away, galloped back. He stopped his horse inches from them. "You need a wagon and mules, tents, muleskinner," he said. "I'll look around. We leave Monday!" He shouted something to the Indians, who nodded. "Don't worry about the horses! They won't cheat you!"

Next day they rode the ten miles to Independence. They passed many wagons, clustered in groups and a few singles. A huge encampment had been set up on the prairie outside Independence and new trains were arriving. Over a thousand people were already there. Parkman and Shaw stopped for a while to listen and observe. It was a town meeting gone mad. There was great confusion. Meetings were being held, resolutions introduced and passed, suggestions offered and denounced, but there was little agreement on leaders or on plans of organization, and when these subjects were brought up, wrangling broke out.

Parkman and Shaw rode on into town. A steady hammering and pounding came from a dozen blacksmith shops. Children were underfoot, horsemen were everywhere, some selling wares from wagon to wagon. Parkman was particularly struck by a full-figured lady in a black dress on horseback, vainly holding a tattered parasol above a complexion already overbaked and coarsened from travel. There seemed to be more families and fewer of the adventurers than they had observed before. It was frightening. What would become of all these people? Some had to die, but there would be no stopping of this great beast until it reached the Pacific Ocean.

"Glad we're not part of that, eh Frank?" Shaw laughed.

Parkman grunted. Shaw was right, of course. But were they right to feel superior?

They started back to the relative quiet of Westport. The day was quite beautiful. The road was ridged and muddy from the passage of so many hooves and vehicles, but alongside it spring flowers were growing, and the grass was up. Even where the refuse and the wheels of man made it difficult for other plants to grow, the sunflowers were up, pointing the way the wagons would be going, westward toward the afternoon sun.

They were out in the open prairie, with no buildings, wagons or riders in sight. But they were not quite alone. Shaw nudged Parkman and pointed to the top of a nearby hill. An Indian, stripes on his face, a necklace of bear teeth around his neck, almost naked, sat astride a mustang. The Indian was heavier than most Plains warriors. The red man raised his hand, revealing a tomahawk. He seemed to want to talk to them. An Indian like that, here, so close to the settlements and wagons? Suddenly three other Indians, in similarly garish dress, appeared. Two had Spanish saddles, like those they had seen in Westport—in fact, much like the one Shaw had except that, in the full glare of the sun on the slope, theirs seemed newer. All started down the hill. Parkman's horse, catching the scent and sound of other horses, raised his head and danced a step or two forward. The Indians spread out and broke into a gallop. What could they want? Shaw's horse too grew restless and pulled at the bridle. Shaw's horse reared, and before he could bring it down again, the Indians had surrounded them.

Three had tomahawks raised; the fourth had his bow out, the string stretched, and a metal-tipped arrow held in such a way that he could easily have hit either man he chose. One of the Indians grabbed Parkman's bridle as his horse, nostrils quivering, started to plunge. Another Indian hooked his arm under Parkman's, holding his tomahawk at the ready in the other hand, and yanked him out of the saddle to the ground. Parkman landed heavily, stunned. His horse, pulled forward by the Indian holding the bridle, leapt away and galloped along after his new master. The same thing happened to Shaw, who shouted, "See here! See here!" before he was forced off his horse.

Parkman heard the Indian with the bow shout, in passable English, "Off! Off!" They thundered away out of sight around the side of the hill.

Shaw, not as stunned as Parkman, helped his friend up. "You all right, old man?"

Parkman nodded as Shaw went off to look for his pipe in the beaten grass. Parkman felt weak and his ears were ringing, but the blood was back in his face and he could feel his head clearing.

Parkman knew from his Indian studies that the feathers their attackers wore were chosen and arranged in a Crow pattern. He also knew there were no Crow villages for hundreds of miles. True, Indians of many tribes came into Independence and Westport. But it did not seem likely that they would make up raiding parties around there. Beckwith had worn such feathers, and he was supposed to be some kind of Crow chief.

Shaw came back with his pipe. "All right? Able to walk? No broken bones, eh?" Parkman shook his head and stepped forward limping. "Yes, you *are* hurt!" This time, for the first time, Parkman was able to smile and pointed toward where his boot lay, a few steps ahead. He had lost it in his fall from the horse. It struck him suddenly that he was quite lucky. He chuckled as he pulled on the boot.

"Don't see what there is to laugh at. Bloody scoundrels!" Shaw said.

I've got both my legs, and my scalp, Parkman thought. That's what there is to laugh about. "You still have your money belt?" he asked.

Shaw quickly slapped himself about the waist. "Why, yes. Dastards didn't think to look for it. May have thought we had our money in the saddles."

"Well, that's another thing to laugh about. And you still have your scalp."

"I still don't see how you can be so gay. They stole our horses."

"But we still have our money and more in the luggage. We can buy other horses."

"We could have been killed!"

"That's why I'm so gay, as you call it." He looked around for his hat and found that, too. "Did it strike you, Quincy, that those Indians were extraordinarily bold, so close to the settlements?"

"Yes. Dressed strangely, too."

"Did you notice anything at all familiar about them?"

"None dressed like that in Westport." He kept staring at Parkman. "You saw something?"

"The feathers on the leader."

"That savage on the hill." He puffed his pipe a moment, then he stamped his foot and hollered, "Yes!"

"I expect," Parkman chuckled, "our horses may turn up again at that livestock auction. After a decent interval, of course."

They had to walk the rest of the dusty way back, about five miles. After two miles they came upon an emigrant encampment. The people invited them to stop and rest.

"Why not stay and come along with us?" a stooped elderly man with a gaunt, greying daughter seated next to him asked them.

"Very sorry," Shaw said. "Have our own plans, you know."

Parkman added, "No, we're sorry we can't. But thank you for asking."

They were drinking something the man called coffee. They put down their tin mugs. The man got up and hobbled to the fire to get a coal for his pipe. Parkman hoped that there was a more able-bodied man to lead his wagon, but he saw no one else nearby.

The man puffed on the pipe. "Be proud if you stayed for supper. Not much, but welcome."

"No . . . really . . . have to get back. . . ." Shaw, then Parkman, got up—Parkman with a certain amount of regret because the time seated had stiffened his legs.

"Man died this morning," the elderly man said. "Good man. Died this morning and they already buried him." He pointed the pipe toward a nearby cluster of wagons. "We have to leave in the morning. Part of the Colby train."

"Have to?"

"Leader says so. Worried about the mountains." He puffed again on his pipe. "Not only leave, but keep up. Woman, girl, three sprats." He lifted his contemplative gaze and looked directly at them. "Need a man. Men here got their own wagons. Be a Christian service. Maybe money in it."

Parkman thought he knew who the dead man was. The children and girl they had met. She had said something about her father being ill. The small boy had seized Shaw's bachelor hand.

"Can't. We have arrangements," Shaw mumbled. And in an unusual burst of loquacity added, "If we find somebody, we'll send him out."

The old man nodded. His eyes moved downward and into his own thoughts. The daughter remained as immobile as she had been all along. They wished them good-bye. The old man nodded again. Then they left.

They got back after dark. The next morning they found Captain Collins, who expressed sympathy and indignation at the story of the robbery, his red beard bristling. He said he didn't know where Beckwith was and didn't want to know. He also said that he had met an American army man with a similar taste for hunting, and would be leaving with him in a day or two. They went to the tavern together, and Collins got drunk again.

They didn't want to meet Beckwith again either, but they did, on the weekend. He was sporting a new buckskin jacket and a Stetson instead of the feathers. His rage and indignation when told of the robbery was even more excessive than Collins'. He screamed. He threw down the new hat in the dust, then picked it up and beat the dust out of it, swearing. "Do not be afraid! I swear I will find those horses for you. I swear I will avenge this disgrace. We will go buy new horses, and I will guide you to the mountains and I will ask all my Indian friends, and my Crow tribe, and we will hunt them down, and we will leave whenever you are ready."

Parkman noted Beckwith's new boots, softened with bear grease, complete with cavalry spurs, not available in shops.

That night Francis Parkman wrote in his journal that Beckwith "is a ruffian of the first stamp; bloody and treacherous, without honor or honesty."

Chapter 2

As they passed through the saloon on their way out of the tavern, the older trappers smiled knowingly and a few laughed openly. There was also a minor stir on the street among the loungers when they passed by. The shopkeepers also seemed to share a secret joke concerning the Bostonians. "Damn it all, they're laughing at us!" Shaw said. "Laughing at us as though we had been taken in by a college prank! Thievery is just a joke to them! Murder too, I guess!" He bit his pipe, having made his longest speech on the trip. "Let's get out."

"We'll need a guide," Parkman pointed out.

"I will not hire that scoundrel!"

"We'll ask for advice."

Shaw glared at him. "From whom? These mountain men? They're laughing hard enough now!"

"There's an army base close by, Quincy, if we need it. But more to the point, you did notice the office of the American Fur Company? I believe that the district manager would be a reasonable man."

Shaw was quiet, but the end of that pipe was between his teeth. Would the representative of a local business corporation think, as apparently some others did, that robbing a traveler of his goods was funny? A traveler who might be carrying furs, for instance? In fact, wouldn't such a businessman perhaps help identify the robbers? "I think we can stand a smile or two, Quincy." He began to smile himself.

To get to the fur company office, one had to walk up steps to the sidewalk planks, then another two wooden steps to the door. At each step was a scraper, and on the door itself a wooden sign marked "Wipe Your Feet." From the amount of mud on the sill, it didn't look as though any of the trappers could read.

They went inside. There were benches on both sides of the door against the wall, and a potbelly stove, unlit but bearing a cracked coffeepot. Straight ahead was a long counter which held balance scales, weights and a small pile of skins. Beyond were two chairs and a table with a wooden yard rule and an abacus.

A man sat on one of the chairs. He was dressed in a tight-fitting jacket and ruffled shirt. He was tall, well built, heavily bronzed, with black hair parted in the middle and tied with a bit of red yarn behind. His mustache and beard were closely trimmed.

"You're district manager here, sir?" Parkman asked.

The man looked at them calmly. No, he wasn't; the manager had just stepped out and should be back in a moment. Would they be so kind as to take a seat?

He spoke with a French accent—not the strong, blunt accent of the French Canadians, but a slighter, softer one, as though he had been in this country a long time. Much of the fur trade was under the control of people of French extraction and this district was led by Pierre Chouteau Jr., from St. Louis.

Parkman explained that they weren't there on business, but to ask a favor.

"I'm sure that Mr. Carlin would be delighted to help, and I think it would be best if you waited for him."

Heavy footsteps and vigorous boot-scraping sounded outside the door. The door was flung open with such vigor it banged against the wall. A big man in a Stetson hat, wearing a grey blanket coat came in.

"Gentlemen, gentlemen," the big man said. He rubbed his hands together as though he were cold, or perhaps, Parkman thought, anticipating money. "Sit down, please. Now, what can I do for you? Furs to sell or buy?"

"You're Mr. Carlin?"

"Yes, sir. Yes, indeed." He proceeded to the counter.

"We were just speaking to your assistant—"

Carlin laughed. "Well, I guess he is my assistant, at that. Yes, indeed, I guess so." In a good humor, he looked at them more closely, stroking the ends of his handlebar mustache. "Don't I know you gentlemen? Of course, I've seen you on the street. I think you gentlemen are actually somewhat famous in this town."

"What, sir?" said Shaw. "How do you mean, sir?"

"*Comment*?" the man behind the counter asked.

Carlin spoke to him in French. Though Parkman knew the language, this was not the French he had learned at Harvard, or used in Paris. But he was saying something about the robbery, and Parkman stiffened.

The man behind the counter made a soothing sound, shook his head, and when he looked at the two Bostonians, stiff in polite outrage, there was sympathy in his face.

"Well, I'm very sorry, sirs. Uh, please—I'm afraid I didn't get your names," Carlin said.

Each bit off the single word of his own name: "Parkman." "Shaw."

"Ah, Messieurs Parkman and Shaw. Well, I'm very sorry, and I certainly didn't mean to make fun— or seem to. The fact is, you aren't the first people who had this kind of thing happen to 'em. Those wagon trains—well, if they don't get good guides who know their business, men who keep a sharp lookout, well, they lose a lot of livestock. Of course, most of it isn't worth much. Indians don't have much use for oxen, for one thing, and thieves—and they ain't always Indians—won't usually attack wagons sticking together, with lookouts."

"If it's so common, why isn't something done about it?" Shaw said.

"Oh, kind of hard to prove, and bands of Indians come in and out all the time. They don't exactly sign the register. And no regular courts. Be a month or so before anybody could be tried. Kind of a live-and-let-live place." He nodded toward the back of the room where a rifle lay across a pile of pelts. "Keep our own guns back there."

Parkman said, "You think it only involves Indians?"

"Can't tell." He started to smile again and controlled it in time. "Well, gentlemen," Carlin said. "What is it that I can do for you?"

Parkman assumed his usual role as spokesman.

"We thought, sir . . . well, we'll be traveling to Fort Laramie and maybe beyond. We had certain things in mind we wanted to see and do and we haven't been over the route. We thought we'd ask your advice about engaging a guide. Someone who might know about hunting buffalo and other game, and about the tribes on the way, as well as the trail."

"A guide? Why, I thought you'd already talked to the best guide and one of the best hunters in the business!"

"Sir!" Shaw exploded. "Are you suggesting that we hire that scoundrel and go with him all the way to Laramie?"

Carlin's eyes widened. He exchanged glances with the other man who looked equally puzzled. "I beg your pardon?"

"To suggest . . . I knew that this town was . . . was . . ." Shaw had to stop, teeth digging into the pipe.

Carlin looked at the man behind the counter. "Are you saying you think that Henry Chatillon . . . is a . . . what did you say? A scoundrel?"

Now Parkman and Shaw were silent, staring at Carlin, who glared back. The silent standoff was broken by the man behind the counter, who began to laugh. Carlin relaxed. Then he too began to laugh. He turned toward the counter and beat it with his palm, in time to his guffaws.

The man behind the counter stood up. He was taller than Carlin, as heavy in the chest and shoulders, but thinner in the waist. "Maybe I'm the one should beg your pardon. I am Henry Chatillon."

Chatillon went on, "I am a hunter, trapper, and sometimes a guide. Mr. Carlin knew you had been talking to me, and so he thought—" The laughter rumbled for a few seconds in his throat again, then was brought under control.

Carlin took out a red bandanna and wiped his eyes and mustache. "I'm the one to blame, I guess," he said. "Gentlemen, this fellow behind the counter is not some ladies' man who walked in off the street, and Lord love me, he's not some bookkeeper sent up from St. Louis who never stepped in buffalo chips. He's Henry Chatillon, the best hunter and guide on the Oregon Trail, and I don't think he's killed anybody lately. He hasn't stole any horses either."

"I have been to see my mother in St. Louis," Chatillon said. "And I will be ready to leave tomorrow. If you gentlemen will still be looking for a guide, I will be pleased to work for you. Or do you have a previous arrangement with Jim Beckwith?"

"No!" Shaw said loudly.

"Well," said Parkman, "I think he may have that idea, but we never agreed. And when you consider the circumstances—"

"That's good," Chatillon said. "I don't want to interfere with anyone's agreement."

"On the other hand," Carlin said, amusement returning to his eyes, "Henry don't entirely trust Beckwith, I think maybe with good reason. Or so I've heard. That right, Henry?"

"I think that's right," Chatillon said. His manner was mild; nothing seemed to disturb him, but the tone was definite.

"That's just your experience," Carlin said, "your personal experience. Now, you wouldn't want to go spreading any scandal around for other people, would you?"

Chatillon smiled, but did not reply.

Carlin turned to them. "But Henry wouldn't recommend Beckwith to anybody."

Parkman said, "Do you think—are you hinting, sir, that Beckwith had anything to do with stealing our horses?"

"Well," Carlin drawled, "you can't really tell with Indians. Stealing horses is a game. This close to town, a little risky, unless it's planned. . . . Actually, what bothers me more is the way some of these wagon trains are being victimized." He slapped his palm down on the counter. "I sure wish they'd stay home! Bunch of sharpers taking advantage of a lot of greenhorns who are going to leave their bones out in the mountains, if they get that far! And they'll ruin the fur trade in the bargain!" He turned toward Chatillon. "Henry, why the hell don't you go out and offer to lead some of those wagon trains, so they don't fall into the river! And lead them right back to Pennsylvania!"

Chatillon took the suggestion as though it had been made seriously. "I want to get back without too much delay. You can't make much time with cattle." He turned his dark eyes back to Parkman and Shaw. They had not yet taken his offer. He waited patiently, politely.

Parkman had been studying the Frenchman and he liked what he saw. The man was calm and strong. He certainly didn't look or talk like the other trappers or mountain men that Parkman had seen. He had trouble imagining this gentleman among the bearded, buckskin-clothed men in the tavern.

Carlin went behind the counter. He opened a ledger on the table. "Slow day," he observed. "Maybe I should go out and do my own trapping. You boys been taking your business to Rocky Mountain Fur,

Henry? Think old Chouteau should open more posts out in the mountains?" He sighed. "Never mind. Have to convince St. Louis bankers, not me." He nodded toward Parkman and Shaw. "Why don't you guide these gentlemen?"

Chatillon smiled, but did not answer. He waited, at ease.

Shaw puffed. He muttered, "I don't see why not. If Mr. Carlin recommends him."

"Well," Carlin vouched for the Frenchman, "I've known him for fourteen years. Since he ran away from the farm. That's what you run away from, Henry, wasn't it? Or was it jail? Yes sir, I do recommend him. Without argument." He pulled out a drawer. In it was cash—gold coins, bills in bundles, two little cloth sacks either of coins or gold dust. He pointed to it, then toward the pelts in the back. "I left him alone here, drawer unlocked, nobody watching. I don't have to count it. Don't know anybody else I'd trust with that. And I didn't worry about anybody coming in and robbing me, either." He slammed the drawer shut and this time locked it. "Yes, I recommend him. Get him out of here." He looked up at them, with level, unamused eyes. "I want to see that nothing else happens to you. And him, too."

Shaw moved his pipe forward a couple of inches. "We'll need new horses. And supplies," he said.

"We'll take care of that this afternoon," Chatillon promised. "And tomorrow morning too, if we have to wait for good horses." He paused. "We are agreed then? I will be your guide? If you desire?"

"Yes," Parkman said. He didn't wait for Shaw's comment; he could serve as spokesman. "We are agreed. Would you like to discuss terms now?"

"We can get what we need. And discuss it then. You'll need a cart for supplies. The kind we call a mule-killer. And mules, and a muleskinner. I know a good one, not far from here. If acceptable to you, we can pick him up when we start. His name is Delorier. A Canuck—French Canadian. Not Frenchman from St. Louis, like me." Once more that smile. "I think you will like him."

"This may not be the usual trip," Parkman said. "I mean, our purposes are different. We're not going to California. We're not settlers or speculators. We intend to hunt. And more than that."

"I know what you want to do. This is one reason I thought I might want to be your guide. You want to hunt. You want to see the trail, the plains and the mountains, and the way people live. And you want to stay in an Indian village for a while. I am friendly with some Indians, I know the villages well, and I think I can tell you that they will make you welcome." He paused and smiled again. "Indians do not always welcome strangers. They are suspicious, or they can fight. Or they can pretend, and lie, and try to fool you."

"How do you know about the purpose of my trip? I don't recall telling anyone," Parkman eyed him curiously.

"The mountain men are not many. And they are something like a family. And they learn to figure things too, to live in the open. How do we know the trail, the animals, the Indians—where they are, where they go, why? Bent grass, a twig in a creek. Little things, hints. You said some things, people watch your equipment, what you buy, who you are. They know you're not settlers or miners. And trappers, mountain men—they look for ways to make money, sometimes to take advantage. This makes them smart. I think so."

"Henry, you're talky as hell today, ain't you?" Carlin said.

Chatillon shrugged. "I just want them to know that not all dangers are on the trail, or come from Indians. People—guides—take advantage. Well, they think, the greenhorns have it coming."

Carlin took a bent plug of tobacco out of a pocket, and a long, ugly looking knife out of a drawer. He cut off a piece of tobacco and put it in his mouth.

"Some of these crazy fellers look more like bears than men," he said. "After a month or so they smell like 'em too. They like it out there. Big sky, clean water, miles and miles of nothin' but maybe buffalo, no houses, no law and no wives or kids. Beautiful. Now the settlers goin' to come out and ruin it all, and maybe even make the squaws wear underpants and go to church.

"Now a few, I think, are even crazier than the others. They don't see wilderness as just a good free place for trappin', shootin', drinkin', whorin' and what not. They see it like—oh, just them and God, just after creation, before sin and the flood. And they might want to share it for a little with some other poor fool who could appreciate it too 'fore it's gone." He took a few silent chews. "Providin', of course, that he don't stay too long—that he's got someplace else to live and enough sense to go there before he turns Indian, like Henry. He spat accurately into a battered brass spittoon. Satisfied, he wiped his mouth and went back to his ledgers.

"Well, then . . . I suppose it's settled?" Parkman said.

Chatillon said, "I'll come to your tavern this afternoon and we'll start to get the horses and supplies."

They got up to leave. Chatillon smiled and nodded like a gracious host expressing humble gratitude that they had favored him with a visit.

Chapter 3

"I'm goin'," declared Nat Gantt, trapper. "I'm goin' back. This child don't want no part of town when there's buffler in the mountains." He'd spent a winter in the mountains, and though the weather was now warm again, he still felt he had to thaw out a little. At his age cold got deep into the bones.

Gantt was the oldest man in the tavern—not counting the owner and his feeble-minded help, who, of course, *didn't* count. His full beard was streaked with white, with two grey swatches down the sides. His mustache and hair were similarly streaked, and he hopped when he walked. The toes of his right foot had been frozen six winters before and chopped off to prevent gangrene, and his ankle and knee were stiffened with rheumatism.

Gantt wanted to be asked to lead some group out, to get a little more of a stake for the supplies he would need for the rest of the year. Trapping hadn't been good this year. Beaver were thinning out and he had to go deeper and deeper into the forests and mountains for them. Even if the trapping weren't so bad, mountain life would be tougher than it used to be. With age, the discomforts and loneliness of the trail tended to grow greater and the compensations were not as compelling. He had no squaw waiting for him. His last, and he realized now, looking boozily in his glass, the one he had liked the most, was dead, killed last year in a Pawnee raid, and he hadn't had the heart to get another. But he would go back. He really couldn't stand it here much longer, and next year he did not intend to come as far east, but to do his trading at someplace like Bent's Fort. Still he dawdled, waiting for he knew not what.

And, he realized, the other men around him had their own excuses for hanging around, even if they weren't as old as he. Maybe they were getting soft. But he knew that one day he would get up, glassy eyed and shaky from the night before, and find two or three gone, and then the others would get the fever and leave within days.

Hardly mattered, though. There were always newcomers. The sheer size of this movement West stunned him. The Indians scoffed at the idea that there were that many *wasichus* in the world. But they would find out. He felt a glow of boozy pride, but it turned quickly into anger. These whites, with their slow oxen and slow minds were his people, but never his kind. The Indians were closer, but not his kind either.

He raised the unsteady glass slowly, like a Dakota making an offering, a propitiation to the gods. Leave it up to God. *He* took the toes. If He liked 'em, He might come for the rest next winter.

The man facing him at the table, a Frenchy, Louis Gravoise, waited for him to make his toast. Gantt said, "This child hates . . . Jim Beckwith!" That seemed a reasonable thing to say.

Gravoise showed no surprise. "Who likes him? You know anybody?" he asked.

The more Gantt considered the proposition, through the whiskey haze, the angrier he became. Beckwith was at home everywhere, even if everybody, in time, learned to despise him. He was at home so much with the Crow as to have been made some kind of chief; he had Indians following him around here because of that big and lying mouth. He even had the fur company fooled into making him some kind of representative out in the mountains so that Gantt had had to deal with him in Laramie. And be cheated. He was sure! And now he had gotten hold of some greenhorns who would pay him too much to take them out on the Oregon Trail, and keep paying him and paying him. And they had already paid with horses. And Gantt and others like him didn't even know if they could get enough supplies to last through next year!

It enraged Nat Gantt. "He's goin' to ruin it for everybody! Ever' trapper, tryin' pick up a little extra, tryin' to get by an Injun village without gittin' scalped, is goin' be in trouble! Safe nowhere 'cause ever'body knows Jim Beckwith lyin' and thievin', an' ain't we his friends?"

His hand came down hard on the table, jarring a bottle of whiskey. Gravoise grabbed it before it fell. "Bushwhack him," Gantt said. "We can kill him. Say Injuns settled him. Many bucks might want to kill him. Say"—his eyes brightened—"I remember, he hit his squaw with a hatchet last year." Not to be unfair, he added, "Flat side."

Nat Gantt's fury mounted. "By Gawd! That man goin' to lie and lie and make Injuns mad till no Injun trust a mountain man! No squaw stay with him! No wagon master hire him to guide!" Beckwith didn't even have to rely on a wagon train, with its creeping oxen and children, for a job as guide. He had those greenhorns.

Just then the door opened and the two greenhorns came in. The smaller of the two had a trimmed, jet-black beard, and a slightly underslung jaw. He was pale and Nat Gantt could see, with his experienced eye, that he had the bowel gripes already starting, and that he would be sick on the road. And when he had to drink the alkali water, it would get worse. The other greenhorn, huskier and with a permanent angry look on his face, had a fuller brown beard and a short pipe jammed between his teeth. The two looked around a moment, then started toward the back stairway. The heavier one was carrying new saddle blankets.

As the greenhorns passed his table, Nat Gantt lurched to his feet. "Now, hold it there!" he yelled. "Hold it there, gents!"

The man with the pipe said, "Yes? Yes, fellow!"

"Be you . . . looking for a guide?" Gantt asked. "I . . . be a *honest* guide!"

The room grew quiet. Louis Gravoise stared at him. So did Shaw and Parkman.

"We have an honest guide," Shaw snapped, and marched off.

Parkman hesitated a moment. "Yes, we've already engaged our guide." Civility was never out of place. Though the man was crude in his speech, he had asked a reasonable question and deserved a civil answer. "Yes, we're satisfied with our guide. He seems an honest man. But we appreciate your interest." He passed on toward the staircase.

Nat Gantt sat down abruptly. He wasn't quite sure what had happened, but he knew he hadn't handled it right. He thought about it a moment, his mind groping toward some recognizable trail in a fog. Then desolation burst on him. Jim Beckwith had won again! He had those greenhorns where he could squeeze them good!

He sat and brooded for a while, thinking about life in the mountains, life with the Indians. "Damn these settlers!" he shouted suddenly to Gravoise, who seemed incapable of being surprised by anything. Once more he seized the endangered bottle as Gantt rose to his feet and pushed the table away. Lurching on his chopped and stiffened foot, he almost upset another table. He told the heavy men who rose in complaint, both younger than he, "If you don't like it, c'mon out, and show me what you got!" He made it to and through the door without anybody following him, which confirmed his low opinion of those who hung around in towns.

The sun dazzled him. He squinted until his vision returned and then looked about the busy street. Among the many colorful sights that greeted him was one more colorful than the rest. A truly red man. Not just a redskin—no skin was ever that red. It was a brave wrapped, in spite of the warmth, in a flaming red blanket. His face had been painted an equally bright vermilion. Some of the Indian's other decorations included the tail of a prairie cock—a prairie cock!—worn on his head, and something yellow in his ears that was probably shell. He was armed for a one-man war with arrows, bow, knife, and in his hand a sword that he probably had gotten in trade at Fort Laramie for buffalo skins. He was a dandy, all right. He was an Oglala, a long way from home. What was he doing around here in a get-up like that?

The Indian was on a tan horse. He rode like a king, not deigning to look to the right or left. No doubt he'd ridden like that all the way from Oglala Dakota country.

"It's Horse!" Gantt shouted. "By Gawd, it's Horse! All the way from Whirlwind's village, I bet!"

But what was he doing here?

Nat Gantt couldn't read words, but he could read trampled grass, and wind, the pattern of buffalo chips —and the meaning in Indian gatherings, and dress, and movement. All the years on the trail, he'd learned to pick up these things, or he wouldn't have stayed alive. War was in the wind among the western bands of the Dakota. Their war parties had been beaten, their braves killed and horses stolen. In the villages the people wailed and swore blood vengeance on the Snake and Crow. To make it worse, Whirlwind's own son had been killed and he would not be appeased. The story was that he had called the neighboring Dakota tribes to a council, which meant to prepare for war. You couldn't always trust Whirlwind, Nat knew. He did as much running around as his name implied. But this was his son whose death had to be avenged. And the rest of those tribes had scores to settle, too.

Horse rode toward him. "Hey there, Horse!" he called. "Hey there! Whoa!"

Horse reined up. But he didn't look at Gantt.

"Hey Horse, don't you know me? Nat Gantt! Nat Gantt, by Gawd! I seen you in your village not six months—uh, moons ago. What you doin' here, you heathen savage?" Then he lapsed into Dakota, Oglala dialect, choosing his expressions more carefully.

Horse waited patiently, still looking straight ahead. Those *were* yellow shells in his ears. "Where is Henry

Chatillon?" he asked in English. The horse stamped, but the man, except for a minor blanket adjustment, did not move.

"Well, tell me, you damn painted devil! There goin' be war or not? What's doin' out there?" Gantt persisted.

Horse waited, immobile, unconcerned with anything except what he himself wanted to know.

"What do you want Chatillon for? What's he got to do with it?" Gantt knew that Henry Chatillon was somewhere in town. He knew that Chatillon had a particularly close connection with the Dakota, especially Whirlwind's group. Did they want him in connection with the war? A squaw? What?

Any fighting among Indians cut down the fur trade, because Indians were hunting each other rather than beaver and buffalo. Indians could generally be persuaded to take less for their furs than trappers like Gantt would accept. He stamped his stubby foot. "Consarn you, Horse! Cain't you talk?"

"Where is Henry Chatillon?" Horse asked again.

"Why, blast your soul!" But Gantt recognized that there was not much point in going on. Western Indians, particularly warriors, rooted in their own lands, were not as cowed by white men as those in the settlements. And Horse probably had business that Whirlwind had told him to discuss with no one except Chatillon. If he only had time to get the Indian drunk. . . .

"How'd I know where he is? Try the fur company." Gantt started to turn. But that damn Injun just stood there, waiting for directions. He turned back. "Over there! That building! There, there!" He jabbed his finger. Horse, without acknowledgment or thanks, moved off, leaving Gantt swearing.

But Gantt was not really angry. In fact, he felt a kind of elation. There would be war, but not right away. There had to be councils and powwows, a gathering of the tribes. And passing the pipe and making medicine. And probably the Snake and Crow and Pawnee and the others would be making some kind of peace talk, because it was one thing to ambush an occasional hunting or war party, and another thing to take on thousands of Teton Dakota. He knew that the Snake had already sent old Vasquez, the trader, to Whirlwind to try to talk about the death of his son, saying they hadn't known it was his son, and offering compensation. But Gantt was pretty sure Whirlwind wasn't buying that.

Anyway, there would be war. And Gantt had time to get ready. He wasn't as young or fast as some of the others and maybe couldn't stay on the trail as long, but he had something for his years of experience out there that they couldn't buy for millions. For one thing he knew that Beckwith was a chief among the Crow, and one reason their raiding parties and ambushes had been successful was because Jim had been advising them. The reason Beckwith had been kicked out of the U.S. cavalry hadn't been because he wasn't a good soldier when it came to fighting. Did Chatillon know all this? Probably. If they were squared off against one another. . . .

"Yahoo!" he yelled to the street, stamping his feet. "I'm goin' back! Hear me? This child's goin' back!"

Chapter 4

A flood tide of Indians spread across the broken, barren plain, washing toward Laramie Creek. It was a mile from front to back, and broader across than anyone could see. In the gloomy distance the high ridges of the Laramie Mountains stood like sentinels protecting their flanks. There were heavily laden pack horses and dogs, some pulling travois and carrying lodgepoles, being urged on by desiccated old women wearing fragments of tattered buffalo robes. Able-bodied young squaws and magnificently muscled warriors rode on horseback. Children and dogs ran in and out of the mass making a racket. The male elders of the tribe, wearing their white buffalo robes with great dignity, strode along in a body.

Whirlwind's camp was on the move. The chief himself rode out in front, a large strong man, nearly naked, on a white horse. Next to him was his youngest and favorite squaw, a slender girl with a spot of vermilion on each cheek. She rode a large, gentle mule decorated with white skins, bits of metal that tinkled as she rode, and a blue and white beaded blanket.

Whirlwind had spent much of the past week in council with the other chiefs and the wise men who could advise them. In response to Whirlwind's call for revenge against the Snake and Crow, tribes and groups of the Teton Dakota were starting to gather at the camping ground on La Bonte's Creek. Oglala, Brulé, Winniconjou and the rest. But Whirlwind had decided that he and his warriors would not go directly to the camp, but would travel through the mountains they called the Black Hills and hunt first, to lay up meat, lodgepoles and other provisions his village needed for the winter. They would send an experienced and able war party to the campground.

It had been a hard decision to make, and since it involved so many others and so many considerations, Whirlwind had often deferred to the advice and the arguments of the others in the council. He knew it made him appear as one who vacillated. Many of the braves were restless for action. He could almost hear their thoughts. What kind of chief was this whose own son had been killed, who talked of war and revenge and stirred up the people, and then himself rode off to hunt? Their relatives had been killed and scalped in raids, their horses stolen; they had been challenged and humiliated. Sometimes, when they rode on what were their own tribal lands, they saw markings on the barks of the trees with written insults from invading Crow, Snake and Pawnee who had brazenly entered Dakota land without punishment and left written gibes. The braves, especially the younger ones, were eager for war. They had reputations to build, coups to count. They rode arrogantly in the moving mob or as guards on the outside. Whirlwind, though he did not look to left or right, could sometimes feel their eyes on him.

The high, barren plateau on which they moved began to descend gradually as they approached their

goal. It was not visible yet, but like horses that smell
the hay of home after a long workday, the Indians
sensed it and pressed forward. Soon they could see
the steep descent to a broad, spreading green meadow
below with Laramie Creek, shallow and swift, at the
bottom. In minutes the plain was swarming with Indians.

Whirlwind rode along the stream with his squaw.
Old women began raising the lodgepoles, while others
were getting the leather coverings off the horses to
cover them. Large groups were crossing the stream to
set up family lodges in the green meadow on the other
side. The families began to drift together around the
rising tepees, even the howling dogs and romping children. Stray horses, colts and mules broke away and
ran through the crowd, chased by screaming hags.
Along the bank, painted, younger squaws held the
spears of the heads of their households aloft to call
the members together. Temporary shelters of buffalo
hides were stretched across poles to keep the sun off
the master of the house while he reclined, perhaps with
a favorite squaw, with his rawhide shield, his lance
and pipe, bow and arrows and medicine bag set up
on a tripod before him, while the lodge went up
swiftly around him, supervised by an older squaw.

After the horses had been watered and rested,
allowed to eat some of the bottom land grass, the
warriors mounted them again. The young men wore
war eagle feathers on their heads and on their shields.
Some had the scalp locks of enemies on their tunics.
The face of a tall, scarred one was blackened, to show
that he had taken a Pawnee scalp.

The leader of one group was Mahto Tatonka,
Bull Bear, son of the great and legendary chief of
that name who had ruled so ruthlessly and so long

until murdered by his rivals in the tribe six years previously. The younger Bull Bear, showing every indication of becoming like his father, raised his lance and started his gallop. The others fell in and charged ahead on the two sides of the stream, singing their war songs, swinging in wide arcs through the plains and hills around the camp to see what game could be found, to scout out what enemy parties or settlements might be in the vicinity. Some carried lances, some guns. All had knives and bows and deerskin quivers. Soon they left only dust on the hill. Whirlwind watched them with satisfaction. They were ready for war. The Pawnee and Snake were not their equal! But he also felt some unease. When would his village, low in food and supplies, be ready for war?

Whirlwind walked among his people, a tall man, vermilion streaks on his cheeks—heavy with experience and care, if not yet with years. There were scars on his arms from old battles, and on his chest and back from the manhood trials of his youth—the wooden stakes, weighted with buffalo skulls, had torn the flesh—to prove his courage and justify himself to his people and the Great Spirit. Other than that there was little in his dress or in the fittings or furnishings of his lodge to distinguish him as a chief. Among the Oglala, the chiefs were not kings, distinguished by great luxury or delegated power. They ruled by example and respect, or by force of personality and arms, as the elder Bull Bear had. Whirlwind could, of course, have dressed as he pleased, to the extent that he could personally afford, but he was no dandy. Let the foolish, like Horse, who had not even won particular distinction in battle, spend all their substance on dress.

The elder Mahto Tatonka had been dead a long

time, but his victorious and tyrannical rule and assassination from within had left the Oglala divided. The simmering hatreds and widening schisms among the warriors made organizing for war very difficult—against other tribes and, he was afraid, against the more formidable white men as well. They could not use their strength against others if they used it against themselves. And this was one reason why their hereditary enemies had dared to invade their territory, defy them, and often defeat them.

Bull Bear was dead, but his family was still exceedingly important. He had left thirty children. His son Bull Bear was the band's most ferocious warrior and he followed his father in other ways, too, such as taking whatever maiden he wanted, whenever he wanted her, and refusing to pay any bride price. Still, Whirlwind thought, the younger Bull Bear might make a great chief in time. And Whirlwind, when he was sure the boy was seasoned and less hotheaded, might be glad to step down.

In the meantime though, to show respect for the band's most distinguished family and in hopes of bringing more unity to the feuding factions, he moved over to their lodge to extend his greetings and good wishes. He also wanted to inquire about the health of Blue Eagle Speaks, the elder sister of Mahto Tatonka.

The skeletons of most of the tepees were up and the leather covers were going on. The old women were shrieking at the dogs and children as they did the major part of the work. Some of the lodges were finished. The shields and emblems of the masters were easy for Whirlwind to see and recognize. He greeted them with their titles and expressions of respect, and his greetings were solemnly returned. "Counter of many coups," he said to a rather pompous middle-aged man sitting regally before his lodge while the women bustled around inside. "Taker of Pawnee and Snake scalps."

The man's eyes glittered. He returned the greeting and began a long recital of Whirlwind's accomplishments, to return the compliment. Whirlwind grew impatient. At this rate he would never finish his rounds.

Whirlwind's squaw, by his side, was also impatient. Was a chief always wise to take a young squaw? "I wish to see my brothers and sisters in my father's lodge," she pouted. Being the favorite, having priority and authority over the older women, had spoiled her. She was a beautiful child. But still a child.

He nodded. "Go." She smiled with delight, a girl turned loose to play. Now she could show her family her beaded moccasins, the trim on her white deerskin tunic, her chiming brass ornaments. Her eagerness gave him a twinge. "Be back in time to cook the meat," he called after her. She was the favorite and others could do the cooking, but he wanted to tame her a little.

He reached Bull Bear's lodge. He did not have to, but he asked permission to enter. It was gloomy inside. Old scalps, war trophies, decorated the walls, but other than that there was little to reflect the reputation and power of the family. Inside were three women, and a little girl whose skin seemed to shine in the gloom. She was half white, the daughter of Blue Eagle Speaks. He had seen the half-white son, naked and barely able to walk, stalking one of the family dogs outside with a tiny bow and arrow.

Blue Eagle Speaks lay on a buffalo robe, a rich, good one, and another covered her, for these days she was always cold. Perhaps it was the dim light, but her eyes and cheeks seemed a little more sunken than they had been when he had last visited her, only a few days ago. Women had mysterious illnesses that came and went, but he knew now that she would not be better soon.

She greeted him, "Welcome." She spoke clearly enough, but not with a great reserve of strength. Whirlwind felt a twinge. She had been the most beautiful squaw in the village until recently.

Her sister, younger but a grown woman without a mate, laid a robe down for him to sit on. He put his lance against the leather wall and sat down cross-legged. The woman, named Many Flowers because she had been born in late spring when the plains had been covered with flowers, kept her head shyly down as she moved off to one side. She was as graceful as her sister and would have been as beautiful except for the scar on her upper lip that had kept her without suitors equal to her station.

"The evil spirit must be leaving you," Whirlwind said to Blue Eagle Speaks. "The health seems to be coming back to your cheeks." He kept watching her, thinking that this last trip must have been torture, dragged along in the travois over the rough ground. Young Bull Bear, of course, wouldn't have helped much, not when he had a fast horse to try out.

She smiled faintly. "We are honored that you have come. Your presence brightens my face." It struck her as unusual that a chief would have come to visit a woman, even the daughter of a great chief. "None of my brothers are here. I am sorry."

"I shall see your brothers always in the front of the war party, in the battle, making coups, killing our enemies. When we fight, or ride, I shall see them often there. But to sit and talk quietly in the lodge of the great Bull Bear with his daughters and grandchildren is an honor I do not often receive." Solemnly Whirlwind took off a glass ring a white trapper had once given him, which he carried tied to one of the fringes on his breeches since it was too small for him to wear. He offered it to the light-faced child. With equal solemnity she took it, tried it carefully on each finger and finally put it on her right thumb. It wobbled but stayed. Her face broke into a bright smile. "She is fortunate," he said, "in grandfather and father both. And uncles."

He raised his eyes speculatively to Many Flowers. The thought of his own squaw chattering with the other children in her family came to his mind. Would he have been wiser to have allied himself with the family of old Bull Bear? He certainly had enough station for her, and a chief can do as he pleases without damage to his prestige. He could certainly have used the respect and support of the biggest faction in the tribe, the greatest warriors.

But then that would have meant taking sides, acquiring the bitter hatred of the old chief's enemies, perhaps open fighting within the tribe. Besides, the woman's eyes were not submissive under his gaze. They returned his glance coolly and his eyes lowered first, coming to rest on her sick sister. It was not the slight harelip that put him off but something about Many Flowers, something imperial, cold and unyielding.

He said to Blue Eagle Speaks, "I have come out of respect, and to see if I can help you in any way."

Blue Eagle Speaks smiled again. "Your good will already lifts our spirits and makes our way clearer and lighter."

What help could he give her that she did not

already have? A Dakota chief had no more wealth and little more power than the average brave, unless he chose to take it ruthlessly, and she had all the material support and protection she needed from Bull Bear and her other brothers. But that was not what he had in mind and she probably knew it.

She would not say anything, however. The Bull Bear family treasured its privacy and its freedom to act without consulting others.

"There is someone who is missing," the chief said.

She became quiet. Her daughter nuzzled close to her mother, holding out the glass ring for her mother to appreciate. But, though Blue Eagle Speaks put her arm around the child, her eyes did not leave Whirlwind.

He decided it was time to speak. "You know we must hunt now for a time, to dry meat, to get poles and robes and leather for our lodges, clothes for our children, for the winter. You know, though, we must make war," he went on. "The Snake, the Crow, even the Pawnee have invaded our grounds, attacked and killed our hunting and scouting parties, taken what should have been our buffalo. They have marked challenges and left taunts on the trees. They grow ever more bold. Some braves have died. Your brother. My son. We must drive them from the land. We must avenge this or die."

She said, "I know the chief thinks of his people."

He said, "Little escapes the daughters of Bull Bear. You will have noticed that Horse is not with us. He is not off to seek a wife in another tribe, or to carry a message to the other Dakota at La Bonte's Creek. He is not dead in some foolish attack." At least he didn't think so, though the way was very long, through the territories of many enemies. Horse was vain, but he was also strong and clever.

He said, "I have sent Horse to him for whom you wait."

Her face grew still. But he thought he saw a flash deep in her eyes. Women did not question a chief once an action was taken, but it was understood without argument that some things were not done.

She said, "I had not wanted him to know. Yet."

He nodded. "Horse does not know. I asked him to come for the war councils."

He got to his feet. The little girl became frightened at the towering figure and moved closer to her mother. Suddenly she remembered and hid the thumb that held the ring behind her. His face did not change, but he felt like laughing, suddenly, in this place of sickness.

He made the signs appropriate for departure. "I sent greetings, and said all was well. It is true; you will be well, shining among the women as your brothers do among the warriors. It is a long journey, but he will come sooner than he would have otherwise, and I think he will come straight. We will hunt now, with our village staying on these green meadows, by these clear waters, where the buffalo and the antelope come to drink and feed, and there is food for horses and people. I think he will come after we have finished much of our hunting and have rested, and are ready."

The Great Spirit ruled over all, but should be called upon only for the greatest requests. Silently he wished her well by the spirits of the forests and of the stream and called upon the Grandfathers for help.

When he left the lodge, he saw the oldest of the medicine men approaching. His whistle, made from the wing bone of the war eagle, was tied into his topknot, his pouch of charms held in his hand. Whirlwind waited until he was sure that the other was headed for Bull Bear's lodge. He knew what the medicine man would do. He would beat a drum next to her head in that close space. He would howl, yell and dance. He would pound her with both fists to drive out the evil spirits. Whirlwind did not move from the entrance, so that the old man had to stop and greet him before going in. Whirlwind did not have much patience with him, and the other knew it. Whirlwind did not believe, himself, that he had ever been helped by such medicine.

He said, "You will not beat her. Hear me clearly. Make what medicine you want, but do not beat her." He turned and strode off without waiting for a reply.

Whirlwind sat before his lodge as the sun sank down toward its own lodge behind the mountains. His squaw had not returned. He would take care of that when she did come. It would not happen again. The fires were lit, some smoke curled out of the valley. He heard a distant rumble like drumming, perhaps shouts. He looked toward the north end of the village and saw that the lookouts on the heights were standing, straining to discern the cause of the commotion. From the sound, he knew it was their warriors returning.

A wild yell sounded from the hill. They came rushing over it, a crowd of horsemen like a torrent, at full gallop. They entered the village two by two at top speed. Each warrior sang his war song. Whirlwind watched them with pride. They wore splendid dress for war, great crests of feathers, antelope-skin tunics fringed with the scalps of enemies. They carried shields with feathers from the war eagle, bows and iron-tipped lances and a few had guns. In front, the most splendid of all, Mahto Tatonka, rode a bay horse, and his cousin, White Shield, was on a black and white.

They circled the village three times. As each of the more noted warriors passed, the tireless older women screamed out his name to honor him and to inspire the younger warriors who had not yet built reputations. The young boys ran after them, shouting, brandishing whatever weapons they had. Even toddlers, large eyed, holding their toy bows and arrows, were caught up in the excitement.

As abruptly as the procession had entered, it rode out of the village. A half hour later the warriors returned, more slowly, to drop off in ones and twos around their own lodges and fires. The horses were put out to graze in the meadow.

Whirlwind's squaw had returned and was busy preparing the meal with no argument about whether she or someone else should cook. She cast furtive glances at him, waiting for his rebuke, trying to appear busy and virtuous to stay his hand. He would take care of her later. Now, with the sun behind the mountains, he watched the sky change from light to deep blue to purple. It was a time for pride, for presenting accounts to the Grandfathers for their approval. The young men were ready. First there would be preparation, training, the storing of goods, the mobilization of allies. Then they would sweep the plains.

At his age he often thought more of peace, of hunting, building better lodges, of long days in which he could teach the children the old ways and the old beliefs. If the other elders felt the same way, they did not often talk of it. Mostly they were full of talk of old exploits, telling the same old lies. The young were not for peace. And their enemies were not for peace. And there was his murdered son. He stood up. There would be war. And he would lead. Their plains would be clear of Snake and Crow. Even the white men would have to respect them. Then maybe, with the plains full of grazing buffalo and antelope, there would be peace and glory.

and maybe all of it in the mountains themselves." He explained this to some of the travelers. Some of the women, seeing their prized possessions threatened, looked distraught. Some men, convinced that they were, indeed, passing through savage lands full of cannibals and thieves, gripped their guns tighter and would not respond. But Delorier got his mules, one of them only slightly lame, from a group of travelers who became convinced by Chatillon that they should get rid of their surplus weight and stock where they could still get a good price, and have cash and seed that would help them get what they would need later on.

They moved toward other wagons, to see what supplies they could buy, mostly from those Chatillon recognized as being overloaded.

"He could cheat them if he wanted to," Parkman said to Delorier. "Couldn't he?"

Delorier's eternal smile grew a little broader. "There is no need. He knows more. He never thinks to cheat."

"He is a lucky man," Parkman said.

Then they returned to the Kansas Indians, and Chatillon got the horse he had wanted, quietly refusing the bay, which they kept urging on him, and which, to Parkman's eyes, looked to be the best of those offered.

The long, orange-tinted twilight had set in by the time they were finished with their most important purchases, and they decided to call a halt. They escorted their horses and mules to the log stable where Chatillon kept his own grey Wyandot pony, and he and Delorier set to work feeding and tending the beasts. Parkman's horse was a large brown, rawboned gelding named Pontiac.

It was time for dinner. Parkman asked their two employees if they would like to eat with them. Delorier seemed at a loss. He said that he really had not had time to get supplies, to get things ready. Making a campfire in town might not be desirable—

No, no, Shaw interjected. They meant that Chatillon and Delorier would be their guests in the tavern or perhaps some other place, more convenient and no doubt cleaner.

Delorier pulled his mustaches nervously and conferred with Chatillon. Chatillon, bent over to examine the horses' hooves, straightened up and smiled. It suddenly struck Parkman that the problem revolved around what Delorier thought was the proper relationship between a muleteer and his employer. Parkman started to protest, to say that they would be happy for the company. After all, they would all be living together out on the trail.

Chatillon spoke. He said that they appreciated the invitation very much, but they still had work to do, and they, Delorier in particular, felt it would be more fitting to go ahead with it and eat later, according to arrangements they had already made. For one thing, after they brushed and examined the horses, Chatillon wanted to ride them to give them a little exercise under saddle. He particularly wanted to give his own pony a run, as it was growing restless in the stable. Delorier's smile broke into full flower again and he nodded vigorously, then turned and smacked one of his mules on the rump to establish immediate control and familiarity.

Parkman and Shaw were satisfied as they started down the main street toward their tavern. When they reached it, they heard Jim Beckwith's loud voice from within. Hooting and laughter by his fellow patrons accompanied it. Parkman and Shaw paused. The door flung open. Beckwith came out, still roaring, with two rather bedraggled Indians clinging to him. They were whiskey Indians, Indians who'd exchanged life on the plains for life in towns and saloons. Beckwith saw Parkman and Shaw and stopped.

He was a large man. They had not really appreciated his size before. Parkman suddenly remembered the ease with which Beckwith had thrown Captain Collins over his shoulder and carried him down the street.

Beckwith and his Indians standing in the doorway abruptly silenced the crowded saloon. Some men came up to see what was going on. Parkman recognized the man who had accosted Shaw and himself when they had come through at noon—the older man with the streaked beard, who hobbled as he walked, and the dark-skinned trapper who had been with him. Others crowded in behind. Now Beckwith had an audience.

Beckwith smiled. In the dying light, facing west, the silver tooth glistened. "Gepmen! I been waiting for you! Why so long? We got work to do!"

As usually happened in time of crisis, the customarily silent Quincy Shaw was the one to speak. "We want to pass, Mr. Beckwith. Please step aside," he said firmly.

Hoarse laughter came from the doorway. "I'm sorry to be late, gepmen," Beckwith said. His face contorted with accommodation and reasonableness. "But I did wait . . . I did wait for you. These men can tell you that Jim Beckwith waited and waited, willing to do anything to help the men he's supposed

to guide. I am sorry that you did not come sooner.
But we can still do some of the things necessary to
prepare for the trip."

"We've done what is necessary," Shaw said. "You
are not involved. Now let us pass." Shaw started forward. Parkman put a restraining hand on his cousin's
arm.

"I heard," Beckwith said. "You have horses and
you have mules. You even have a muleskinner. Delorier isn't the best, but he'll do. I want to be agreeable. Well now, this makes it easier, much easier. I
would like to look at the horses and equipment to
make sure that they are all right—that is my job, to
make sure. Then I think we should be ready to leave
in . . . oh . . . day or two? Is that right?"

"You scoundrel!" Shaw cried. "We want nothing
further to do with you! You . . . you . . . think we
would let you guide us anywhere?"

There should have been some way to avoid this,
Parkman thought. There ought always to be some
way to avoid unpleasantness. But now the loafers on
the muddy street had all been alerted and had come
closer, and the men from the tavern were all around
Beckwith, avid for entertainment. Beckwith's eyes
narrowed as Shaw approached him.

"You've been mistaken, Mr. Beckwith," Parkman
said. "We never hired you to be our guide. We have
someone else."

"First you want me to be your guide, and I give
up other jobs. Now you want to steal away the money
you promised me. And now this little man wants to
beat me. Beat me! I ask you"—he turned to the Indians—"have I done anything to these gents from the
East to be treated like this?" The Indians looked at
him blankly. "For somebody to steal from me, beat

me? No?" He turned back. The two Indians separated from him, spreading out on both sides, so that, with the group moving in from behind, there could be no escape. "Come ahead, little man." Beckwith motioned to Shaw and took a step to close the gap. "Come ahead. Oh yes, you will pay what you owe me. You think you can cheat Jim Beckwith?"

"We don't want any trouble," Parkman said.

The crowd roared and Beckwith lunged at Shaw. Shaw stepped nimbly aside, and before Beckwith could turn, Shaw kicked his moccasined foot out from under him and hit him on the head.

Beckwith went down heavily on his knees. The crowd roared again.

To Parkman's continuing surprise, Shaw began to dance around his opponent, thrusting out his left in a series of swift jabs against the unresisting air. Then Parkman remembered that for weeks before they had started on the trip, Shaw had been taking instruction in pugilism from a broken-nosed English boxer who held regular classes in a local gymnasium. He'd told Parkman such knowledge might come in handy on the trail.

Beckwith regained his feet and Shaw gave him two or three carefully calculated blows to the face, then jumped back quickly before Beckwith could grab him. A dot of blood appeared on Beckwith's face. The crowd roared again. Beckwith crouched and began stalking Shaw.

Parkman tried to step between them. "Please, gentlemen!" he said. But Beckwith shoved him aside with a massive shoulder. Shaw had dared to strike him and hold him up to ridicule before his fellows.

The crowd pressed in, shouting for more blood. Shaw, dancing out of Beckwith's reach, found himself stopped by a solid row of laughing, jeering spectators. Beckwith charged him. Shaw jumped aside, but tripped over an outstretched foot. More jeering and laughter.

"Don't be so bashful, greenhorn! Go on, kiss him!" someone yelled.

Shaw managed to keep his feet and dodge Beckwith again. But he was sweating and starting to look around for help. Parkman tried to intercede again, but a brawny arm closed around his neck and he was pulled away. Someone also grabbed Shaw from behind. He struggled, having lost all dignity.

"Let him go," Beckwith said. "I don't need no help. The man try to cheat me out of my money. I can take care of him myself."

"Go on, greenhorn! Kiss him!"

He was thrust, headlong, toward Beckwith. He ducked down and the top of his head rammed into Beckwith's gut. Beckwith grunted in pain and Shaw was able to twist away and gain a moment's respite.

Wild yells and pistol shots, which seemed to come from the other end of the street, distracted the crowd for a moment. The arm around Parkman's throat relaxed and Parkman twisted away and ran to Shaw's side. Beckwith, too, hesitated a moment to see what was happening.

The roar of a buffalo rifle deafened them momentarily. A window above the entrance to the tavern seemed to explode, showering glass upon the men before the doorway. The crowd broke up and ran.

Parkman looked through the dust and saw Henry Chatillon on his grey horse, his rifle across the saddle, apparently trying to stop some runaway mules violently careening down the street, their heavy cart banging behind them. On the cart, the reins firmly in his hands, was Jean Delorier. He made a clucking sound and moved his hands on the reins, and the mules, which had been fighting the bits, shaking their heads and charging wildly, stopped suddenly, and with gentle shivers stood alongside the astounded Parkman and Shaw.

"*Sacre bleu*," the muleteer said calmly. "These animals are hard to control."

Beckwith, who had not run with the crowd, was not to be distracted from his anger at Parkman and Shaw. He started threateningly toward them. Chatillon was off his horse in an instant. He passed his rifle to Parkman and stepped in front of Beckwith. Beckwith stopped.

The effect of this new drama on the crowd was electric. If the fight between Shaw and Beckwith had been exciting, the impending clash between two such giants was better than an Indian raid. The circle closed and tightened again.

"Jim," Chatillon said, "I must care for the safety of these men, so don't come closer. But if you have any complaint against anybody, make it now. We'll listen."

"You," Beckwith growled. "You . . . Henry Chatillon. I know you, you damn liar. You're a cheat! A thief!" To make sure the insult struck home, he added, "Squaw!"

"You going to prove I cheated you?"

With a movement so rapid that Parkman didn't even see it, Beckwith jerked a bowie knife from his belt. He lunged at Chatillon, who stepped quickly aside.

Beckwith turned, ready to attack again. But in that moment Chatillon had moved to Parkman, took back his rifle and shoved the long smoothbore barrel into Beckwith's stomach. Beckwith stopped cold, the knife still clutched in his hand.

Some members of the crowd muttered. It didn't seem fair, a rifle against a knife. They had come to see a fight, and though all sorts of dirty tricks were accepted, even applauded, this one robbed them of their fun.

Chatillon's voice was as deliberate as before, though it had taken on an edge. "I didn't come to fight. And I will kill only if I have to. There will be no lying or cheating by me or the people I work for. Make your complaint!"

"Brave . . . rifle against knife," Beckwith sneered. "All right. Drop the knife."

Beckwith hesitated. The rifle barrel jabbed into his belly. "Drop it! I'll get rid of the rifle," Chatillon said.

Beckwith let the knife fall. Chatillon kicked it away and passed the rifle to Parkman. Then he turned to face Beckwith again. "All right. Again. Who cheated you? And don't keep us here all day."

Beckwith had never heard that Chatillon was good at wrestling, whether bears or men, and Beckwith had had to wrestle both, using the knee in the groin and the thumb in the eye with the men, and an ax with the bear. He had not lost. He took a step forward.

Chatillon warned in that same calm tone, "If you try to fight me I will break your arm. If you try a knife or gun I will kill you. Are you going to talk or not?"

Beckwith stood stunned, and then shook with outrage. "I am their guide! I am! They hired me. We agreed! I helped them buy horses!"

"You helped steal those horses!" Shaw piped up.

"Who says that? Who says that to Beckwith? Say that to my face!"

Again, Chatillon moved between Beckwith and the two Bostonians. "Did you tell Jim Beckwith he could be your guide?" he asked the two men.

"No," Shaw said. "You know we hired you for a guide."

"Before you hired me, did you agree Beckwith could lead you?"

"No!"

"I have witnesses," Beckwith boasted. His eyes rolled. His sweeping arm seemed to include more than half the press of onlookers. "I have dozens of witnesses who will swear!"

"We have a right to take who we want," Shaw said.

"I would not interfere if you had promised some-one else first," Chatillon said.

Parkman looked at him with surprise. "What if we changed our minds? Particularly after what happened to our horses?"

"Then you would have to settle with him first. I would not break an agreement."

"We never promised him anything," Shaw insist-ed. He turned toward Parkman for confirmation.

Parkman wanted to be fair. "He may have un-derstood—"

"We did not hire him! And after our horses were stolen by those Indians who knew—who I'm sure were told where we were going to be. . . ." The enor-mity of the whole idea overcame Shaw. He shook. "Scoundrel!" he yelled at Beckwith.

"Liar!" Beckwith shouted back, shaking his fist.

"Why should you want to go with them, if they don't want you?" Chatillon said reasonably.

"I don't need them! I don't need anybody!" Beckwith kicked up dust with his feet. He raised his fists, this time to the heavens. "But I will not be cheated! I want my money. They promised! They lied about me to Captain Collins, so I have nobody now! I will have my money!"

Parkman felt his bowels griping. He hadn't been feeling well before. Maybe it was the food or the dust. And then today's excitement, the walking, the heat, the arm around his throat. Wouldn't it be easier to make an arrangement of some kind? Perhaps the man really thought. . . . Rather than stay around and have this sickness, this unpleasantness. Then he remembered the new boots on Beckwith, and the stolen equipment from Collins . . . the horses. . . . "He has been paid enough already," Parkman said. He turned to Chatillon. He was pale and sweating, and afraid that he would be sick openly, in some particularly unpleasant way. "Please . . . Mr. Chatillon . . . can we get out of here somehow?"

"Then you are convinced that you made no arrangement with Beckwith?"

"No!" Shaw shouted. Parkman's answer was softer, both in wording and in tone, which was starting to waver: "No. I sincerely believe we did not."

"Because they lie, will I get no justice?" Beckwith was carried away by his own performance and the drama in his mind. He shook, but he controlled his gestures. "Chatillon, I'll kill you. . . ."

Chatillon watched him steadily. "If I thought you told the truth, I would not lead them. I would advise them not to take you, but I would not go myself.

But I know you, Jim. And I have not seen them lie yet."

The two faced each other again. The old tableau, Parkman thought, like watching some repetitious nightmare of his childhood. He did not know if he could stand it. But Beckwith looked more dangerous now than he had before.

On the edge of the crowd Delorier made a small clucking sound, and a strap slapped softly on a rump. "Excuse me," Delorier said, and the cart moved forward into the crowd. One man reached for the small Canadian, but the others parted, rather than have crushed feet. In a moment he and his mules were in the inner circle, close to the antagonists. Beckwith had to step back to avoid the cart. "I am sorry, but we have much work to do, and little time," Delorier said.

Beckwith's oath blistered the air. While the crowd moved restlessly and laughed, Beckwith jumped for the heads of the mules to grab the reins. Delorier twitched his straps and the mules jerked their heads up and turned away from Beckwith, who had to jump back to avoid the cart's wheels again.

The cart now separated Beckwith and Chatillon. Beckwith was still swearing, but Parkman thought it unlikely that he would try anything very serious. He didn't try very hard to get around to Chatillon. And, of course, there was little to be gained: Beckwith would have realized by now that there was little money he was likely to get, at least by argument and threats. He might want revenge, but a head-on fight with Chatillon was not the best way. If they could avoid humiliating him before this rough audience. . . . If they could get through the day. . . .

He closed his eyes at a stab in his bowels and

he could feel the sweat breaking out on his forehead. When he opened his eyes he seemed to be looking through a fog. I'm not that sick, he thought. The sweat is in my eyes. He saw Chatillon looking at him. Beckwith was threatening Delorier, while the muleskinner was rolling his eyes and shrugging. The cart managed to hold the trapper off. Delorier was in no immediate danger. Chatillon came over to Parkman and took the rifle from him. He said, "All right. We will leave. There is no more we can do here."

He began to shoulder his way through the crowd, holding Parkman's arm, like a good shepherd. Shaw marched on the other side of Parkman, glancing fiercely on both sides.

"You run away?" Beckwith called from the other side of Delorier's cart. He tried to get around. "Coward! You run away from Jim Beckwith?"

Jean Delorier swung the cart quickly around, leaving Beckwith blocked off behind it, and followed the others. The crowd parted more quickly before his mules than they had before Chatillon.

"Coward!" Beckwith called. "You will not fight Beckwith?"

Parkman turned toward Chatillon. Even through the beard he could see the muscle ridges from the man's clamped teeth. But the guide said nothing and kept on. Delorier had tied Chatillon's horse to a post and they closed the distance toward it, Parkman thankful for each step. He felt Shaw stiffen and start to turn. He muttered, "Forward, Quincy, please!"

"Cowards!" Beckwith called and began to laugh hoarsely. One or two voices in the group took up the cry. They were still unwilling to be robbed of their fight.

Chatillon unhitched his horse and swung onto it

with one easy motion. He turned and surveyed the crowd calmly. The momentary anger had apparently subsided. He was analyzing the situation, coolly and quickly. It would be a rare rage that would sweep him into foolish action.

"You will not stay here tonight," he decided. "We have a place. You will go to your rooms and get your belongings. We will watch."

They did not go directly through the crowd, but went along its fringes. Chatillon rode closest to the edge, his rifle on the saddle. Delorier swung his cart close to the railings before the shops, so that it could carry the luggage. Chatillon stopped before the tavern door.

"Most of our belongings are still at the docks," Parkman said. It would not take long to vacate the rooms.

"All right. We will get those later."

"Cowards! Run away!" Beckwith repeated.

Parkman and Shaw went into the tavern and up to their rooms as quickly as they could without seeming to run. Through the window they could hear more taunts from Beckwith, and a rising response from the crowd. They hurried down, paid their bill and then hurried out.

The crowd had moved over to Delorier and Chatillon. Beckwith was still shouting defiance. "I will have my money. You hear me, Chatillon? I will be paid! I will find you. Hear me?"

Shaw and Parkman hurriedly put their belongings in the cart. Shaw helped Parkman into it and then climbed in too.

The crowd pressed closer. Chatillon lifted the rifle and fired it into the air. In that narrow street, in the brief space between the crowd and the building, the big buffalo rifle's roar was earsplitting. The crowd stepped back. "This gun has two shots," Chatillon threatened.

They began to canter down the street, not rapidly, not in flight, but faster than the crowd could follow. "We won't go where Beckwith can find us," Chatillon said. "We'll choose another place." The cart jolted. Parkman wondered if he could ask Delorier to stop or to take it easy.

They came to the small log stable where the other horses were being held. They went inside and closed the door behind them. Chatillon and Delorier examined the horses and conferred in a low tone. Delorier nodded and went out. They heard him cluck to the mules, and then the cart creaked away.

Parkman sat down on the straw-strewn floor, leaning against the rough log walls, while Chatillon and Shaw tended and saddled the horses. They had to wait for what seemed to Parkman a long while. Sometimes they heard voices outside, or hoofbeats and horses neighing. Chatillon lit a candle. There was little chinking between the logs and he was afraid that the light could be seen outside, so periodically, when the noises came close, he shielded it, and once put it out altogether. He seemed to know which noises might pose a danger and which would not.

Perhaps Parkman dozed. He wasn't sure how long they'd been in the stable when he heard the mules outside. Delorier was back. He came in and he and Chatillon conferred for half a minute.

Parkman rose. Delorier came over to him. "All your luggage is in the cart. I think it better, though, that you ride the horse."

His horse, Pontiac, had a Spanish saddle, with high, stiff edges, front and back, and when he had been helped into it he was grateful for the extra support it gave.

They came out into the dark, fragrant with spring flowers and the smoke of distant campfires. They picked their way down a hillside, leaving the mayhem of the town behind them. Parkman's horse made its way, without direction from him, around a boulder he didn't see until they were brushing against it. At the bottom of the hill they waded across a creek and then climbed up another hill. They drifted on, in limbo in the moonless night. Suddenly campfires and people appeared in a little valley before them. He realized where they were. It was one of the emigrant encampments that he and Shaw had passed on their trip to Independence.

The wagons had been drawn up in a circle to keep the livestock from straying. Their tents were inside the circle, out of sight of people passing on the road. They went to the tents and unloaded. Most of the people in the camp nodded to them but paid little attention, being busy tending the livestock or the children, preparing food, or loading the wagons and tying their belongings down if they were due to leave in the morning. A few of the men came up to them. One touched his sweat-stained hat with a gnarled forefinger and said to Delorier, "These the Christian gents you talked about?"

"Ah, *oui*," Delorier answered enthusiastically, "these are the gentlemen from Boston in the East!"

The man took off his hat. The one next to him took the hint and removed his also. The flickering firelight brought their gaunt features into sharp relief.

"We'd be mighty pleased if you'd eat with us." The rough voice was suddenly apologetic, "Such as it is."

Their food would be coarse and probably unclean,

and Parkman's stomach rebelled at the thought. He looked, with pale appeal, at Chatillon. Chatillon nodded. What did that mean?

Chatillon said, "Thank you, sir. We accept. And we will bring some of our own food to make sure no one goes hungry. You did not expect so many guests."

The men made noises of polite protest, but Parkman felt that if they had eaten without contributing, somebody, perhaps children or the men themselves, would have done without.

"Mr. Parkman," Chatillon said, "is a little ill. Perhaps he should rest."

The men insisted the food would be good for him and so they ate at one of the fires outside the ring of wagons. The food, a kind of stew, mostly beans, was dipped from a ladle from a black pot on a tripod over the fire. Delorier tasted it, then rose to give advice and directions to the woman handling the ladle. She paid no attention to him, so he shrugged and left her alone. Shaw and Chatillon ate well and presented gifts of food to be cooked later. Parkman ate little. Delorier sighed again, added seasonings from a small box and ate a moderate amount.

"Goin' to California or to Oregon?" one of the men asked.

They were going to neither place. How to explain that to these people, without causing needless complications? Parkman wondered. They would certainly never understand his desire to live with Indians—unless, of course, he was traveling as a missionary. They waited for his answer. "We're going on the Oregon Trail," he replied at last.

The man closest to him smiled and slapped his back. "We travel with you then!"

Parkman looked in alarm at Chatillon, who raised

his finger to indicate that he should keep calm.

Finally, the meal was over. They gave their thanks and could leave. They went outside the circle into the bushes to relieve themselves. They washed hands and faces in a nearby brook that Parkman was afraid might be polluted from so many people.

He went, or was led, to the bigger of their two tents. Chatillon said he liked to see the stars and would sleep outside. He arranged his blankets and put his gun beside them. Parkman asked him, weakly, about what the man had said about traveling with them. Chatillon told him not to be concerned. They were the ones who decided when and where they went.

Parkman said he was sorry that he couldn't help more. He hadn't been able to think clearly lately.

It had all been taken care of, Chatillon said, or could be taken care of at Fort Leavenworth. What was most important now was to sleep. Chatillon lay down himself. He didn't take off his moccasins and his gun lay in easy reach.

Shaw was fussing around in the tent with a small, shaded lantern. He came to the entrance to see where Parkman was and then held the flap open for him.

There were the blankets, the familiar hard, grey bolster, waiting for him. Shaw put out the candle. Parkman started to slide into sleep as soon as his cheek felt the bolster, and he was fully asleep after one long, slightly shuddering sigh.

Chapter 6

He felt as if he had just closed his eyes, that he had
hardly slept at all, when he was awakened by Chatillon. It was still dark.

"I am sorry, Mr. Parkman. I think we should
leave now," Chatillon said.

Parkman got up on his elbows. He was a little
dizzy, but surprised that he didn't feel any worse. There
was a muffled oath, quickly stifled, as Shaw was wakened close by, and he heard Quincy heave to a sitting
position. Parkman sat up, too. The air smelled of the
clear chill of morning, clean, without campfire smoke
or dust.

He put on his boots, got to his feet and held
on to the canvas flap at the tent entrance to be sure
he was steady. Shaw bumped into him and said, "Oof!
Sorry, old man."

He heard the muted shuffling of hooves and a
mule snort. The air filled his lungs. He shivered slightly,
found his coat in the cart and put it on. Delorier, in
the cart, bade him good morning. "I'll go in and pack
your blankets." The muleskinner returned a moment
later with the blankets. Shaw went into the bushes and
Parkman followed.

When they returned, Chatillon was waiting silently with the horses, saddled and ready to go. Parkman
drank the air in long drafts. He was still a little unsteady, but the illness and nausea of the night before
seemed past, at least for the time being. Why were
they leaving so suddenly and so early? Well, he was
sure Chatillon had his reasons.

Parkman could see only one fire, and one sleepy
guard sitting by it. He could not quite see Chatillon's
face, but he saw that it was turned toward that guard
and he thought he could see the head shake a little.
The emigrants would have to do better than that on
the trail.

The tent came down quickly and silently and
was folded and put into the cart. Shaw mounted and
Parkman mounted immediately after him. Chatillon
moved ahead a little, rose in his stirrups to look down
the road, and then, in the opposite direction, toward
a path through the bushes. The guard, finally hearing
a noise of some kind as one of the horses stamped
and gave a soft neigh, looked toward them, saw that
it was only the strangers, nodded and turned back to
the fire.

Chatillon moved into the narrow path and they
followed, the cart rocking with a slight creak on the
uneven ground at the rear.

Once more they traveled on ground he could not
see, yet with purpose and confidence. They went down
a hill, then up another. The stars seemed close; a quarter moon descended in the sky before them. They
seemed to be going west, but he couldn't be sure.

The branch of a tree stung his cheek. They were
following a path, cutting back and forth down a long
hill. Chatillon, in the lead, not only had to find the
path, but make sure that the others, particularly a

loaded cart drawn by mules, could follow. Behind him Parkman could hear Delorier reciting, in soft sing-song, his litany of French curses at the mules.

Behind them, dawn began as a soft glow on the horizon. Soon it was lighter around the travelers.

They waded into a shallow stream, one of the minor tributaries that moved toward the Missouri River. They moved upstream so that no trace of their progress would be left behind even for the experienced eyes of trappers or Indians to detect. It was slow going. Trees hung over the water, sometimes cutting off their view of each other. It grew light. The stream turned left and at the bend had built a little pebbled beach and sandbar. The cart stuck in the mud. Delorier's curses were no longer whispered. Chatillon and Parkman rode back, tied ropes to the tongue at the side of the straining mules, and helped to pull it out. They pulled up on the sandbar, then moved off, in the brightening light, west into the plains.

Parkman fell back to talk to Delorier. "Why did we leave so early?" he asked.

Delorier shrugged. "I didn't ask. I think, I think Henry wanted not to be in camp in daylight."

"Was Henry worried? I mean, thinking that Beckwith and his gang might find us?" Parkman asked.

Delorier smiled and shrugged again. "There might be many unpleasantnesses." He lingered on the s's. "Henry might be thinking, would Monsieur Parkman and Monsieur Shaw like to stay with that wagon train and sing hymns all day? Marry that man's ugly daughter? And then, you know, we could meet Indians, like you did, funny Indians close to Westport?" He tapped the mules' rumps gently with his strap and they stepped up the pace a bit. "My beauties, eh?"

The sun was up, but it was not hot yet. The trees

were thinning out, and the great seas of grass seemed to stretch unbroken before them, undulating in the wind. The stream had doubled back and they were not far from it. Trees, except for a very few solitaries, grew only along the water on the Great Plains, and you could tell the paths of streams—and the presence of water and of good camping ground—miles away by a line of sycamores and cottonwoods winding through the grass.

Delorier broke into song and then became garrulous. "I think Henry feels, Why have this Westport unpleasantness when we can have"—he waved his free hand toward the horizon—"this pleasantness? Better to get up a little early, get an early start. *N'est-ce pas?* Especially since I think he is in a little hurry."

"In a hurry?"

"I think, you know, he wants to get back to Laramie. Important reasons. I think he hear something." He retreated a little. "I think. Don't say I said."

Other responsibilities began to concern Delorier. He glanced at the line of trees that they were gradually leaving behind and frowned. He was the cook and he hadn't been able to cook for them yet. "It has been a long time. I think we should eat while there is water and shade. Yes?"

Chatillon had apparently concluded the same thing, because he had stopped. His heavy rifle had been on his arm, ready for use. Now he let it rest against the high pommel of his worn saddle, and trotted back toward them.

He and Delorier understood one another. They pointed, almost simultaneously, toward a copse of trees around a pool formed at a bend in the stream. They turned their horses in that direction. When they arrived, Parkman and Shaw dismounted stiffly. Delorier raced around, building the fire, greasing the skillet. Soon the smell of frying made them all sit up. It was a quick meal, fresh eggs and milk and bacon. They rested under the trees as they ate their first meal on the trail. Parkman that night wrote in his journal, "All the trees and saplings were in flower, or budding into fresh leaf; the red clusters of the maple-blossoms and the rich flowers of the Indian apple . . . and I was half inclined to regret leaving behind the land of gardens. . . ."

He had, before coming on the trip, spent a lot of time hiking through forests and mountains. He had written of "the restlessness, the love of wilds and hatred of cities." The next few days, when he looked back at them later, seemed to him a particularly golden time—the sun on the waving grass, the fellowship, the sense of increasing well-being as he recovered health, the feeling of floating in time and space on this grassy sea.

Of their guide and hunter, Parkman wrote, "He was a proof of what unaided nature will sometimes do. I have never, in the city or in the wilderness, met a better man than my noble and true-hearted friend, Henry Chatillon."

Shaw followed close behind on a little sorrel horse leading a larger horse by a rope. He and Parkman were dressed for comfort and long wear: red flannel shirt belted around the waist, moccasins to replace the worn boots, buckskin pants made by a squaw in Westport and picked up by Chatillon as most serviceable. Each used a plain black Spanish saddle, carried holsters with heavy pistols and had a blanket rolled up behind.

Toward evening a hare, about twice as large as

the jack rabbits that Parkman knew from the East, broke from cover and ran across their path. Chatillon spurred his horse after the animal, cut him off as he tried to double back and shot him. "Not exactly like shooting buffalo," he said. He gave the carcass to Delorier for skinning.

They had the rabbit for supper. "That was great riding and shooting," Parkman said as they ate.

"Not me," Chatillon said, and nodded toward his horse. "All done by Five-Hundred-Dollar."

Parkman had heard Chatillon call his horse by that name before. He could not possibly have paid that much for him. "Why do you call him that?"

"Damn good horse. Worth that much to me." He looked out toward the twilight. The sun had just set. All afternoon, of course, the sun had been ahead of them, almost in their eyes. Parkman reflected that one of the least pleasant aspects of the trip might be that in the hottest part of the afternoon, they would be facing the sun. Chatillon continued, "Maybe we stop too early tonight. But this is good campground. Tomorrow we start early. Better always start early."

Parkman was already nodding. "We certainly started early enough this morning. Was there any particular reason?"

Chatillon kept looking toward the west. "I did not think we should wait. Caught in the crowd. I wanted to get clear early." He gestured toward the darkening vista ahead. "Many miles yet." He got up, laid out his blankets and then sat smoking awhile, humming softly.

In the morning they met their first Indian—a middle-aged man riding alone. His blanket and tunic were rather tattered, but he rode erect and with pride. He did not seem surprised to see them.

Delorier, walking alongside his beloved mules with a long cottonwood switch, brought his cart to a halt. Chatillon spurred ahead and called out a friendly greeting to the Indian.

They heard him laugh. Then he returned with the Indian who asked Chatillon a question. Chatillon smiled and pointed to Parkman. The Indian rode up and looked at him closely. The Indian smelled of heat and leather, nothing worse, and Parkman endured his close scrutiny.

The Indian straightened, his disdain for Parkman evident in his expression. He said to Chatillon, "No good! Too young!" And without another glance or word rode on his way.

Chatillon grinned. "He asked, who is my boss? I showed him you," Chatillon explained.

"Quite a compliment," Parkman muttered.

Shaw's face crinkled above his beard and his pipe. "Could be worse, Frank. Your face got any redder, he could've shot you for a Pawnee."

Parkman was not as ruddy as Shaw, but he realized that his face had felt hot all day. He wiped his brow, dampened his face with water from the canteen and pulled his broad-brimmed hat forward to do a better job of protecting it from the sun.

They traveled through a sea of grass, broken only by ravines, and barren, rocky areas caused by the recent drought. There was no shade or protection from the sun on the trail. A beautiful land, but with little mercy for the unprepared.

Parkman was used to the forests that covered the eastern third of the nation. This open country was different. He had seen nothing like it before—not in New England, not in Canada, not in Europe. Again he wondered about the wagon trains and those who rode with them. Most had been farmers or shopkeepers. Such people would have trouble facing this unending sun, the open plains in which they would be constantly slowed down by the grass, the hub-deep mud in the hollows and creek bottoms, while they remained open and visible to any Indians around for miles. Of course there were some hard experienced men. He had seen a number of leathery, hard-eyed Jed Smith types with their long strides and long rifles, but they, too, were creatures of the forests, where game, cover and rain were plentiful. How would they manage out here, where there was practically no game?

Parkman found he was not prepared for the weather either. They met their first prairie thunderstorm—and their hoped-for relief from the sun—that afternoon. They were riding serenely over a free and open prairie. The clouds were wispy bits of cotton. There was no breeze. The horses hung their heads in the heat. Then black thunderheads rose above the horizon. He watched them with a kind of lazy interest, wondering what they meant and why they seemed to be growing so fast. There came distant thunder and their horses snorted nervously.

The clouds rushed with spreading wings, shrouding half the sky as Parkman watched in astonishment. Ahead the prairie grass thrashed restlessly, and turned purple in the inky shadows. Then from the densest fold of clouds, lightning flashed, followed by a deafening blast of thunder. A cool wind, precursor of what was to come, struck them, smelling of rain, and the grass around them flattened as before a scythe, while the horses turned their backs and the men held on to their hats.

Chatillon, in front, waved toward a clump of trees around a muddy pond to their left and started for it. "Ride for it!" Shaw shouted, and rushed past at full speed, the horse he was leading tossing its head and snorting alongside. The whole party broke into full gallop, Delorier on the cart, lashing his mules.

They reached the trees and the meadow beyond, leapt from the horses, tore off saddles, and hastily hobbled the nervous animals before turning them loose. The cart came wheeling in, Delorier's curses adding to the general din. They got the tent poles up and then fought to anchor the canvas against the wind. They were able to get inside just as the storm struck. The rain fell in such torrents that the nearby trees disappeared from sight. The canvas flapped and strained and it seemed to Parkman that soon it had to give way. The earth could not carry away all the water and it began to leak in under the tent. They sat on their saddles and shivered together. Water dripped from their hats down their cheeks. Parkman had managed to get his India rubber cloak on, but Shaw's blanket coat soaked water like a sponge.

Delorier was the last in, having had the most to do. He stuck his head in first. His broad felt hat hung down around his ears at the same angle as his mustache. "Supper, messieurs?" he asked.

"Never mind supper, man! In out of the rain!"

He crouched in the entrance. "I do not think I could make a fire right now, but I could try."

The thunder, Parkman noted, was not like the tame thunder of the East. It was like all the world's artillery trained on their one little tent.

But it ended as quickly as it had come. The black clouds rolled past. A bright red streak appeared close to the western horizon and the low sun streamed through to make a thousand small rainbows on the dripping trees. The puddles in the tent began to recede, to soak into the ground. Distant thunder still grumbled, unforgiving. Above the horizon the clouds turned purple and began to break up.

Delorier was the first out. They found him already at his cart. His hat still dripped on his wet shoulders, but he started to haul his utensils out. He grinned. "Dinner, now, eh?"

They tended the shivering horses and mules, then came back to try to get warm and dry around the growing fire. Delorier's skillet began to sizzle.

In the morning they were on the way again. But much had changed. On the trail there seemed to be, especially in the low places, as much as six inches of mud and slime, through which they plowed and dragged the cart. They crossed one stream. It was swollen and running fast, but the cart got stuck in quicksand, and began to sink very rapidly. Chatillon, waiting on the opposite bank, rode back, and they hitched their separate horses to the tongue and the traces and pulled the cart out.

When they were finished and Delorier had washed some of the mud off the wheels and examined the load for damage, they sat a moment on dry rocks on the bank for a smoke. Parkman asked how dangerous quicksand was.

"Only once have I seen any creature die in quicksand," Chatillon said. "Every other time I have always seen them pull out. It is not a great danger. Only it is—what do you call it?"

"An inconvenience?"

Chatillon nodded.

"What about the one that did die?"

"That was not people," Chatillon said. "We got them out. It was oxen." He puffed a moment. "Oxen are very sad, I think. You think it may be because they are stupid? Would an ox be more stupid than a cow? I think they are sad, like they despair of their life. Maybe that is why the Indians do not like them. They do not fight the quicksand, like other animals. In the river quicksand is not deep enough to kill if you fight." He shook out his pipe and got up. "Not a great danger."

Pontiac nuzzled Parkman's hand, looking for a little of the brown sugar or a small slice of apple, but there was none. Parkman put his foot in the stirrup and mounted him. The horse was refreshed after its passage through the stream and eager to move. He let him gallop for a moment, running out ahead of the others, before reining him in. He waited for the others to catch up. The horses were dry by now and only part of the leather of the saddles was still damp.

Since the horsemen usually had to go a little slower than they would have liked because of the cart, Chatillon, as guide and security guard, often rode back and forth in front, looking for vantage points from which to examine the country around. It was obvious that he was on the lookout, probably for Indians. He had said that they could start looking for Indian trouble when they entered Pawnee country, but they hadn't yet reached it. But now, as they waited for Delorier and the cart, Chatillon remarked that it might not be a good idea for Shaw and Parkman to get far ahead or behind.

"Then you *are* afraid of Indians around here!"

"Not afraid."

Parkman was immediately sorry he had said it; Chatillon would probably not be *afraid* of Indians.

"Kansas Indians around here," Chatillon said. "They wait to rob. They prey on people alone. Not like Pawnee, Dakota or the others. Not anymore. They are very poor. You saw them in Westport. Often they beg or steal."

"But they wouldn't attack me with a gun out here," Parkman said.

"Maybe not. But if they thought you didn't know your way, they might." The cart caught up. Delorier waved his hat and they were off again. "Some of them, sometimes, I think they follow the wagon trails, maybe rob." Like wolves, Parkman thought, looking for a straggler.

"Don't the Pawnee and the rest also kill and steal?"

"Yes." Chatillon grinned. "But more like warriors."

And what he also meant, of course, was that their party was traveling close to the wagon trails, and the Indian scavengers would tend to gather in the neighborhood, alert for whatever pickings might be available.

Chatillon touched a strap to Five-Hundred-Dollar and moved ahead toward a slight rise from which he could look out over a wide swath of open prairie. Chatillon began to sing a sad song about a maiden lost and alone in the city. An odd thing to hear out in the open prairie.

Chapter 7

"This child's goin' back."—He no longer shouted the words. He repeated them quietly and they acquired a deeper, richer taste, like that liquor he had drunk in a fancy St. Louis hotel years before, the end of his best year. Labeled bottle with a wax seal. You remembered things like that. Goin' back. . . .

He had been thinking about it for a while. He could see in his mind's eye the white mountains, passes deep with snow and barely open, the frozen springs —and maybe the tracks of some bird or antelope he could eat or maybe a beaver shelter. There was something about sitting in a warm saloon and knowing it could be different that changed the way you looked at things. He straightened his stiffened leg. You could even admit things. Things like he was afraid of losing the rest of his toes and he was afraid of getting stuck and not being able to get to shelter or food. And he didn't give a damn who knew he was afraid. He was goin' back. But it would be different.

There were the good memories. Oh God, he remembered that night, bedded down in those soft, warm buffalo robes with that young squaw, naked as a jay-

bird and chirping like one too . . . the warm smells
. . . the snow outside . . . Oh God.

For a man like him, that was home, if there was
a home for him anywhere. He couldn't think of that
squaw's name now. If still alive, she would probably
be one of those hags in the Indian villages, scolding the
dogs and the children, building the lodges, carrying
wood and pounding pemmican. Old men were usually
honored in the villages, sitting in their lodges, telling
tales and smoking while the squaws did the work.
Well, it might not be altogether like that for him.
But it would be all right. It wouldn't be like being
sick and old with the white men where you could be
thrown sick and drunk out in the mud and the cold
and they'd let you lie there!

That Indian village. The rest of his life. A stake
to keep him going and enough skins for extra money.
All he needed. Just working enough to keep busy and
self-respecting. A new squaw. His own lodge.

Louis Gravoise tried to sit down with him but
he waved him off. He didn't belong here. He wanted
nothing here, except to be left alone.

Nat Gantt was waiting for Beckwith. Sooner or
later that son of a bitch would come. He had something Beckwith wanted, all right, something he'd be
sure to show up for—money. Beckwith would come
out of need, but also out of meanness.

Beckwith might be a little late. After the way
Chatillon had stood him off and then had slipped away,
it might not be such a good bragging time for him.
But he could always make something out of it that
would make him look good, Nat knew.

It was getting hot and hard to breathe in that
damned tavern. He got up and stamped out. The

thought struck him that Beckwith might have left town, but he would have heard about it. He was sure of that. Nat thought to catch up with Horse after the Indian had talked to Henry Chatillon, then get him drunk and pump him for information.

But the next day, when Nat didn't see Horse, he went out looking for him, and there wasn't a smell. Disappeared. Hole in the ground maybe sucked him straight to hell. Must have talked to Chatillon, then went right back. Never stopped to show a squaw how that fancy blanket looked spread out on the ground.

He went back inside the tavern. But this time he kept his glass before him and only sipped from it occasionally. He had to keep a clear head.

Beckwith came in late. Louis and most of the others had gone. Susie, one of the whores who worked out of the back rooms upstairs, was sitting at a corner table. The smoke was starting to thin out, though the stench hung on. Beckwith came in with two Indian friends. One, like Beckwith himself, was some kind of half-breed with a little mulatto thrown in. Beckwith told the man behind the bar to give the Indians what they wanted, but no more than two drinks. When the drinks came, he took bills, including some goldbacks, out of his pocket to pay for them. Goldbacks!

"Hey! Jim! Jim Beckwith!" Gantt called.

Beckwith didn't respond. He took his drink and went with the Indians to a table. None had been cleaned off, so he swept about half the contents off with his forearm. Bottles and glasses smashed on the floor. The owner yelled. Beckwith cursed him and began talking to the Indians.

The Indians reached for their drinks, but their hands stayed suspended until Beckwith had finished speaking, as though waiting for permission. He nodded and they grabbed their drinks.

"Jim Beckwith!" Gantt repeated.

This time Beckwith frowned a little. But now Jim was paying the two off, counting bills out on the table and Gantt didn't want to interrupt that.

The Indians had drunk the first drink fast, then gone back for the second. They had held up drinking that one to watch Beckwith count the money, though their hands kept straying back to the shot glasses. They snatched the money and fingered it, but it didn't seem to Nat that they really knew what they were getting. One had a breast pocket and jammed his few bills in. The other put his in his waistband. They threw down their second drinks and staggered to their feet. Then they waved at Beckwith and walked out.

He grunted a farewell. He left his money on the table in front of him. It was not usually a safe place, but Beckwith didn't seem worried that anybody would try to take it. He began to count, moving his lips.

He had *his* stake!

Nat spat on the floor. He waited. Beckwith finished counting, rolled the bills together bending over so that what he did wouldn't be obvious, tied them with a buckskin string and slipped them carefully into a small, blackened deerskin pouch. He looked suspiciously around the room and Gantt looked elsewhere. Beckwith would now, he knew, go through that business of hiding his poke in his secret place. Everybody knew it was hooked to his belt and dangling into his crotch and they could usually see it when he sat, making him look like a freak.

Gantt didn't wait to be summoned. He only waited until the poke was stowed. Then he got up, carrying his own drink, and walked boldly to the table. He sat down facing Beckwith. "I think I know where Henry Chatillon and them others went," Gantt said.

Beckwith examined him silently. "Where all the greenhorns go?" Beckwith guessed. "Oregon Trail, Platte River, maybe Fort Laramie." He shrugged his heavy shoulders.

"You think that's all?"

Once more that stolid, unwavering look. "What else?"

"You think Chatillon's just hangin' around Fort Laramie, huntin' buffler?"

"He'll be around. I'll catch him sometime."

Although Beckwith would fight Chatillon face to face if he felt he had to, as he had offered to do in the street outside, Nat didn't think he'd go out looking for that kind of fight. A shot in the back maybe, or lead a Crow raid on his camp. Sooner or later he would try to get his revenge.

"I hear them Dakota is gatherin'," Gantt revealed.

Beckwith looked up sharply. His eyes cut into Gantt. Gantt held the gaze, but he was worried. Maybe he'd said too much. Beckwith was no fool, he could figure it out as well as anybody. But then Nat relaxed a little. Sure, Beckwith would know something, but he wouldn't know much, and he wouldn't be able to figure out what it meant since he hadn't seen Horse.

"They could sure raise some hell among them Crow and Snake," Gantt added.

"What do you know?"

"Don't know everything. Have to get out on the road a little and look around some."

Beckwith snorted and looked away.

"Well, I wouldn't have to know much more. I

know the fur trade ain't gonna be worth the fleas in a donkey's ear if them Injuns fight. There won't be as many furs to buy from 'em, and with not so many furs, Bill Sublette ain't gonna be hirin' nobody to represent him in the trade." He took a deep breath. "But a war would help somebody. With less pelts around, them that there is is gonna be worth a whole lot more. Be the best years ever for somebody. Could be for us—I know where the beaver is, back in them mountains. If I got a stake, I'd get the furs. Be our best years."

Gantt eyed Beckwith, trying to judge the latter's reaction as best he could in such a whiskey haze. He seemed to have Beckwith hooked. But Gantt had another lure for him besides money—a chance to help his adopted tribe, the Crow. "Now a war between the Crow and the Dakota might help us, but I'm not so sure about the Crow . . . but then the Dakota, they drink and fool around a lot sometimes. Maybe if we was lucky, the Crow'd make out all right . . . and so would we."

Beckwith just glowered at him. "What you know?"

Stubbornly he said, "Where to find beaver."

"What else?"

He shrugged. "Dakota tribes comin' together."

"What Chatillon got to do with that?"

Nat smiled. "I ain't sure. Maybe nothin'."

Beckwith appeared to be calculating. "Where Chatillon goin'?"

"Where those greenhorns goin'. First."

"They say they just want to hunt buffler. Visit an Indian village."

Nat stretched his legs, as though making himself comfortable for a long stay. "Then I guess that's where Chatillon's going. First."

Without warning, Beckwith brought the flat of his hand down hard on the table. The glasses jumped. "What village? Whose?"

If Beckwith knew that Horse had come to see Chatillon, he would know what village Chatillon was going to. Knowing the recent history of Whirlwind and his dead son, and the rumor that the chief had called the other villages of the Teton Dakota to council, he would know why, and if not exactly why, close enough. Particularly if he remembered Chatillon's connection with that village.

"I guess he'd be going to Laramie first." That was safe enough, Gantt thought. But the word "first" rung in his ears, like a cracked bell, and he wished he hadn't said it.

Beckwith studied him. "We go back to Laramie tomorrow," he said suddenly. "You know where beaver is, I'll get you a stake there. Tomorrow morning."

Gantt exhaled slowly and smiled. It seemed a friendly smile, the kind that fixes agreements between partners.

"I'll be ready," he said.

Once they got to Fort Laramie, and Nat Gantt had his stake and the arrangement for the furs he brought in, maybe directly with the Rocky Mountain Fur Company, he didn't care what Beckwith did. Let Beckwith know the danger to the Crow; let him know that the man he hated might be helping the Dakota—a nation already larger and more warlike than any combination of Crow and Snake—become an efficient striking force. And let him know what village Chatillon was in, while it still might be vulnerable.

Nat Gantt would be in the mountains, among the beaver in this, his last year. War would not interfere with trapping, nor with the trading posts. But it would sure play hell with the competition.

"If he goes by the trail, by the Platte, maybe, on horseback, we can catch up to him," Beckwith said.

Nat hoped not, not before he got his stake at Laramie. But he nodded and smiled.

Beckwith usually traveled alone with an extra horse to carry his goods. He didn't pay anybody he didn't have to. Nat said, "My friend Louis Gravoise is goin' out too. We were goin' together." He hadn't asked, or more accurately, told Louis yet, but the Frenchy was almost always agreeable. He added, with a little belligerence, "He brings his own food."

Beckwith seemed to have lost interest. He merely nodded.

Nat had counted on Beckwith's greed to assure that those half-Indians he used in Westport didn't tag along, but he told Louis to be on the lookout, and that one of them would have to be awake at all times. Beckwith alone was enough of a handful.

"Why you worry?" Louis said one night in the tent on the trail. He was cleaning and oiling his Hawken rifle. "They'll be drunk for a week. I saw them already." He wiped off the front sight with spit and pointed the rifle at a fly on the wall of his tent. For a moment Nat thought Gravoise was going to shoot a hole in the tent, just for one of his Frenchy jokes. "See that fly? Could be a bison on the hill. Antelope. Maybe even Beckwith. Or a Pawnee scout, maybe a raiding party. They might attack, no?" He blew on a rust spot as though it were dust, rubbed it with his thumb and then raised the gun again. "Smart man take chances?" That front sight still followed the damn fly, and Nat was sure he was going to blast the tent. "You worry too much," Gravoise said. He lowered the Hawken.

They'd been making such good time—Beckwith and Gravoise both on horses leading young mules that carried their goods—that Nat, on his old mule, had been having trouble keeping up. Chatillon and his bunch had a start of at least two days. Gantt had been sure they would not catch up, but now he was less certain. Delorier had a slow-moving cart, and it was probable also that the greenhorns would pause to hunt and explore.

Nat spat. He had a chaw that he gummed where his back teeth used to be to fight the dust. The plain shimmered green and yellow before them. Clouds scudding before the wind threw shadows that sailed like swift ships, distorted by the waving grass.

Gantt was sure Chatillon wouldn't lose any more time than he had to. Unless Horse had told him there wasn't any particular hurry. Which could mean what? Whirlwind wasn't ready yet? But in that case, why did Horse risk the trip? The greenhorns wouldn't argue too much about getting to Laramie as soon as possible, if that's where they were going. At least that would be their jumping-off place if they meant to follow the Oregon or California Trails farther.

"Wah-hoo!" Gantt shouted, just to see if he could scare up any varmints out of the grass. If there were any rabbits, maybe Louis would shoot one. No use. If the horses, mules and Louis' singing hadn't scared them, nothing could.

He hadn't been trying to pick up Chatillon's trail, but on the second day, in a muddy creek bottom, he found unmistakable signs. Mules do not leave the same hoofprints as horses and oxen, and Delorier's cart left different tracks from those of the broad, steel-rimmed wagon wheels. Beckwith saw them too. They had stopped to rest and water the horses and chew on a little dried beef. Nat made an elaborate act of looking away, and then squinting as though the sun had injured his one good eye. For a moment he thought to walk over the marks, but that wouldn't get rid of them, and it would only attract Beckwith's attention. Not that Beckwith would have missed them anyway, especially not since Louis had chosen to stand right by them while urinating into the water, whistling through his teeth. Beckwith studied the marks a moment, but said nothing. He turned back to his chewing. He was almost as good an actor as Nat.

So they had found the tracks. From then on he could see Beckwith looking for signs as he rode, and every so often changing direction very slightly, following something.

Nat began to feel sore right where it would keep getting sorer. This blasted mule was getting as old, tired and ornery as himself, and as skinny. It had a back like a picket fence. He shouted, "Hey, how 'bout stoppin' awhile!" Beckwith paid no attention.

Actually he stepped up the pace. Louis, as Nat might have expected, appreciated the change because he was bored. He bawled out Nat for holding them up. "Ride that Nellie! She's not for making love!"

They reached the ford of the Kansas River at noon the next day. The river, though still swollen, was down from the high mark caused by the recent heavy rains. They could see more than two feet of fresh mud on the usually dry, grassy banks. This was the easiest ford on this part of the river. Even so, some of the wagons had had trouble. There was debris around, including an abandoned barrel and some planks. Downstream was a broken wagon, partly submerged, and a dead ox, partly eaten by varmints. Older prints and marks had been largely washed clean by the rising water, but there were plenty from the recent passage. That must have been a sight, Nat thought, all them greenhorns hollering and whipping their mules and oxen in the wrong direction, and the women screaming and falling in. He saw some sodden cloth, brown with mud, hooked on a snag. Looked like a petticoat.

Beckwith rode up and down on one side of the river, looking closely for markings. He then crossed the river and took up his search again. Louis Gravoise was only a few feet behind him. They had to wait a while for Nat. The old mule, having shorter legs, had to flounder about in the current for a longer stretch and Nat thought he might sink. The cool water soothed his tortured flesh at first, but then the grit got into the seams and irritated it more. When he came out on the other side, Beckwith was sitting erect in his saddle watching him. The look was steady and cold.

"I don't think Chatillon crossed here," Beckwith said.

"Well, where else would he cross on this cussed and blasted river!" The pain from his sores gave his words an added fervor.

"I don't know." He kept looking at Nat.

"Well, what consarn fool would try to cross anywhere else, and this mudbath so high? Tell me that!"

The logic might have been perfect, but the red eyes were still hard on him. He had gotten half of his stake from Beckwith before starting out because he needed supplies and traps. Beckwith had said he would get the rest only when he came back to Laramie with some evidence of beaver and information about Chatillon's whereabouts. At least Beckwith had parted with *some* money and would have to come up with the rest in time or lose the beaver. But now, under that gaze, on the pretext of adjusting his moccasin, Nat reached down to his right foot in the space where his toes used to be to check for what he had left of the stake. The little pouch felt sodden, but it was there. When he glanced up, Beckwith had turned his back and was moving on.

Beckwith called a halt early that evening. Following a detour he knew, they had come onto a pond surrounded by a small forest. It was a little off the main trail. The greenhorns probably hadn't seen it, so it ought to be clean enough. Nat was glad to get off Nellie and she was glad enough for him to get off. Like the horses, once the saddle was off her, she lay down and rolled over and rubbed her back in relief. Nat had some tallow in his bag. "This child sure wishes he had bear grease!" he said. He would use the tallow on his own sore spots once he got his breeches off and ready for the night.

The lowering sun picked up some white specks on a rise visible through the trees. He closed his left eye and saw that they were whitened buffalo skulls arranged in a rough ring. It was one of the old circles the Indians had set up as medicine to bring the buffalo herds back. The white man had driven the buffalo away from this part of the territory some time ago, but it indicated that this camping ground had not been used much. He told himself that if he ever came this way again, he would stop here. But why should he come again? He wasn't going to come back. He was going to lie out in the open tonight, rub that tallow around his sore thighs and family jewels, and think long thoughts about that Indian village, its hunting, its buffalo meat and its squaws.

Beckwith had a tent he slept in every night. Nat had crawled into it the one night it rained, but Beckwith threw him out in the morning when he found him there. Beckwith didn't smell so good anyhow so, all in all, he would much rather sleep in the open on fine nights, with his blanket and his waterproof under that. By God, a fellow who used to sleep in a buffalo robe in a trench dug in the snow on the lee side of a bluff didn't need any Westport white canvas tent! The old fellow ain't gone yet! In the morning there might be dew on the robe and his face, but that was all right, it was the only really fresh water and wash he got, and he wished Jim Beckwith would get at least that much.

Louis Gravoise came over and squatted down by him after they had eaten and while he was rubbing himself down with the tallow. Beckwith had gone to his tent. The Frenchy leaned on his Hawken and watched him solemnly for a minute or two. This annoyed Nat. Out on the trail, sometimes for months, you watched out if a partner started looking at you like that, though he had never heard that Louis had any leanings that way. Still, he wasn't an American.

"Like what you're lookin' at?" he snapped. "Never seen none before?"

"What you think?" Gravoise asked.

"What I think about what, you damn foreigner?" He was tired, his wounds still smarted, he'd sat through a lousy meal in which Beckwith wouldn't say a word, and he wasn't going to put up with anything.

Gravoise touched a forefinger to his lips. Nat dropped his voice. "Well speak up, you damn fool!"

" 'Bout Jim Beckwith."

Now that he thought about it, Nat decided he really didn't know much about Louis Gravoise. He was a drinking friend, a man that fixed him up with a squaw once, but not much more. For one thing, the man had strange nocturnal habits. He didn't seem to sleep much. Often Nat would wake up in the night and see Louis sitting on his blankets smoking a pipe. Nat would tell him crossly that any half-blind Pawnee or even Kansas could see the glow half a mile away. Often he would be off prowling among the animals. Frenchies had funny habits. When asked, he said he liked to look at the night and somebody ought to be standing guard. Sometimes Nat caught him nodding in the saddle, catching up on his sleep that way.

"What 'bout Beckwith?"

"You think he's acting funny?"

"Just mean as usual."

"I don't know." Silence again. Leaning on that damn rifle.

Nat suddenly kicked out, knocking the rifle stock out from under Gravoise's arm so that he fell forward.

"Hey! You could kill me!"

"Then talk, damn your Frenchy soul! What're you worked up about Beckwith for now? You know somethin' you ain't tellin' me?"

Once more Louis touched that dirty finger to his lips and dropped his own voice. "I don't know. Somethin's happenin'."

"What?"

"Don't know. Don't feel right."

"You must know somethin' you ain't sayin'. Now don't give me any of that magical stuff, Louie."

Louis sighed. "You think you could trust him this whole trip? I been waitin' to see him like a rattler."

He thrust out his hand with a whiplike motion, then yanked it back quickly. "I think we better go some-where, Nat."

"Go? Where, consarn you?" Get up and go again, at night, tonight?

"Somewhere. Maybe close. Just wait and watch."

Nat shook his head. "You worried about Beck-with, mean like a snake? And how he's gonna be when he wakes up and finds we're gone? How's he gonna be then? You're tryin' to make him mean and crazy as you!" He was up on his elbows now and Louis raised his whole hand to his mouth in alarmed warn-"Go on if you want to! Go on!"

Louis Gravoise looked at Beckwith's tent, then at the pond. He got to his feet. "Better if you come, Nat. Not far. Just sleep someplace different, someplace he don't know 'bout. Come back in the mornin'."

Nat turned his back in disgust. He didn't even want to talk about it. Just because Louis couldn't sleep didn't mean that Nat couldn't. The Frenchy just want-ed to walk around all night and wanted company. He sighed heavily. He knew all about Beckwith and never trusted him, of course. But he had a few things Beck-with wanted and he was all right until that mean bas-tard got them.

Louis was quiet in those moccasins, but still Nat heard him fool around a little, waiting, before he finally left. But Nat knew he'd be back, shaking him awake again at dawn. Frog son of a bitch.

So he wasn't surprised when he was shaken awake. But it was too soon and too hard. Something cold and sharp pressed against his throat and his eyes popped open. Beckwith had a knife pressing firmly against his throat.

Somebody was yanking his loosened breeches off him roughly and each tug brought that knife deeper into his skin. Nat could feel the blood starting to trickle down his neck.

"Got it?" Beckwith growled to somebody.

Nat heard the voice of one of Beckwith's half-Indians saying, "Not in pants."

The knife bit deeper, and unable to speak, he opened his mouth in a silent cry.

"Where's that stake?"

But he couldn't speak. The knife bit deeper. He pointed toward his right moccasin. They had taken it off to yank down the breeches. His foot was dropped. In a moment the guttural voice said, "Here."

He heard Beckwith swear. He was probably angry because there wasn't more left. "All right, I take everything else, too. Where's that beaver? Where!"

Nat tried to point toward the knife, to signify that he couldn't speak, but somebody trampled his hand into the ground. Beckwith must have gotten the message because he let up a little.

"Where!"

"Co-Co-Copper Lake."

"Okay. Now." The knife pressed tighter, then loosened to let him speak. "Where's Chatillon goin'?"

Blood ran down Nat's neck and reached his chest. His voice grated. His throat felt like scraped meat. "Whirlwind."

"Whirlwind? Whirlwind village?"

He tried to nod. Maybe Beckwith understood. The fuzziness from his eyes was spreading and tightening across his brain.

"Where is Whirlwind village?"

He shook his head to mean he didn't know. The

knife cut into him and the warm blood soaked his chest. He gulped for air and could still get some down, but it didn't seem to matter much.

In the distance, no longer of great importance to him, that familiar gravelly voice said, "You got the Frenchy?" followed by some kind of answer that resulted in "Good!" from Beckwith. "Not hard, was it?"

Another voice asked, "Scalp him?"

"Leave'm to the Pawnee."

But they must have tried because, when the fog in his brain was so thick that it seemed impossible that anything could come through, there was a flash over his half-blind left eye. Then no more pain.

Chapter 8

Chatillon was scouting ahead as usual and had ridden to a slight rise. Delorier and his cart were stuck in a hollow and the muleskinner was trying to use persuasion, rather than a whip, on his mules. Shaw and Parkman circled around him, shouting encouragement, but giving him little real help.

They heard Chatillon shout and Parkman was able to turn fast enough to see him fire his rifle into the air. Then he and Five-Hundred-Dollar disappeared beyond the rise.

Parkman whipped Pontiac and he and Shaw went pounding over the small hill and down the other side after Chatillon. There were two wagons by a creek, one apparently stuck in the mud. It was a small party, consisting mostly of women or girls. Three Indians were mounting their ponies quickly, trying to get away before Chatillon arrived. Two were already kicking their ponies, but the third, who was trying to lead another horse by its bridle, was having more trouble getting started.

Chatillon yelled something resembling a Dakota war cry. He was bent low, holding his rifle out ahead, and charged down the hill like a flying arrow.

What the Indians had been doing before Parkman saw them, he could not be sure. One of the females and what looked like an old man were on the ground. The woman got up and reached to help the man. The Indians did not go straight ahead, but bore to the left. Chatillon rode in a wide curve in that direction in an attempt to head them off.

The two in front might possibly have been too far ahead of Chatillon to be caught, but the one in the rear had made a slow start and, pulling another horse behind him, was having trouble catching up. He kept glancing fearfully back at the bellowing Chatillon. Parkman started shouting and Shaw's bass rumble took it up, so that they must have sounded like the advance guard of the cavalry. The last Indian released the stolen horse, kicked the sides of his pony and rode as fast as he could straight ahead. The Indians split up and Chatillon slowed his pursuit. He contented himself with picking up the stolen horse. Parkman and Shaw reached the wagons just before Chatillon came trotting up, leading the horse by its bridle.

Parkman leapt off Pontiac, shouted "Whoa!" and kept hold of the reins to control the surging animal. He saw that it was a young girl who was helping the fallen man to his feet. Both were smeared with mud. They turned and he saw with mild astonishment that it was the same girl who had rescued Shaw from the clutch of the small boy in Westport. And when the old man got to his feet, Parkman saw that it was the same bent and limping old fellow they had met after their horses were stolen and who had asked them to stay to help a family whose male head had died. Their guess at the time, that the family consisted of this girl, her mother and the other children, was obviously correct. The faces of two girls appeared in the opening at the back of the nearest wagon. A woman got down from the front. She was carrying a squirrel rifle with a barrel longer than she was and was holding it with difficulty. She pointed it at Parkman and Shaw, moving it shakily from one to the other.

Shaw, too, had gotten down from his horse and started toward the wagons. When he saw the gun pointing at him, he stopped abruptly. "I say!"

"Madame," Chatillon said, "these are the gentlemen who rescued you. And I have a bigger gun." He slid off Five-Hundred-Dollar as she brought her rifle around toward him. He ducked under it and pushed it into the air. She pulled the trigger, but it was an old flintlock and it didn't fire.

"You didn't load it properly," Chatillon explained. "And with flintlocks, you must be sure the powder is dry. I'll show you." He had hold of the long barrel. Her head came up to his shoulder, but she still tried to wrestle the gun from him. He said, "I will show you later." In the struggle most of the powder fell from the pan. He knocked the rest out and let her have the gun.

The old man was on his feet, though he still leaned a little on the girl. "It's all right, Mrs. Fleshner. I know these fellas." Apparently he had been trying to speak for a while, but no one had heard him. "I know 'em! Met 'em back there in Westport. Told you 'bout 'em!"

"Strange way to greet people who want to help," Shaw muttered.

"Gun wouldn't fire," Chatillon said matter of factly. "I could see."

The woman appeared to be in her thirties. They married young in the country, Parkman remembered.

Her oldest child was about seventeen, he guessed. But there was a streak of grey in the woman's hair, which she wore in a bun, and deep lines around the mouth. She'd lost her figure to children, marriage and the years. She seemed suddenly to come apart. She fell against the side of the wagon and her daughter rushed to her side to help her.

"It's all right, Mrs. Fleshner," the old man repeated. "It's all right."

"Could have used that gun against those savages, 'stead of us," Shaw grumped.

Although he was closest, Chatillon didn't try to help the woman. Instead, he motioned Parkman to do so. Parkman held Mrs. Fleshner up on the other side so that he and the daughter were able to walk her forward. There was no place for her to sit in the trampled mud and so they just stood there, holding her awkwardly.

Parkman's old boots, such as they were, were back in the cart, because moccasins seemed more logical for riding. Now he could feel his feet sinking damply under him. He noted that the woman on the other wagon, obviously the old man's daughter, the same gaunt woman they had seen in the encampment back at Westport, had come down. Silent as ever, she stood back and watched.

"Now madam," Parkman said to the woman he was holding, "it's all right now. The Indians are gone."

The old man had regained his composure and come over to them. Bent and feeble as he was, he only had to say "Liz!" to the silent daughter and she came over and took Parkman's place.

The girl had been speaking softly to her mother. She now said to Parkman, "Thank you. We'll be all right now." They helped her onto higher ground, where the other wagon was, and Liz got a stool down for her.

"I'm sorry," Mrs. Fleshner said. She leaned back against the mud-encrusted wheel of the forward wagon and closed her eyes. She didn't cry.

The recovered horse had, in the disturbance, made another getaway. Chatillon jumped on Five-Hundred-Dollar and recaptured it in minutes. He tied the wanderer to a peg on the back of the rear wagon.

"Woman had a hard time." The old man slowly shook his head. "Her husband, Mr. Fleshner, he died just before we left. You knew."

"We knew," Parkman said. "Terrible mess."

"You have it easy, yourself, old father?" Chatillon asked. "Relatives of yours?"

"Did you stay behind to help?" Parkman asked.

"Well. Christian thing, maybe. Not exactly. Had trouble keeping up, too." He squinted up at the sky. Some patchy clouds had moved in front of the sun and their shadows scattered across the plains. The grass beneath the shadows started to move in the freshening breeze, so that shades of yellow, and then purple, were traveling along the waves. White tendrils of the old man's hair waved also. He was suddenly shaken by a rage that, for a spasm, seemed stronger than his weak frame could stand. "Damn Indians! Damn them Indians!"

"What did they try to do?" Parkman asked.

"Why they"—he moved his shaking hands forward and around as though words alone could not begin to carry the burden of what he had to say— "Why they hollered . . . and they stole the horse . . . and things! And they pushed . . . me and that little girl . . ." The hands moved and trembled. He stopped.

Chatillon nodded slowly as the man spoke and said nothing until he had finished. "Did you try to fight, old father?"

"Why . . . why . . ."

Chatillon's voice was soft. "I don't know, but I don't think they would have tried to hurt you. They were stealers, you know? Not warriors. They only want to steal. Scare a little, only. *If* you don't fight."

"They certainly seemed brutal enough," Shaw put in. His ire had now turned toward the Indians.

"Only steal, I think. Most times. You don't count coup against women and old men. Most times."

Chatillon looked toward the small cluster of women. The younger two had put down a box for Mrs. Fleshner to step on and were helping her over the back, through the parted canvas. She was trembling.

The daughter went inside with her mother. Standford's daughter, Liz, watched them a moment, then turned back toward the old man, her first responsibility.

Chatillon put his hand on the old man's shoulder. "You did fine. The Indians will be afraid to come around again." He motioned Liz to come and take charge of her father. She took his arm and muttered something. The old man nodded and went with her. "Go on, rest now," Chatillon said. "We got mules to pull the wagon out of the mud."

Delorier, clattering up behind them, had avoided the mud. He had gone some distance upstream to find a shallower, sandy ford and was now standing by them with no more ill effects than damp moccasins.

"Jean," Chatillon called, gesturing toward the wagon. "Unhitch. *Comprends?*"

Delorier nodded and went to work. Chatillon

looked at the far wagon and shook his head. He spat neatly between his moccasins. "To let such innocents go out alone in this wilderness. Is it not madness?"

Why were they alone? Parkman wondered. Hadn't they started out with a train, the Colby train? Maybe the others had gone on without them. The weak had to keep up—or fall behind to the scavengers.

But other questions bothered him. Why had Chatillon, who had had the major part in rescuing the travelers and saving their goods, given the credit to Shaw and Parkman? And why had he refused to help the mother, but had motioned Parkman to help her? Parkman asked him about it.

"Most emigrants are mad at hunters and trappers. They think we don't want wagon trains on the prairie. They think we side with the Indians." The dazzling teeth showed briefly. "Call us French Indians. You know that? So there you are."

Chatillon went forward to consult with Delorier about how best to hitch the mules to supplement the oxen. Parkman joined Shaw at the back of the stranded wagon.

Parkman had occasionally wondered why it was that Shaw, one of the most congenial and peace loving of souls and given to so few words, should so often be involved in confrontations. There he was, having some argument with the two girls, biting his pipe. The boy, Jeremiah, was there too, trying to elbow in alongside his sisters. His skin was flushed and both jaws were swollen. My God, Parkman thought, mumps! He tried to recall if he and Shaw had been exposed, avoiding panic only when he remembered that both had been isolated together because of the disease when he was ten.

"But you have to get out," Shaw explained with rising irritation. "We have to lighten the load. Don't you understand?"

As though Shaw were Medusa, the girls had turned to stone. The smaller moved closer to her sister. The boy achieved a blissful smile in spite of his puffed cheeks, making him look like a pumpkin.

"Here, now. Come. I'll help you." Shaw reached for the larger girl. Both moved backward.

"Now see here. You'll have to come."

Jeremiah held out both his arms, straight as poles, ready to be taken by Shaw. The younger sister turned to him quickly and tried to push them down, and they struggled briefly. The boy was not only very young, but weak from the disease. He started to cry.

The younger girl turned on Shaw as though her brother's tears were his fault. "Now, see?" she reproached.

"Well, why won't you listen?" Shaw was on the point of exasperation.

"Let me try, Quincy," Parkman offered. He turned directly to the larger girl, who, in the absence of her mother and elder sister, was obviously the spokesman. "What is your name?"

"Rebecca," she said proudly.

"Well, Rebecca, did your sister or mother tell you to stay right there in the wagon without moving, or something like that?"

She still did not answer, but the small girl was not made of such stern stuff. "Lucy said to stay right here!" she piped up.

"What's your name?" Parkman asked her.

"Ruth," the older girl, Rebecca, answered for her. "Her name is Ruth, and she's only six."

"How old are you, Rebecca?" Parkman asked.

"I'm ten."

"You're not supposed to be talking to them," Ruth said to her sister.

"Well, you're talking to them," Rebecca retorted. "Besides, they ain't Indians." She turned the same defiant expression on the two men. "You go on now!"

"If your mother told you not to talk to the Indians—"

"My sister, not my mother. My sister Lucy," Ruth corrected.

"Well, when your sister Lucy told you not to talk to the Indians she didn't mean us. Now we're trying to help and you're making it very difficult," said Shaw.

Rebecca stood straight and spoke loudly and clearly, as though reciting a lesson. "Lucy said, 'Now don't you talk to no Indians or no other strangers less'n I say you kin. Mind now or I'll wale you.' Now that's what she said, an' I'm not lyin' a bit!"

Parkman began to laugh. Shaw joined in.

The boy held out his arms again, sweat and tears on his face. Shaw reached for him and before the girls could object, lifted him over the back rail.

"Now you—" the older girl started to threaten.

"Quincy," Parkman said mildly, "I hope you remember whether you had the mumps."

Shaw stopped abruptly, holding the boy at arm's length. He thought hard.

Parkman waited a moment, then said, "Twelve years ago. Both of us. Your house."

"So it was." Quincy started to put the boy down, but the child clung to him, so he held him on his arm a moment longer. "Why didn't I notice that?" His professional pride, especially as one who had hoped to woo Indians with his homeopathic skills, was wounded.

The girls were leaning over the tail of the wagon and shouting at them when the wagon, deep in the mud, gave a jerk. Parkman heard the snap of a whip and Delorier's command to the mules and oxen.

Rebecca pitched head first out of the wagon and Parkman caught her. She started to fight, but he had her on the ground before she could do much damage. Ruth hadn't been leaning out as far and caught herself in time. But she was the last survivor on the ship, which began to pitch her about perilously, so they took her out, too. They carried the two smaller children and led the larger one to dry ground.

Delorier's curses became encouraging. He cracked the whip triumphantly above the backs of the straining beasts. The wagon rocked, then lumbered up the bank to dry ground, shedding gobs of mud with each turning of the wheel. Delorier stopped it and began to sing.

Parkman and Shaw followed, trying to knock some of the mud off their moccasins and ankles. Shaw still carried the boy and held the small girl by the hand. The boy had refused to get down. "Hot as a furnace," he told Parkman. "Poor shaver. Have to get him back inside and under cover." The professional manner had returned. The child seemed content. He lay against Shaw's blanket coat, his face almost as red as the wool, and closed his eyes. His lips parted and he was asleep.

When Shaw tried to put him down he woke with a little cry and clutched the coat. Shaw had to straighten up again. Parkman laughed. There in the wilderness, Shaw was caught in the domesticity he had avoided so successfully in Boston.

Up ahead, the oldest daughter, the girl with the muddy dress, Lucy, was talking earnestly to Chatillon, who had taken off his hat and was listening politely.

The wagon pulled alongside, the mules out ahead, and Delorier got off to unhitch them. Parkman and Shaw plodded up toward the group, bringing the children. Rebecca broke away to run up to Lucy and Ruth went after her, shouting, "I didn't want to!" She was now close to tears and wanted to get her protestations of innocence in before the other side was heard.

"What?" Lucy said, turning toward them.

"Oh," Rebecca said, "she just talked to them when you told us not to!"

"Why, that's all right. You mean—well, I meant that for strangers and Indians."

Now Rebecca felt, apparently, that she might be put in the wrong. "Well, they are strangers! Look at . . . that. . . ." She gestured toward Delorier, who, with the mules, was starting to shamble past, his clothes hanging baggy and loose over his small frame. He raised his eyebrows.

"All right," Lucy said, "now that's all right. No arguin' now! These gentlemen wanted to help us. But all right, you couldn't know."

Chatillon gave Rebecca one of his dazzling smiles and leaned forward to shake her hand, but she turned her back on him.

Parkman and Shaw came up, the boy fast asleep on Shaw's shoulder. Shaw looked in the wagon. Amid all the household goods and packages, a small pallet of blankets had been made for the boy. "I think we ought to get him back to bed," Shaw advised.

Shaw tried to pass the boy over the back of the wagon, but the boy, without even waking up, tightened his grip and would not let go. Lucy came up close and started to take the boy from him. The child fussed a little with a sickly tone.

"Now you just come on, Jeremiah!" The child didn't seem as happy as he had been against Shaw's coat, but he settled down on the pallet. He was soon asleep once more.

"Thank'ee," she said to Shaw with a nod as correct as a trooper's salute and turned back toward Chatillon. Her face was determined in spite of how tired she was.

He said, "He has the mumps, you know."

"I know. We all had it." She went back to Chatillon, whom she took to be the leader of the group. "I was explainin'. That's all."

"I am glad you weren't hurt," Chatillon said. "I think all they wanted to do was steal. It's easier if they frighten people."

"I wouldn't let them take my locket." She pointed to a scratch on her throat. "I tried to fight. That's when they pushed me."

"They took it," Chatillon said kindly.

"Yes." Her hands touched her neck again.

It seemed to Parkman that she changed before his eyes back and forth from girl to woman. She was no more than seventeen, the flush from the wind and excitement still on her cheek. But she also was a careworn woman with underlined eyes, muddy and bedraggled, trying to hold her shoulders straight and wondering what to do next to take care of those who needed her.

"I wish we had come earlier," Parkman said.

"Thank'ee. But others can't help always."

"There are times not to fight," said Chatillon. "Especially for women. Unless they have guns."

"Maw had the gun. She just didn't have it loaded and ready. An' she didn't see them when they came from behind."

"Yes. We saw that gun," Shaw said. "Would have scared anybody."

Chatillon smiled, recalling that the gun wouldn't fire. "There are times not to fight even when you do have guns," Chatillon added.

The two smaller girls had taken positions one on each side of Lucy, each holding a handful of muddy skirt. They had the same round-eyed defiant expression they had had in the back of the wagon. The smaller girl, Ruth, put her thumb in her mouth, but when Shaw started to smile at her she removed it quickly.

"How is your mother?" Parkman asked.

"She's restin'. She'll be all right. Just took Paw's death hard."

"How did you come to be left behind?" he asked.

"Well, like I just told this gentleman," she said, pointing to Chatillon, "we couldn't keep up. One thing and t'other. Then gettin' stuck. They kept sendin' back people to help. Then they said they had to go on and we could catch up. Maybe when they camped." She looked up. The shadows under her young eyes were quite pronounced. "Had some trouble yesterday, too."

Shaw motioned toward the old man, sitting on his stool and sipping water from a tin dipper that his daughter had brought. "That the help they sent?"

"Oh, no. That's Mr. Standford. He just stayed with us. He tried to get some fellas to go with us when Paw took sick, and said he'd stay with us, we'd go together. A Christian man." But her tired eyes held a flicker of amusement. "Don't know how far he'd be ahead if he hadn't stayed."

"You're going to have to rest awhile," Parkman said. "The boy's asleep. You three girls go rest by your mother." Till we figure out what to do with you, he added silently.

"Yes," Chatillon said. He put two fingers in his mouth and whistled briefly and piercingly. Delorier, fitting the mules back in their traces, raised his head. "Jean!" Chatillon called. "Bring the wagons and the cart close. Then let's make a fire in the center. It's time for lunch, eh? Gold old salt pork and beans."

They had not often had a formal midday meal on the trail. They'd eaten biscuits or dried beef as they rode or when they had to stop to rest or water the horses. Generally, they did their heavy eating when they stopped for the night and built the campfire. But Delorier didn't argue. "*Tout de suite!*"

"Oh, no," Lucy protested.

"Why not? He is an excellent burner of bacon."

"No. Now, listen—"

"We're men and we're hungry. We always eat now. If it bothers you, you and the tall lady can help out." He addressed Parkman, "I'll help Jean. Monsieur Parkman, would you mind? Would you help her?"

Parkman nodded and went to her to take her arm. "No, I can walk all right!" she said.

Parkman nodded and smiled. Her unsteadiness was not due so much to physical fatigue, though there was plenty of that, as to the accumulation of shocks. They often caught up to one when the pressure was off. But the dangers were not really past for her. She would have to be ready again for them tomorrow. Or later today. At seventeen years of age.

Delorier's whip cracked and the wagon lurched by them to pull up parallel to the other wagon so that they could eat between them.

Delorier got a good fire going, got it down to coals and then concentrated on making one of the great meals of his career. Liz Standford came over to help. She said that her father, Mr. Standford, could not eat everything, certainly not food too strong on garlic, foreign oil or Indian spices, so she would have to keep an eye on what went into the pot. Delorier rolled his eyes, but welcomed her amiably. Women were always the best cooks, he told her.

The wagons had small barrels of beef and fish in brine and bottled preserves, which made a welcome addition to Delorier's stores. Delorier and Liz worked well together and when Lucy came over to see what she could do, Liz told her that everything was under control. Lucy could concentrate on setting plates and serving, if she wanted to. At that moment Delorier was explaining the superiority of coals to flames for cooking and was starting to hint that garlic had more virtues than she knew. Their heads were together.

While the meal was being served, Chatillon asked Delorier about his efforts at diplomacy. He shrugged. "I nevair make dispute with a tall woman." Then he took his plate and sat down next to her.

Mrs. Fleshner came out and also sat down. She ate little, though Liz scolded her gently and told her she had to keep up her strength. At first, she couldn't look directly at the men. Then, in a rush, she said that her daughter had told her all that had happened, and she had been so confused and frightened when she came down from the wagon, and was so ashamed, so ashamed—

"Nothing to be ashamed for," Chatillon tried to

bolster her spirits. "People often take me and Delorier for wild Indians." Delorier, at his name, looked up quickly from his intense conversation with Liz, who was seated demurely on a rock nearby, knees tightly together.

No, she never thought that, Mrs. Fleshner continued. She'd been just so frightened and confused. So much had happened lately.

"Be assured, madame, that we were even more confused."

Jeremiah came to the back of the wagon with a weak little cry. He was taken out and seated next to his mother, but he kept looking at Shaw.

"Quite a conquest you've made, Quincy," Parkman teased. "Perhaps you should do something about it."

Shaw sighed and got up, taking his plate with him along with a blanket, and sat on the blanket next to the boy. Parkman rose too and took his plate and sat down on the damp ground next to Shaw. "So you won't feel abandoned in an enemy camp," he said.

"The nuisances of being a father," Shaw groused, "with none of the privileges."

They sat around Delorier's fire as at a picnic. The brassy sun had passed its zenith and was on its way down. Dark clouds were gathering to the west and Parkman watched them. The gathered wagons and cart made a little alcove like a nest, but it wouldn't protect them. Chatillon was chatting calmly, sometimes directing remarks to the old man or the mother, but mostly talking to Lucy, who had moved to be able to speak to him more easily. He seemed to have all the time in the world. Parkman understood that he felt the women needed rest and reassurance, and some help at getting started again with more confidence and more instruction. But this was the same Chatillon who had roused them before dawn back in Westport, who got them on the trail early and usually kept them riding till late, who kept glancing toward the western horizon, and who, at least according to Delorier's hints, had an urgent need to get to Fort Laramie. Yet there he sat. The emigrants had been left behind by their wagon train because they couldn't keep up. They'd been delayed further by the Indians, and if they didn't catch up soon they might be left alone on the prairie, at the mercy of the Indians, the weather, time and their own inexperience. Yet they too simply sat.

The food was the best they'd had on the trip, but Parkman didn't feel particularly hungry. He resented the time and effort they spent eating the meal. Chatillon's casual attitude especially annoyed him. He glanced at Shaw, who was bound by the child, even if he didn't want to be, and wouldn't be able to get up now without some upset. He rose to his feet. As he passed Delorier, the Canadian thought he came to get second helpings and put his ladle in the pot, but Parkman shook his head.

As he reached Chatillon, the hunter was getting to his feet. Had he had a nice chat with the pretty young girl? An uncharitable thought, Parkman said to himself, but he needed some relief from his irritation. Should he now remind Chatillon that he was a hired hand, working for Parkman and Shaw, rather than someone who could do as he pleased?

Chatillon addressed Lucy. "I think you should see how your mother feels. She doesn't have to drive the wagon. One of us can. But we should use the daylight."

"You think we can still catch the train by the time they make camp?" the girl asked.

"Maybe not today."

"Well, couldn't we go a little longer, maybe after dark?"

"I don't think that's wise. But we can see."

"Well, that's all we want. Just till we catch up."

"We'll see."

"Well, we don't want to be beholden to you too much. We can do it ourselves."

"It's no trouble. It's on our way. Your family is better company than bearded men."

Parkman started to speak, but Chatillon raised a cautioning hand, invisible to the girl.

"Well," she said, "we never been beholden to anybody before. That's the way we was raised, what my paw always said. And we'll pay."

Again he swept his hat. "We can discuss all that later." He moved the hat gently toward her mother.

Lucy rose, but her dark eyes stayed on him. "We don't want to keep you from your trip. But you see how it is." She motioned, not toward her mother and the children, but to Mr. Standford, who had just been informing Parkman how independent he was.

"I understand," Chatillon said. "You have responsibilities. I don't think we'll have trouble." She turned away, glanced back over her shoulder at Chatillon and went to her mother. Chatillon drew aside, ostensibly examining the oxen, who cropped occasional mouthfuls of grass but otherwise stood almost immobile.

"You're the boss," he said. "I think we had better talk together."

"You've reached some kind of decision," Parkman said. Perhaps the slight irritation in his mind had reached his voice. "Why don't you tell me what it is?"

Chatillon glanced at him. "It isn't up to me to make the final decision."

"Well . . . I'm sorry. You have something in mind."

Chatillon slapped the closest ox. "You see how they are."

"You are afraid of the Indians?"

"Maybe. But these Indians aren't the greatest worry. Not yet."

"Well, Henry?"

Again a pause. "I don't see how we can leave them alone."

"You aren't thinking of taking them all the way with us?"

"No. I don't think so. Even if we could, I don't think it would be wise."

Chatillon continued. "Even if we took them all the way—if we could, and they didn't slow us down too much—they would be at Laramie, and have yet to go to California." He sighed. "You see how they do on the flat prairie. They would yet have mountains."

"Well, once we catch up to the train—"

"I don't think we will catch that train. Most of the other wagons have horses and mules. And young men."

Delorier called to him and said something in rapid Canuck patois. Chatillon nodded gravely. Delorier became busy, packing up. "And if we did catch the wagon train and left them. What then?"

"But when will they get to California?"

"Even with the best, they couldn't get to California this year. The way they go, they would find the passes blocked with snow. Even if they could get through with good weather. And they couldn't go alone. I've been there."

"Then what do you think?"

"I think it would be best to take them to Fort Leavenworth. In time another train, maybe a better, slower one, with more oxen, will come through. And they may be more ready. And the snow may be melted, with spring, when they get to the passes. South Pass."

The matter was settled, of course. But he had to make some objection. "But Leavenworth is out of our way."

"A little. Not much. We have to go north for the Platte anyway."

He paused. "Did you tell them?"

"No."

"Will they know?"

"Not right away, I don't think."

Parkman thought about that for a while. "Then you are proposing taking them to Leavenworth when they think that we will be taking them to Laramie or at least to the train?"

Chatillon was silent.

"You won't tell them?"

"For a time at least. I won't bring it up. I don't think I'll lie, though."

"We'll have to tell them before we get there. They'll have to be prepared."

"Yes. We will tell them. If you agree."

"Oh, I agree." Yes, Parkman thought, I'm the damned boss and I make the decisions, don't I? But how could he argue? Even if it did delay them and involved responsibilities they didn't want. "Quincy is also a boss. I'll have to talk to him."

He found Shaw telling Jeremiah the story about the church full of people, using his interlocking fingers to illustrate it. The boy was delighted.

Shaw rose to meet Parkman. "Go on to Mama now," he said to Jeremiah. Parkman motioned Shaw to join him out of earshot of the women. "Henry thinks we can't leave them out here," Parkman said.

Shaw lit his pipe. "Certainly can't. What then?"

"Have to lead them."

"Till we meet those wagons?"

"He thinks there's not much chance of that. And they couldn't keep up then, either."

The smoke rose up around Shaw's face. "Saying we're stuck with them? Rest of the trip?"

Parkman looked around, trying not to be too obvious, to make sure none heard who was not supposed to hear. "He thinks we should let them off at Fort Leavenworth. Wait for a later, better train. Thinks they're asking for disaster if they try to go to the coast now."

A short, smoke-filled silence. Finally, "Seems the best of a bad bargain. If he's sure."

Who could be sure about anything? Delorier had finished loading most of the items onto the cart. Ordinarily he shoveled dirt on the coals to put them out before they moved on. This time he took a bucket and went down to the stream. Liz, looking back at him, now was trying to convince her father to go inside the wagon while she handled the oxen.

Parkman said, "Chatillon wants our permission."

Shaw closed one eye as though in thought, or it could have been a wink. He nodded. Then, as Parkman started to turn, Shaw said, "What if we said no?"

Parkman smiled.

Shaw said, "Who's going to tell them? They think they're going to catch up, you know."

"Better if they don't know just yet. Might not be politic."

Chapter 9

Just as time had seemed to be of no importance earlier and during the meal, now, suddenly, all was efficient hurry. The horses and mules were taken to the stream to be watered and the casks were filled. Chatillon asked Parkman and Shaw if they might be available to take over the reins of both wagons, to spell the others in the hours ahead. He pointed out that they, too, might sometimes want to get out of the sun and sit on a proper seat.

"You drive the second wagon, with the children," Shaw told Parkman. "That feverish little devil'll make my life miserable."

"Quincy, I don't know why you try to avoid your fate." But, back on Pontiac, Parkman rode up to the wagon, now loaded with supplies and children, and, touching his hat, spoke to Lucy and her mother. A trunk, softened by a folded blanket, provided a back rest for the older woman.

"I don't think you ladies better tire yourselves too much after that scare. I can relieve you after a little while."

Lucy held the reins. Her back was straight, her

fists clenched. "We're fine. Now we're just fine. We come this far."

The mother, he thought, looked dragged out. "Well, I'll relieve you a little later. I'll want to get out of this saddle for a while anyway."

He rode back to Shaw. "The boy may want you, but the girl wants Henry."

Chatillon was speaking to the two on the seat of the first wagon. "Fine, fine, never better!" Parkman could hear Mr. Standford say.

"Well, old father," Chatillon said to Standford, "you've been fighting Indians, and you're going to need to rest a while, for the next Indians. Somebody will take your place later." He looked closer, with some concern. "You still dizzy from that knock on the head?"

"I'm fine. You just take care of the women in the back. Liz can spell me. She always does." Parkman glanced at the quiet Liz. With her big bones and steady, competent hands, she was probably the strongest and most able person in the two wagons. Standford ran his free hand through his scant hair. "Ain't worth no Injun's time." Then he almost collapsed in laughter. "Go on now!" he said.

Chatillon winked at Parkman and then rode out in front. The small train followed, the two ox-drawn wagons next and Delorier and his cart bringing up the rear. Parkman and Shaw rode on the flanks.

Jeremiah sat or knelt in the back, looking out, trying to keep Shaw in view. Rebecca took a place next to Jeremiah and stared at him also. He rode up. "You still mad at me, missy?"

"No!" she shouted, and turned to the side, exposing a profile as sharp, delicate and uncompromising as a cameo.

"Never had any luck with the pretty ones," Shaw called to Parkman.

The afternoon was moving on, but it was still plenty hot. The sun burned down a little more from the left side than it had the day before. Lucy called to Parkman once, as he rode up to see how they were doing, "Ain't we goin' a little different?"

She would not be easy to fool. In a sense that was encouraging, since it meant that she might be more self-reliant than they had thought. "We have to catch the trail at the Platte River," Parkman answered, and then rode ahead before she could ask more questions. He joined Chatillon and they rode together for a while. They were in a sea of Kansas grass, so tall it reached their shins.

"We're visible out here, moving so slowly," Parkman complained.

"No Indians around here make much trouble, not with mounted men carrying guns around."

"I could ride point for a while," Parkman suggested. "Why don't you go back and help the women out? You could use a proper seat yourself. I'd like to take the lead for a while." He paused, then added, "If you think I can."

Chatillon smiled, raised his gun aloft in salute, and turned back. Parkman watched him trot back to the second wagon, tie his horse to the back, toss the saddle inside and climb aboard. He took the reins from Lucy and sat between her and her mother.

Parkman urged Pontiac forward and let him trot freely. It occurred to him that Chatillon, with his horse unsaddled, might not be able to come to his aid quickly enough if Indians appeared, and the thought briefly unnerved him. But then he felt a strange exhilaration.

Occasionally he looked behind to see that the plodding, boat-shaped wagons, rising and dipping on the waving grass, didn't get too far behind. When he saw Shaw riding up to meet him, he fell back.

"Anything wrong, Quincy?"

"No. Jeremiah has a new friend, so I thought I'd join you for a while."

"Everything seem to be going all right?"

"Swimmingly, I'd say. Especially between Henry and the women. Family needed a man."

"Well, I hope they don't think they've got one."

Shaw's little sorrel nickered softly to Pontiac, who ignored her. "May take some self-control on Henry's part," Shaw said. He trotted forward to take a turn as point man.

Parkman wiped the sweat from his brow and readjusted his hat. He'd been up front for a while and he decided to let the wagons catch up to him. He trotted alongside the Standford wagon. "How do, Miss Standford," he said to Liz.

She nodded. She seemed to have thawed. It paid to be polite, even out here.

The old man did not respond or even open his eyes, so Parkman didn't speak to him. "Everything all right?" he inquired.

She nodded again, with no change of expression. She was determined never to intrude herself or try to attract attention. They rode in silence for some time and Parkman figured he'd had all the conversation with her he was going to have that day.

"This ain't the trail, is it?" she asked abruptly.

He was startled, but recovered himself quickly. "It's a little easier traveling over new ground, sometimes. Henry Chatillon knows the best ways." He smiled and touched the brim of his hat. They moved slowly past him, like pictures in profile.

Things were a little livelier at the rear wagon. He could hear Chatillon intoning his favorite song about the sad little *oiseau.* He wondered whether the women and children had been treated to all of the words and implications of that somewhat bawdy ballad. But when he got alongside he realized that the hunter was confining himself mostly to the opening verses, as though the lady were a real *oiseau,* and the constant repetition of the simple refrain—the poor little bird, all alone—like the chorus of a child's song had brought on off-key, birdlike pipings from the back. Mrs. Fleshner seemed a little more rested. Lucy, without the burden of the wagon and its occupants on her shoulders for a little while, had closed her eyes and seemed more at peace.

"Goes well up there?" Chatillon asked, breaking off his lament.

"No Indians," Parkman returned. "Don't see any hills or problems. Quincy is out in front now."

At the new voice, heads popped out of the canvas opening. Little Ruth giggled and then pulled her head in quickly. A front wheel struck a stone, the seat and the front of the wagon pitched and Chatillon twitched the reins to make the rear wheel miss it. The mother turned to see if the children were all right. It all seemed so natural, the women looking after the children now that the leaven of the baritone voice and the male hands on the reins had been added.

"Well, I better saddle Five-Hundred-Dollar," Chatillon said.

"Stay there," Parkman said. "I'm enjoying myself riding point."

Chatillon hummed a bar of his song, adding "Same heading, *n'est-ce pas?*" as though it were part of the lyrics.

Parkman nodded and responded. "*N'est-ce pas.*"

He rode up to rejoin Shaw. "Want to take Henry's place, Quincy?"

"And have that young devil on my back, mumps and all?"

"Well, how about seeing if the Standfords need any relief? The women aren't as pretty there, but they get just as tired, I expect."

Shaw saluted and fell behind. When Parkman glanced back, he saw that Shaw had passed up both wagons and was talking to Delorier, who'd gotten out of his cart to stretch his legs and was walking alongside the mules. Shaw had made his own arrangement. Delorier was sitting between the Standfords, chattering away and guiding the oxen with an occasional crack of his long whip a yard or more above the backs of the oxen.

The pace of the small caravan had quickened. Parkman wondered again about the rapport between the short, vivacious and uncouth Canadian and that gaunt, shy woman. Mr. Standford made some remark and then chuckled as Delorier took it up with delight, embroidering on it in his bastard French-English. Parkman didn't know what the remark had been, but he saw Liz color. He also saw that she was content.

Shaw had tied his sorrel behind the cart and was taking a leisurely ride in it. He'd rooted around in the baggage till he'd found an Indian pipe he'd bought in Westport with the intention of inaugurating its use when he encountered an Indian who would share it with him. He had decided, apparently, to try it out and break it in first, and was lazily puffing away in the cart in full bachelor contentment.

Parkman watched the usual clouds gather in the west and wondered if they would be wet again in the late afternoon. Chatillon called to him that they would have to make a rest stop. He felt guilty. Why hadn't he thought of that?

They turned the wagon toward the next copse of trees, but before it got there the children were out. The women quickly followed. Jeremiah simply relieved himself in the grass, which almost covered him, and the girls, not much taller, began to squat close by. Then they saw the men high on their horses, and tore off toward the trees and the women.

Delorier used the occasion to gather tinder and dry wood for the evening's campfire. Chatillon re-saddled Five-Hundred-Dollar. "Think we might camp here, as long as we're stopped?" Parkman asked.

"A little longer," Chatillon answered. Now he seemed eager again to get on, despite the delay for lunch. "We cross the Kansas River tomorrow, I hope early."

Parkman rode with the Fleshners for the hour and a half before they did stop for the night. He'd expected that they would ask him about himself and he'd prepared a story about where he was going that he thought might make more sense to them than the truth. Instead, they asked him mostly about Chatillon. Perhaps, thought Parkman, it was easier for Midwestern farmers to understand someone who lived in the open with a rifle in his hand than an educated Easterner like himself.

"He talked about his mother," Mrs. Fleshner said. "He seems to have been very good to her." She wanted to know more. How often had Chatillon seen his mother in the last several years? How often did he even come to St. Louis, to that village close by where she still lived?

"I know he visited her on this last trip," Parkman said loyally.

"Well, he seems a thoughtful person."

"A fella that won't settle down," Lucy said scornfully, determined to show her indifference and independence. "Seems to me, a man shouldn't go runnin' around lookin' for excitement, like a boy." She glanced sideways at Parkman and her face suddenly got a stricken look. "Well, I mean no offense, sir . . ."

"No offense taken," Parkman answered, a little stiffly. "But he does his job very well. Now, you must admit that."

"He doesn't act like a married man," Mrs. Fleshner said. She had made it a statement; the question was only implied.

Parkman made no answer. He kept his eyes on that thunderhead building up on the shimmering horizon ahead.

"Hardly seems likely . . ." she prodded.

The fact was, he realized, he didn't really know. True, it didn't seem likely, but what did he know about the personal lives of these hunters, trappers and guides? "Well," he ventured, "people like guides and hunters, they're a lot like sailors. They have homes sometimes, and families, but they leave for long trips, maybe for years. You can't always tell."

"Marryin' ain't everything," Lucy announced.

Chapter 10

"We are a pack of women," the young Mahto Tatonka said. He didn't speak as others spoke in council, solemnly or in brief, rapid argument. He spoke either harshly and demandingly, as if giving orders, or with an impatient insistence, like a headlong horse. Now he was harsh. "We are women. Our brothers, our sons, are killed! Can we live if we do not revenge their deaths? When will we be men and fight?"

He spoke like his father. But his father had been a chief. He was a young hothead who wouldn't have been in council at all except that he represented his father's family. Whirlwind had thought it unwise to keep him out, but now he was paying the penalty for letting him in.

There was silence. Some of the others in the circle around the coals took covert glances at Whirlwind. He sat rigid and erect, his face set, mouth a straight line. They were waiting, he knew, to see what he would do. To call a warrior a woman was a deadly insult. This is what a warrior shouted at his enemy when he wanted him to come out from fortifications and fight hand to hand. But when a warrior shouted it at a member of his own tribe, particularly a chief, and particularly before his elders, there had to be a death.

And then what? The civil war between Bull Bear's family and followers on the one side against all the others—again and forever? It would be the greatest of the warriors fighting and killing one another, just as they had done after the deceit that had led to the assassination of the elder Bull Bear—and that, of course, had happened after *he* had taunted and humiliated his enemies by calling *them* women and cowards.

But this Mahto Tatonka was cleverer than his father. He really wanted to fight the Crow, not his chief. He had said "We," not "You." He was criticizing everyone, including himself.

"The young Bull Bear, like his father, is brave and rash," Whirlwind said. "He wants to kill and count coup on his enemies until they are like a field of trampled grass." That is not the only way he is like his father, Whirlwind thought. He will go out of this meeting like a fury, and I will be hearing complaints in the morning about men insulted, a squaw taken with defiance and without payment. "He wants war. And so do we all," the chief added.

Whirlwind had the gift of visions and now he had a vision. He saw plenty to eat, piles of buffalo meat and antelope, dried corn and squash, the squaws preparing more to store for the winter. The winter sicknesses were almost over. The warriors were sleek and strong, keeping themselves sharp by hunting and contests. The children were running and laughing, playing at hunting buffalo, or war. Even the old women now rested sometimes, and were beginning to fill out. In his vision the morning was greeted with laughter and song. Prairie Cock chanted to the singing girls who paraded around and followed him, and even Mad Wolf was assuaged for once, calm and almost content. It was a vision without hate. War was necessary to life, to their safety and revenge, but he saw a war that would bring that vision of peace.

"This is no war for the sake of war," he said. "We fight to drive the enemies from our land, to stop the insults, to be strong. To live in peace." He had to add something. "There are wars fought for coups and glory. There will be plenty of coups and glory. But we must be sure of victory."

"Hey!" the elders said. "Hey, hey!"

So he had support again, at least for the time being. Young Bull Bear knew, of course, that Whirlwind had sent for Chatillon. Did he know why? Apart from consideration for the sick? Horse had been back a while already. He said that Chatillon would follow, but that Chatillon had made a contract—a solemn pledge that could not be broken—and he would come as soon as he could. But when would that be?

"We are almost ready," Whirlwind said. "The hunting has been good, the lodges have been built, the people are happy. We have many arrows, long lances, skillful bowmen, good, fat horses. And some rifles. We are making or getting what we need. We are almost ready." As chief he consulted with his elders and warriors, but he made the final decisions. "We'll send out a war party soon." Individual war parties could precede the main thrust, to seek out and strike quickly at the enemy, to scout the situation, and to be sure the village was safe.

Bull Bear said, "Our brothers and cousins—the Brulé, the Winniconjou, the other Oglala—have been gathering at La Bonte's Creek camp. How long will they stay and wait?" He looked at Whirlwind.

"They are not all there yet," the chief replied.

"We will join them. Our war party will leave in no more than eight days." That promise was a little rash. But he had to make it. Maybe Mahto Tatonka and his complaints would go with it.

In the meantime though he had been forced to make a promise that he would send out a war party in eight days. And he would have to fulfill that promise, though he hadn't the knowledge and the plans yet that he needed. Well, a war party had narrow and definite work. Sending one out didn't mean that he was tied into a strategy. It even might be a good thing. As keen as the braves were, they could inflict damage and make the Crow and Snake worry about their own stragglers and villages, and so keep their warriors close to home. Whirlwind began to feel a swell of pride. His warriors and horses were the bravest, the swiftest, the strongest. His war party would strike like a storm, lay waste and be gone. They would be called after the name he had been given—Whirlwind.

"Many are there already," Bull Bear spoke again. "They stay there idly, restlessly waiting for a leader, waiting to do what they came for. And so some are starting to fight brothers. And some have got white man's whiskey." He waved his arm. "Is this how it will end, in drunkenness and quarreling? Does the council know about the whiskey?"

He said "the council," but he meant Whirlwind.

"I have known of the whiskey," Whirlwind answered. "It comes from the wagons of the *meneaska* coming through Fort Laramie. There is an enemy who brings it to the rendezvous to unman us, to make us attack too soon."

Sometimes he thought that an evil spirit must be guiding the white men, their ways were so cruel and strange. There was a feeling of doom around them that would affect not only themselves but those who came too close. At the same time they were often like willful children who needed punishment and control, but wouldn't get it because they were too strong and would strike back without pity. How else explain some of the things he had heard and seen? The people in the wagons carried what looked like whole white men's houses with them, as though they could move worlds to wherever they were going. He had found their broken remains on the prairie and at Laramie.

The fact that Whirlwind's warriors were not yet at the rendezvous made no difference. Had they been there, he feared they too would have gone in for drunkenness and brawling. Whiskey was part of the doom brought by the *meneaska* that might yet finish all the people—along with the sickness called smallpox and the sickness that the women got from lying with white hunters and that they then passed to the braves. Like any other sickness, the whiskey would finish in time. But not if someone was carrying it to them, bringing more and more.

"It wouldn't help if we were there. Worse, we too might have fallen to become drunken animals fighting brothers in the mud. But we are not. See! Look! Our warriors are strong, battle ready still." He stood and raised his eyes and his arms. "Hear me! Let it be so! Oh powers, let them remain straight and fierce as our flying arrows! Let them rise fiercely among our brother Dakota till all are one great lance flying toward our enemies who have torn our fathers from their resting places and broken their bones! Oh let them fly not wild but true!"

He remained with his arms lifted. Silence was all around the fire.

The council broke up after that. Whirlwind stopped Mahto Tatonka and said, "Stay a moment. I have a thing to say to you."

Bull Bear waited with surly impatience.

Whirlwind spoke, "I have said I will send a war party. We will start to train and get ready at first light. I want you to lead the training. But mock fight without wounds if possible, and no ordeals. We cannot fight with crippled warriors. There will be plenty of chances to count coup, prove manhood and tear flesh in battle." His eyes narrowed. "And no challenges that must be answered by fighting to the death by anyone. Oglala must not fight Oglala."

He waited a moment, arranged his thoughts. "You may lead that party if you want. I give permission. But I would rather you did not. White Shield, your cousin, would make a good commander, with your advice and your training." White Shield, though perhaps not as athletic, was less hotheaded. "I would rather that you stayed for the broader plans, for all the warriors, that I have in mind. I need you for that. But the choice is yours." He also wanted him to stay for his sister's sake and to confer with his brother-in-law. But he could not mention that. To suggest that Bull Bear hold back from combat to comfort a woman, no matter how much he loved her—and he did love her—would be to invite a fury that even Whirlwind couldn't handle. His other plans, or hopes, couldn't be revealed yet, at least not to Bull Bear.

"Broader plans?" The young man stood for a moment indecisive—a rare posture for him. That moment was very brief. He would always rather act than think and to him uncertainty was intolerable. Whirlwind knew that sooner or later that rash quality had to kill him, although it had in the past saved his life, as in the fight that had left the slightly whitened scars under one eye and on the high bridge of that nose so like his father's. He was a beautiful young man, not quite as tall as White Shield, but broad and well formed, with every muscle hard and as fully outlined as though carved. Whirlwind noted that except for that body, and the arrogant expression and demeanor, there was no way to tell who and what he was. The feathered headdress, the trinkets and badges stayed in his lodge to be brought out only for ceremonies. He wore a breechcloth, moccasins and a spot of vermilion on each cheek and that was all.

"I ask that you talk this over with your family, all the children of Bull Bear," Whirlwind said. "Then let me know your decision." His tone changed. "Now tell me, how is Blue Eagle Speaks? Does she take more nourishment? Fresh buffalo meat is good for most illnesses, and you and your brothers have provided her with much meat."

Bull Bear frowned, as though to admit weakness in a seriously ill sister was as bad as to admit it of himself. "She isn't better than she was yesterday," the young man said.

"Carry my message to her. Tell her she is much in my thoughts and in my wishes. Carry my greetings to all your family."

Bull Bear inclined his head, made the appropriate gesture of respectful farewell and went out.

Whirlwind waited the time it took to walk several paces and then left himself. Just outside his new squaw was crouched. He put his broad hand on her shoulder. She didn't move away, but she was watching Bull Bear's naked back move through the flickering yellow of a campfire, and did not respond. She was finding, he knew, that being the squaw of a chief of the Oglala was not all that she had hoped. She had finery, but not as much as some. The Hog, who had thirty horses, was the richest man in the village. His ugly daughter had more shell and gold bracelets and beaded garments than Whirlwind would ever be able to afford for his young wife. Maybe, the chief thought, she would like to be free again to wander in the woods and let some strong young brave like Bull Bear find her. She didn't respond to his touch. He sighed. He thought that if she didn't start to respond to him in the lodge he might not force her.

When Whirlwind had been a young warrior, he had yearned to be chief because of the things he wanted to do. Now, every day, he felt heavy on him the things he couldn't do. He couldn't make the fierce young Bull Bear or his own squaw respect him. He could not lift the threat from his village. He could not make Blue Eagle Speaks well. He might not even be able to keep her alive very long, no matter how much he wished it and hoped for it.

He couldn't even trust his own judgment. Had he waited too long to call Chatillon? Was he wise not to have told him about Blue Eagle Speaks? He believed now that he had not been wise.

He breathed deep drafts of the clear air, expanding his big chest, the scars above the nipples giving him slight twinges as they were forced to stretch. He saw the medicine man he disliked moving among the tepees and watched closely to see if he entered that of Blue Eagle Speaks, but the medicine man passed by her lodge.

Whirlwind raised his face, but closed his eyes and silently called on the Grandfathers—not for specific things, but for wisdom, and good, and help for the people.

He pressed his squaw's shoulder and said that he was going inside, and she should come soon. He thought he saw her nod, but felt no response.

Chapter 11

They had become members of a large and demanding family. It wasn't their family but because of it, they no longer had the freedom or privacy that adventuring men should have.

They were riding, an hour before sunset, and except for the small copse they had used for the rest stop, they had seen no trees or bushes, just unending swells of gently swaying spring grass, relieved only by an occasional circling turkey buzzard or a cawing crow. The thunderhead had not dissipated, but it seemed to have moved on toward the east, to rain on other wagons. Parkman wondered what they would do tonight for wood and water. He was sure that the other men, at least, were thinking about it, too.

Up ahead Chatillon shouted, waving his rifle. Over a little rise they could see a spot of green—the top of a tree. Chatillon rode on ahead and the others followed.

A cluster of bushes and low trees surrounded some pools of water in a broad hollow. They pitched camp on top of the rise.

The groups ate separately, the men close to their tents, the Standfords and Fleshners by their drawn-up wagons. They ate quickly. The sunset was glorious—orange and white streamers radiating out from a red sun.

"I must have a bath tonight," Shaw announced suddenly. "Sticky on that saddle." Shaw was finicky about cleanliness, no matter where he was. "How is it, Delorier? Any chance for a swim down there?"

"Ah, I cannot tell, monsieur." The muleteer looked confused, as though he didn't know what to make of such a question. "Just as you please."

"Come. We can see for ourselves," Shaw beckoned to Parkman.

They came down from the rise. But even before they reached the bushes the ground became treacherous, the result of heavy drainage with no clear channel. They had to progress by jumping from one tiny grassy island to another, trying to avoid the muddy pits between. "Could disappear forever," Shaw grunted, nearly missing a jump. "No trace."

"The Slough of Despond," Parkman quipped. "Been trying to avoid it ever since *Pilgrim's Progress* in school."

"Press on!" Shaw said. They followed a stream that eventually opened up into a pool.

Parkman cupped his hands and filled them with water. In the dim light it looked reasonably clear, and when he made a tentative step he found some sand and gravel mixed with the mud on the bottom. Shaw stripped down and waded out. Parkman also took off his clothes and splashed in.

They dove and splashed, stirring up sediment and tadpoles, carefree and refreshed. Parkman heard a stirring in the brush and glanced toward it, but Shaw bellowed and swam out with the flat, overhand stroke and that violent kick he had tried to teach Parkman on Cape Cod.

When the echoes had partially died down, Parkman once more heard sounds from the bank—two rapid splashes, then a hissing, almost like a whisper. He turned his head again, then relaxed. Obviously, small animals would come down to such a pool to drink, and as far as he knew, there were no large or dangerous ones around.

What brought them out, abruptly, was a horde of mosquitoes. In the tent, while Delorier dried and tried to clean some of their clothes before the fire, Parkman entered a description in his journal: "But our ablutions were suddenly interrupted by ten thousand punctures, like poisoned needles, and the humming of myriads of over-grown mosquitoes . . . swarming to the feast."

Still, he felt newly invigorated. So did Shaw who left the tent to get his shirt from Delorier and then paraded up and down, once more puffing on his Indian pipe. Parkman joined him, got his own shirt, still a little damp, and the two strolled over to the wagons to see how the others were making out. The families were around the campfire, Mr. Standford smoking his pipe, Liz tending a coffeepot that hung over the coals. Mrs. Fleshner was doing some washing in a pan, and Lucy had just put down a fresh pail of water for her. The children were in the wagon out of sight although, as they approached, Jeremiah's face appeared over the back.

There was an exchange of "Good evenings." Then Shaw said to Standford, "Feeling better, old timer?"

"Fine, fine. Feel like the saints on Sunday mornin'."

"Now, Father!" Liz said.

Shaw nodded and they puffed at each other a moment in appreciation. "Should make good time tomorrow," Standford said, and once more Shaw nodded.

"Should be at the—at a river tomorrow," Parkman said to Mrs. Fleshner. "Easy to do all the laundry then. Wouldn't want to wear yourself out now."

She pulled a dress out of the pan, wrung it once. He had thought she was washing Lucy's dress from the encounter with the Indians, but this was a lot smaller. She poured out the pan and put in fresh water from the bucket. Parkman wondered where they had got so much.

"Beckie only has the one dress not packed." She put it back in the pan and sighed. "Children are so careless. Playing down by the ponds when I told her not to go there. Says she fell in the mud."

"You got that bucket from that little muddy pond?"

"Beckie found a bigger one further down. Where she was playing."

"Where's she now?" Parkman asked. He looked toward the wagon.

"Sent her to bed, in her shift. You won't be seeing missy out here again tonight, I can tell you."

Parkman chomped down on his own blunt pipe, remembering the sound he had heard in the bushes. He didn't want to see the child. There had been quite enough peeking already.

Perhaps that thunderhead had not gone far off or had doubled back, because that night it rained— not as hard as it had before, but hard enough to create the usual fine mist under the canvas and to make sleep uncomfortable. Parkman laughed softly. They could have had their bath with less trouble and cleaner water. And much more privacy.

Chapter 12

They reached the Kansas River by noon the next day. Most streams in the area, including the rivers, were usually not deep or swift, however wide they might be, but the rains had swollen this one, spread it up the banks and sent large branches and tufts of buffalo grass, riding swiftly, turning and tumbling, down the main current.

Chatillon took charge. He suggested that they build a raft from the fallen trees along the banks to carry the heaviest items, thus allowing the cart and wagons to float more easily. He examined the wagons, boat-shaped for precisely this purpose, to see that they were properly caulked. He pronounced them seaworthy. To be safe, empty casks were tied to the outside as additional flotation devices.

The raft could not be large, so they would have to be careful what they took and to make sure that it was balanced properly. Chatillon first proposed that the men swim across with it, one at each corner, but he changed his mind. Chatillon had thought that the men could all swim back because he could, but then, looking at the river, and again at the men, he de-

cided it might be too risky. He took off his shirt, preparatory to swimming across with a rope.

"I say," Shaw said. "Let me do that. I'm an experienced swimmer. You're needed here."

"I don't know how deep it is out there. And it's
pretty swift."

"Oh, I've swam off Cape Cod. This is only a
river. Frank can testify."

Parkman grew a little alarmed. Last night's adventure had reminded him of Shaw's swimming prowess.
Should he be loyal to his cousin's trust in him to back
him up, or to his own misgivings?

Shaw quickly took the hesitation for support. "It's
settled then. Give me the rope." He too shed his shirt,
a red flannel. He was not as beautifully muscled as
Chatillon, nor as tall, and his shoulders had the droop
of someone who spent much of his time at a table
trying to read by dim light, but he was heavy and
strong. And, thought Parkman desperately, maybe he
is a better swimmer than he remembered.

Shaw kicked off his moccasins and started to
undo his trousers. Parkman stopped him, pointing to
the audience of females by the wagons. "Can't swim
with breeches weighing me down," Shaw snapped.
"Just tell them to look away."

Parkman explained to the women what was about
to happen, and added that Shaw was shy. Mrs. Fleshner looked at him as if all this modesty was nonsense,
at least on her account, but she quickly ordered the
two smaller girls into the wagon, and the three women
followed. Jeremiah resisted. Mr. Standford said, "Well,
if he behaves himself, he can stay with the fellas." He
took the boy's hand and added, "If it's all right with
your mother."

Shaw tied the rope around his waist and Chatillon checked it. Then he dropped his trousers and waded in.

He moved with difficulty upstream, shouting back that he might be carried partly downstream when he had to swim. He had no sooner said that when he stepped off a ledge into the main channel and promptly disappeared.

Parkman ran to help Chatillon with the rope. It tightened and lifted, dripping, out of the water. In a moment Shaw's head reappeared, about fifteen feet downstream. Parkman watched Shaw moving as fast as any other flotsam and he shouted. It looked like Shaw shouted back, or bellowed as he had the night before, but Parkman couldn't hear anything over the roar of the water. In a moment though, Shaw had struck out with a violent kick and his flat, overhand stroke. He began to make progress toward the opposite shore. Chatillon carefully let out the slack, the muscles in his back and shoulders rippling as he moved this way and that. Parkman was afraid that the weight and resistance of the rope itself would pull Shaw downstream.

The head again disappeared, then reappeared in a new place. Shaw had touched bottom on a sandbar. He stumbled, but then got his feet under him and was able to walk a few steps. His chest was heaving. He raised an arm and waved to them. He walked on a few steps and then once more sank, but now the sandbar and a bend in the shore protected him from the thrust of the main current. He reached the opposite shore with a few more steps. He was under an overhanging tree considerably downstream from where he had begun. He flopped down in the shade, waved again and shouted in triumph. Parkman almost collapsed with relief. He ran downstream, splashing in the shallows, hoping to come opposite Shaw. Blocked by a fallen log, he stopped, raised cupped hands to his mouth and shouted, "Are you all right, Quincy?"

Shaw raised his head and shouted back. "Told you I'd do it, didn't I?"

The hardest was yet to come, but it was all anticlimactic to Parkman. He was now sure the crossing could be accomplished. Chatillon apparently had never doubted it could be done, though his fierce concentration with the rope may have betrayed some uncertainty about Shaw.

Shaw, once he had recovered some of his strength, carried the rope back upstream opposite them at Chatillon's direction and snubbed it around a large, rough bottomland sycamore, "that grandfather tree," as Chatillon called it. The other end was tied to a maple on their side of the river.

Chatillon and Delorier, with some help from Parkman and a good deal of ignored advice from Standford, set to work constructing a raft. Mostly they used driftwood and fallen trunks, but they also cut down a tree with a straight trunk and hacked it into sections of even lengths. Their use of axe, hammer and knife was quick and efficient. Parkman pointed out that not all the logs gathered had been used in the raft. "We'll find use for them," Chatillon said.

They launched their makeshift craft and tested it by jumping up and down on it. Then Delorier unloaded the cart and lashed the heaviest items to it. Chatillon and Parkman went to the wagons and after lengthy conferences brought most of the heavy items out and carried them down to the bank. The women and children came out, too. The children climbed down to the muddy temporary levee to see what was going on, while Mrs. Fleshner scolded them. Parkman

looked across the river. Shaw had taken refuge behind
a tree. Chatillon decided that they couldn't load all
the items on the raft just then. They might have to
put them back in the wagons; they would see, he told
them.

"Jean," he said to Delorier, "do you think you
could accompany your lovelies to the other side of
this brook?"

Delorier considered the matter for a time, tugging at his mustaches, then gave an eloquent shrug.
"One can but try."

Chatillon slapped his friend's shoulder and said
to Parkman, "You see? A man of quality."

"One strives to please," Delorier grinned.

The men loaded and lashed objects onto the raft.
Some were still left to be loaded when Chatillon said
there was enough.

"Now Jean," he said, "how do you go, up here
or by the sandbar Mr. Shaw discovered for us? I don't
know, but I think by the sandbar might be better."

"My mules," Delorier said, "like to go straight.
They're lazy."

Chatillon nodded and Delorier got on his lightened cart and eased the mules into the shallows, watching the cart carefully to see that it didn't capsize before it had a chance to float. The mules, their tall
ears erect, stepped into the treacherous mud and cold
stream and stood shivering a moment as Delorier made
sure that everything was ready. Parkman shoved Shaw's
moccasins, breeches and shirt at him. Delorier smiled
and put them under his seat. He cracked his whip over
the mules. The mules twitched their ears. One looked
back questioningly but there was nothing to do but
go on into the river. There was a panicky moment
when, buffeted by the current, the animals turned to

face it and their hooves went out from under them. But they recovered and began to swim. There was another panicky moment when the current began to push the swimming mules downstream before the cart was fully afloat and it looked as if it would overturn. But Delorier leaned his weight on the upstream side, and the lightened end floated easily. The mules struggled to keep their heads above the waves while Delorier shouted encouragement. They sailed on, across and downstream, Delorier cracking his whip like the ringmaster at a circus. In comparison to the long agony of watching Shaw, it seemed to Parkman no more than a tense moment before the mules were digging their hooves into the opposite bank and pulling onto the grass, and Delorier had jumped out and was helping them by steadying the cart, shouting "*Sacre bleu!*" because his feet had gotten wet.

He passed the clothes to Shaw, shivering behind the tree. Then he unhitched the mules and attached them to the rope snubbed around the sycamore.

On their side of the river, Chatillon waded out and attached the other end to the front of the raft. Another rope was tied to the back and snubbed around the maple; then its end was attached to the girth strap of Five-Hundred-Dollar. Chatillon told Parkman to hold Pontiac in readiness, should he be needed for extra pulling power. Chatillon untied the ropes that held the raft to the bank and waved at Delorier. The muleteer clucked at his charges and the mules began to strain slowly at their rope, starting the raft across the river, while Chatillon backed his horse at the same rate to keep the rope taut enough to fight the current.

The raft moved toward the center of the river. The current struck it. It shivered a moment against the pull of the ropes. Five-Hundred-Dollar felt the strain and raised his head, but Chatillon soothed him and held him steady. The raft now began to buck as though trying to throw its load off its back into the stream and some water raced over the logs toward the load. Chatillon signaled Delorier again and began to back up his horse a little faster, while the muleteer moved his mules faster to take up the slack. The raft moved across the current, still bucking, unappeased. Fortunately, nothing fell off. Shaw, decently dressed, came out and into view, and as the raft reached the shallows, he and Delorier waded out, pulled it in and unloaded it.

It would have to come back for a final load. They could see Shaw and Delorier holding some kind of arm-waving discussion. But when Chatillon waved at them and started his horse forward to bring the raft back, it was Shaw who went to the heads of the mules. As the rope pulled the raft away from the bank, Delorier jumped onto it. He lay flat and embraced one of the logs. Chatillon shouted, but Shaw, inexpert with the mules, was already backing them faster than Five-Hundred-Dollar could take up the slack. The raft, with Delorier clinging to it, swung wide, riding high because of the relatively light load, moving toward the channel.

Chatillon pulled his horse faster against the slack. The raft skipped above the current, bouncing up and down like a skimming stone. Delorier was splashed, but he held on. In a few minutes he was close to the bank. Chatillon and Parkman pulled the rope in and went out and held the raft. Delorier got off, smiling.

"You are an idiot," Chatillon said in a conversational tone.

Delorier merely said, "You will need help with the wagons."

Parkman was annoyed. Could the ridiculous little man be showing off for that tall, cold old maid? But then nobody could handle the wagons better than he.

They repeated the transit with the raft, the rest of the load tied to it. Shaw's handling of the mules was not as expert as Delorier's, and it looked for a moment as if the raft would get away from them before Shaw speeded his mules and brought the load to safe harbor.

"You want to use the raft for any passengers besides me?" Delorier asked. He waved toward the line-up, now out of the wagons and on the bank.

"I think the wagons would be safer," Chatillon said. He signaled, then called to Shaw to unload and untie the ropes. Ropes would be needed.

"You want the raft?" Shaw shouted, palms raised to his mouth.

Chatillon shook his head. It would be impossible to untie the ropes and save the raft in any case.

But he didn't say that the raft had to be cut loose. It could have been left on the bank. Perhaps Shaw misunderstood, or perhaps he realized he couldn't handle it alone, or lift it onto land. When he untied it, it was still afloat. He untied the outer rope first and it began to swing around him, to pull him downstream. He got out of the way, but the rope caught him and knocked him off his feet. Parkman ran to Pontiac, but Chatillon shoved him aside and got on in his place. Pontiac, who was always trying to get away if not hobbled and who had hardly gotten used to Parkman as a rider, reared and neighed. But Chatillon rammed his heels into the horse's side and started for the river.

Across the river they saw Shaw rise to the surface. The raft had started downstream, still close in toward shore and out of the current, but picking up speed. The mules, without direction, were backing up, panicking. The rope was close on Shaw. Parkman couldn't see if it was around him or not. Chatillon was starting to breast the waves on Pontiac. There was little chance he could get across in time. There was a good chance he would be swept downstream, with a skittish horse not used to him that was apt to panic. Possibly, by the time the mules hit the tree around which the rope was snubbed, they might be out of control and might be pulled into the water too by the raft, which was gaining speed every second.

Shaw dove underwater, trying to get away from the rope. When he rose he was farther downstream and the rope was still pulling him along. Then Parkman saw that he had a knife in his hand. He had used his knife to cut the lashings on the raft to take off the load and then had shoved it into his waistband when he'd gone out to untie the ropes. He was frantically slashing at it, but the thick rope, slippery with water, resisted the knife, and his feet slipped again.

He was not yet in over his head, but there were holes and roots in the shallows and the rope pushed him faster and faster, too fast to stay on his feet. He rose again, hanging on to the rope, hopping backward. With one hand he'd made a loop in the rope, and with the knife in the other, he was busy sawing away at it. His face went under again, but he kept sawing.

The rope finally parted when it seemed that Shaw could not rise again. The raft, moving into the current, whipped the severed rope out of his hand. He still clung to the other piece. The mules, frantic, relieved of the pull of the raft, started to run. They pulled against one another, so they were unable to go far, but far enough to pull Shaw up against the bank. Delorier shouted at them and cracked his whip like a pistol shot. Across the river they snorted and stopped, stamping their hooves.

Chatillon had almost reached the main current, fighting a rebellious Pontiac. He saw Shaw, dripping, beginning to climb onto the grass. He turned Pontiac back and scrambled up onto the bank about twenty feet downstream.

"Every damn thing go wrong, eh?" Delorier said.

Chatillon got off the horse and turned the reins over to Parkman. He too dripped below the waist. "We still got the easy part," he said. "Only the wagons. And the people."

They watched the raft rush downstream. It moved with surprising swiftness, spinning once over the sandbar and finally disappearing around a fallen tree.

How had other wagons made it?

"There's a better ford upstream that any experienced guide knows," Chatillon said. "But we had to come back to go to Leavenworth. And after these damned rains."

Parkman soon understood the reason logs had been cut and set aside. He and Delorier, with Standford tottering around to show that, as one of the men, he was helping, lifted logs to each side of the wagons while Chatillon lashed them on, providing balance and extra floating ability.

They also wanted to balance the load, human and otherwise, inside the wagons. The packages and bales gave them little trouble, but the people were another matter. The families wanted to stay together, but that meant two in one wagon, five in the other, or, adding the male drivers, three and six. Chatillon thought it might be wise to remove a couple of the children, but Jeremiah and Ruth, the youngest girl, clung to their mother, and Lucy thought she should stay with her also. Parkman leaned over to Rebecca. "Missy, would you ride with the Standfords? I think they need your help."

Rebecca's hands did not cling to her mother, but her eyes did. When Mrs. Fleshner nodded at her, Rebecca marched to the Standford wagon, nose in the air, and got inside.

It was agreed that Delorier would drive the Standford wagon and Parkman the Fleshner wagon, leading Pontiac from the wagon. But Pontiac would be a difficult horse to control, so he let Chatillon swim ahead on the obedient Five-Hundred-Dollar, ready to help if needed. Parkman, coming after Delorier, had only to follow his lead.

The Standford wagon, with Delorier at the reins, moved off first, rocking back and forth as it went off the bank, the wheels sinking into the mud of the shallows. The oxen lowed softly and moved their heads from left to right as the water rose to their bellies. Jean Delorier was not very happy. He'd wanted to be left alone on the seat, free to concentrate fully on controlling the animals, but he had to share that seat with Standford and Liz, who had insisted on being there. Further, because Liz thought that her father, who was exhausted and somewhat irrational from the strain of the crossing, might try to seize the reins "to help out," she had seated herself between the two men, so that Delorier was crowded to one side.

When the oxen reached the channel they almost disappeared for a moment before they struck out swimming, wall-eyed and straining. The front end lifted, floating satisfactorily, and they were launched on the water without encountering rocks or snags. The oxen felt the thrust of the current, shoved their necks forward and up to keep their nostrils above the waves and swam in earnest. Delorier cracked his whip repeatedly over their heads. He turned them to face slightly upstream so that they wouldn't drift too far. It was going well enough, but Delorier was still not happy. These stupid beasts weren't his mules or horses. They had their own slow habits. They didn't understand or obey as quickly. And he wasn't used to them.

The wagon now hit the stronger current. It was caught broadside and rocked, and he had to work with the oxen, while his seat jerked under him, to keep the back from swinging around. He could feel the steadying and stabilizing that the attached logs gave them, and was grateful. Chatillon was a clever man. Old Mr. Standford said something indistinct, but Delorier replied, "We are safe, *mon vieux*. We shall land in time to have an afternoon pipe before continuing this damn trip."

Once Delorier was well out in the channel, Parkman drove his oxen into the water. He had the seat to himself. He could hear the Fleshners talking in the back, the mother starting a story about what California would be like and Lucy taking it up. He had worried about his ability to handle the team. But he had handled it before, and he saw that Chatillon, on Five-Hundred-Dollar, was also in the stream, close by. The oxen were used to following the wagon ahead, he reasoned. Two horses, on long leashes, swam behind. The Conestoga rocked, settled into the water, then floated beautifully. The oxen, at first surprised and recalcitrant in the water, swam, following Delorier's wagon.

The current in midchannel hit the wagon with a force that made his heart jump, but the oxen fought it successfully. They would make it. Up ahead he could see that, though the Standford wagon was still being pushed by the current, the oxen were starting to have an easier time of it.

Delorier didn't know that there was a snag right before him—a water-logged tree limb, caught and held by the sandbar. The oxen were safely past the sandbar. Shaw was on the bank with the mules and the rope, waiting to help if necessary. Then the wagon caught on the snagged limb. The oxen, seeing land and grass before them, kept pulling. The wagon lurched violently to the right and was prevented from tipping over only by the buoyancy of the log on that side. Delorier yanked hard on the reins, then grabbed the canvas to keep from flying off. Liz grabbed him, but Standford tumbled off and landed in the shallow water above the sandbar. He began to drift slowly toward the main channel. Parkman and Chatillon could hear little Rebecca scream as she fell against the canvas inside the wagon.

Chatillon turned his swimming horse toward the sandbar. Five-Hundred-Dollar felt the sand beneath him, tried to stand and stumbled. Chatillon got off and half-swam, half-scrambled toward the old man, who, his clothes now soaked, began to sink slowly as he drifted along.

Chatillon reached him before his head went under, and yanked it up. The eyes were open; the head lolled. Now they were both drifting. Chatillon, holding the old man under the arms, was kicking hard, but the current was growing stronger. Shaw, on shore, had brought the mules close to the bank. He waded out, slipping, and just before the step-off threw the rope as far as he could in Chatillon's direction. Still holding Standford, Chatillon got the rope around his left wrist and forearm. Shaw started to pull, but his feet kept slipping. He dropped the rope, crawled back to the mules and struck them. Surprised, they started forward. The rope pulled taught, jerking the two men toward shore.

Parkman's attention was taken by his own problems. Delorier's wagon was before him and he had to work to avoid it. His wagon was floating nicely, but his oxen were losing the battle with the current and they wouldn't be able to clear the other wagon on the upstream side by much, and on the downstream side lay the sandbar. He tugged at the reins. The oxen raised their heads, but the current carried them relentlessly toward Delorier and the Standford wagon.

Delorier's whip cracked this time not over the heads of his oxen, but onto their backs. The animals jumped. There was a splintering sound and Rebecca screamed. Mrs. Fleshner called out, "What is that? Is that Beckie?" and the wagon shifted a little as she moved forward toward the front. Lucy, with a voice just as anxious, was trying to quiet the children.

The Standford wagon pulled forward. The oxen were digging their hooves into the mud of the shallows, rising out of the water. But the wagon was beginning to sink. That heavy thrust had broken the snag but it had also either sprung the caulked seams or punched a hole in the bottom. Again the whip cracked; the oxen strained. The foremost actually got hooves up on the bank, dragging the heavy wagon behind. There it stuck, in the mud of the shallows. But it was enough.

They wouldn't sink. Parkman saw Delorier turn around and climb inside to get the girl.

Mrs. Fleshner was yelling in Parkman's ear. "Quit rocking the boat!" he yelled at her. Parkman urged his oxen forward through the area now cleared and was able to reach the bank.

Shaw and Chatillon were pulling and guiding the oxen up on the bank. Delorier was carrying the girl onto dry land. The mother jumped down and took Rebecca, who clutched at her. The girl was wet and hysterical, but safe. "Why'd you make me go with them? Why, Mama?"

"It's all right, baby, it's all right now! It won't happen again, I promise, I promise!"

Delorier stood by, ignored since the child had been snatched away from him, as if any further contact with him might be contaminating. He was dripping. He looked as if he, rather than the oxen, had been whipped. He'd gotten them through all right as well as he could, yet somehow he felt all the problems were his fault. He turned toward Mr. Standford, who was stretched out immobile on the grass. He would try to help there too, with nothing probably waiting for him but more blame, his expression seemed to say. And probably richly deserved.

Chapter 13

While the other men took care of the teams and the wagons, Mrs. Fleshner and Lucy comforted the children, and Delorier and Liz Standford worked on the old man. First Chatillon, who had pulled him ashore, and later Lucy, offered help, but they were waved away by the others, busy at their tasks. When Shaw had hobbled the mules, he came over and pointed out that he'd had a little medical experience and somewhere in the pile of goods was his homeopathic medicine kit, which might be of help. They let him come close enough to examine Mr. Standford, who by that time was beginning to breathe with short, soft sobs, his eyelids fluttering. Shaw took the old man's pulse, pushed back his eyelid with a thumb and listened carefully to the breathing. But finally he simply nodded and told them to go on ahead without him.

Liz had wanted to lift Standford to a sitting position but Delorier had said no and turned him over on his stomach. He straddled him and pressed down against the base of his rib cage in a steady rhythm muttering, "*Out,* old papa . . . *in,* old papa . . ." until water trickled out of Standford's mouth and he groaned. Then they knew he would be all right.

"How do you feel, Paw?" Liz asked him. "You hurt? You hear me?" She looked worn.

Delorier began to tremble. He had never felt quite this way before. But then he had never felt before that he had failed his employers to this extent. A little girl and a woman almost thrown into a stream, an inoffensive if useless old man almost drowned. He shivered partly because the escape had been so close and partly because he was cold. The wet pantaloons clung to and tightened around him. He was sorry for Liz. He had thought her ridiculous. These skinny Anglo women who looked as though they never smiled. But she'd harmed nobody, she'd been kind, and even now she didn't complain.

"I am sorry," he said.

She seemed mildly surprised. "Not your fault. He should've been in the back."

"I don't mean that. I am sorry that you suffer so."

She looked at Delorier and frowned. What in her experience could prepare her for such a statement, addressed to her? She didn't answer. She didn't know how to deal with it.

"Let's get him inside," she said. "Have to change him before he catches his death."

"Want me to do it?"

"Oh, no. I done it before. But you can help me get him inside and under the blankets."

Lucy came over to help, saw the condition of Liz's dress, glanced at Delorier, and then went to look through the trunks and packages that had been brought over by the raft.

The Standford wagon was wet and muddy inside and tilting because of broken spokes on the front wheel. They took the old man to the Fleshner wagon. Mrs. Fleshner spread a soft, multicolored quilt that she must have worked on for years. Shaw also helped lift the old man inside the wagon.

"Now, now," the old man said, staring into space. "Ain't nobody can say that to me, hear?"

"Now sit down, Paw," Liz said.

While lowering Standford to the blanket, Delorier felt her tensed thigh against his and their arms crossed. "Thank'ee. I can take over from here," she said to him. The exertion had raised her color, but her eyes also seemed clearer and brighter. She added, "You thinkin' somethin's your fault. That's terrible. I should've thanked you before for everythin'. You done nothin' but what was good."

Surprised, he raised his eyes to hers. She looked down quickly, the red staying in her cheeks.

As he climbed out of the wagon, Delorier saw Lucy standing at the back, holding a dry dress. She glanced at him, then stuck her head into the back between the canvas flaps, said a few words and passed the dress in.

The wagon had to be repaired and recaulked, the clothing dried, the animals tended. Standford was not fit for travel, the children were upset, the women needed rest. Delorier would not admit it, but he himself felt drained and he was pretty sure that Shaw and Chatillon felt something of the same. Of course, with Chatillon, who could know? But they could not go on that day. Chatillon himself made the decision. They had a good camping spot. They would go on the next morning.

Chatillon, usually calm, seemed restless. All the time they were working on the wagon, getting the supplies ready to move on, he kept glancing at the sky to see how much time was left, whether they would be able to travel, if only for an hour or two. Hours had become precious to him.

Delorier, despite his immersion, didn't feel clean. He crept behind a tree, removed his wet pantaloons and went back into the river. He crouched in the back water around the bend beyond the sandbar and tried to soap himself with a yellow bar that felt like sandpaper, shivering all the time. He crawled out, keeping a sharp eye out for the females, and dressed in the last clean shirt and baggy breeches he had. Then he trimmed the wet mustaches so they did not droop so much.

He returned to the others and decided it was time to start the fire. "It is gloomy for *les enfants,*" he said. "We can make a big meal and I can get the Miss Standford to help me." He turned to Chatillon. "Give up the anxiety now. Tomorrow we travel. Tonight— we should make the best of it." Chatillon raised his eyebrows, but said nothing.

The work was done; the wagons were ready. The animals were hobbled and left to graze and rest along the bottomland meadow with its tufts of nourishing buffalo grass. The little band sat up long after dark around the fire. Urged by the women, Delorier, with his thin, plaintive tenor, sang of the sorrows and hopes of *les voyageurs,* so unappreciated. Chatillon did begin a chorus about his *oiseau,* but Delorier quickly told him in patois that it was probably improper for little girls to hear. Mr. Standford was brought out wrapped in Mrs. Fleshner's blanket. He sighed as he was brought close enough to appreciate the warmth of the fire. He mumbled a little, but no one could understand him except his daughter, who leaned close. She wore the dry dress—a little short, since it was Lucy's. The fire smoothed her face and made it rosy, just as it emphasized the lines and ravages in Standford's and the blank, tired look in his eyes. Beckie also was wrapped in a blanket, but kept shivering. She would not leave her mother's side. Her big eyes followed Delorier, except when he turned to her or came close, when she turned her stiff face and moved away.

Eh, Jean Delorier, the monster, he thought. He sighed. Once he offered the little girl a bit of corncake, baked in the ashes, that he thought might be especially tasty, but she merely burrowed deeper in her mother's side. Mrs. Fleshner, smiling with embarrassment, told him to give it to Jeremiah.

What is it with these Anglo children? Like their women, no warmth or smiles? Behave and do like parents say? Not even songs, not even *Frère Jacques,* bad as that is. He popped his eyes and wrinkled his nose at the boy, twirling his mustaches. Jeremiah did not recoil as Delorier had been afraid he might. The boy regarded him solemnly with that pumpkin face, finishing the corncake. Then he too wrinkled his nose to Delorier's delight. But then Jeremiah reached for a rock, stopped only by his mother. Well, Delorier thought, that's something, anyway.

Liz put her father to bed first. Their wagon had been repaired and was reasonably dry. Then the children went, Jeremiah complaining sleepily that he wasn't sleepy. The women stayed up a while, speaking softly together, then bid the men good night and retired to their own wagons. The men sat smoking their pipes.

"How long will we have them with us?" Shaw asked.

Chatillon kept his voice low. Men from the cities didn't realize how well the voice carried in the still night on the prairie. "We will be close to Fort Leavenworth tomorrow," Chatillon said. "We'll camp outside and I'll ride in and see if I can speak with the colonel."

"What will he do?" Parkman asked. "With all the wagons passing through, can he be responsible?"

"They are the people he is supposed to protect. He is not responsible, but he will do something. Wagon trains pass by that route, and they'll be able to join up with one."

The fire had burned down to just coals, rapidly turning grey. But Chatillon liked to dawdle over his coffee, which he liked "right black," and Delorier had kept the pot sitting on the coals, becoming black enough even for the hunter.

"I'm sorry," Chatillon said. "It's all we can do. There are other trains and other wagons like theirs. We must move on." He poked the coals with the end of his pipe. A tone of bitterness, so faint that only Delorier noticed it, came into his voice. "We will see that they are safe. That is more than their train, their own people, took time to do."

In a few moments, Parkman and Shaw knocked out their pipes and went to their tent. Chatillon sighed, told Delorier good night, and went to his blankets in the open. Delorier remained to put out the coals and finish up. He would sleep in the cart. Chatillon would be immediately awake if something unusual occurred, even a twig cracking or an owl's hoot that didn't come from an owl, and Delorier, close to the horses and mules, was just as sensitive to any restlessness on their part.

Delorier went to the cart and closed his eyes, but he couldn't sleep. Finally he slipped on his moccasins, took his pipe and a blanket and went to the river bank around the bend where he had bathed earlier. He sat on the blanket, hidden from the main camp, leaning against an immense oak, and listened to the river.

Delorier thought he heard a splashing that was not part of the river's rhythm. What Indian would swim across this stream at night? Could be a raccoon, trying to catch a fish, or washing its food. Then he sat up and put out his pipe because he heard what sounded like someone singing.

He waited. The song stopped. There was no doubt something—probably somebody—was out there. He relaxed a little, but remained watchful. He was not frightened, merely curious. He was sure it wasn't an Indian.

It was, to his surprise, Liz. She seemed to emerge from a bush between his tree and the bank. She walked silently on bare feet close by him, unaware of any presence but herself. He had been sitting in the dark, and his eyes, trained by years out in the wilderness, had adjusted to the starlight and the barely rising moon. He could see her clearly enough, while he remained in the tree's shadow, invisible to her. Her hair was damp and she had wound it and piled it on the top of her head. She must have been bathing. She carried a bucket with wet clothes, humming a song. She seemed relaxed and free, a Liz that she didn't show to others.

"Miss Liz," he called to her.

She stopped, startled.

"Here. It's Jean Delorier. I'm sorry. I didn't mean to frighten you."

"Oh." She kept staring in the direction from which she'd heard the voice as though she still couldn't see him. "How long have you been there?" she asked.

"Not long."

"What are you doing there?" she continued, a note of suspicion audible in her question.

Delorier held up the pipe. "Like you, I couldn't sleep. So I took my pipe and came here where I wouldn't bother anybody. Nobody see me—and I see nobody."

Liz showed no sign of wanting to leave, so he rose to his knees and spread his blanket out so that it covered more ground. "Sit down a minute. I have a blanket. We're alike, we cannot sleep, we worry. If we talk softly, we won't wake anyone." He sat again and motioned her toward him with the pipe, whose glow made a welcoming arc in the darkness.

She put the bucket down and sat on the edge of the blanket. "I would think," she said, "you, of all people, would be tired."

"Tired yes. What makes one tired can also keep one awake. You know?" She said nothing. Delorier went on, "It was a bad day. If I am in danger, and if men get hurt, or mules and horses . . ." He shrugged.

"I don't know what you mean." Liz turned to look at him.

Delorier bit the pipe. "The girl screaming . . . your papa falling in the river."

"But that was never none of your fault! Why, if 'twasn't for you—why, I don't think we'd ever got across the river!" She appeared genuinely distressed at his self-accusations. "I don't think—why, I never even thanked you enough."

"Me?" Delorier asked in surprise. "Henry Chatillon—you should thank him."

"I haven't thanked him enough either." Now she was staring at him. "But you—well, I sure don't know why you should feel that way—"

He said, "Miss Liz," and reached for her.

Her defenses were rigid, but brittle. Physically, she was a strong woman. He could feel the muscles of her back and the broad, bony hands that pressed against his chest. She could have stopped him. Maybe she didn't know what to do. Maybe she'd been waiting and couldn't control her feelings when they hit her. She twisted and turned, pushed, and said in a strained, hoarse voice that was even now almost apologetic, "Don't. Don't." But she didn't really fight him. She didn't really mean for him to stop.

He didn't bother to analyze her response. He muttered endearments, in Canuck, in English. She was dear to him, he had waited so long, he was so famished. It had been so long since a decent, clean woman had loved him. He sought solace—and oblivion.

She was a virgin. The evidence was on him, on her skirt. Once they had started she no longer tried to resist or hide anything. She responded a little, yet she never really gave. When he came away, she pulled down her skirt and lay still.

He snuggled up to her. "If I hurt you, I am so sorry."

"It's all right."

"I wouldn't hurt you." Delorier weighed what else he had in mind to say, and then came out with it. "I am so fond of you, Miss Liz."

"Are you?" It wasn't a question, only a kind of obedient response. She sat up, straightened her dress and started to rise. He caught her hand. "It's all right," she repeated.

She got to her feet and reached down for her bucket.

Getting to his own feet Delorier said, "Please, I don't want you to think . . ."

She straightened and her coiled hair fell down her neck and shoulders in scraggly wisps. She shook her head and swept it away. "Best be gittin' back. They'll—he'll be missin' me."

"Miss Liz—"

She nodded. The moon was higher now and he could see more clearly.

"I'll carry that for you."

"I can manage it." Liz shifted it to her other hand. "They best not see us now." She went ahead, away from the concentration of trees and bushes on the bank, toward her wagon.

From his cart, Delorier watched. There was no light in her wagon. He thought he heard a fretful whisper, probably her father, irritated at being disturbed. A little later, he saw her open the flaps, fill a pan of water from the cask on the side and then close the flaps again. She would try to wash off what stains she could.

Delorier couldn't be sure if he'd slept at all. If so, he didn't think it had been for long. He found himself awake, his moccasins on. His pipe was cold and lying by his side on the twisted blankets. The moon had crossed most of the sky. It felt close to dawn.

He walked a little stiffly to the clear area before Liz's wagon. He took a tin cup of water and sipped at it, in case anyone looked out and wondered why he was there. There was no sound from her wagon. Other men he knew would talk about something like this in the taverns or at a trapper's rendezvous, describing every detail with laughter. He saw her face again as she picked up the bucket. The moonlight, filtered through the trees, cast his distorted shadow on the rutted ground. He went back to the cart and lay down. He would try to sleep until dawn or Chatillon woke him.

A dot appeared on the horizon. There was sweat in Delorier's eyes and he couldn't make out what it was. It seemed to move. Chatillon was up ahead on his horse and had a better view. He raised his gun to signal Delorier and the others to stay back and then began to trot easily through the high grass.

Parkman and Shaw were driving the wagons, their horses tied behind. Though he usually dawdled behind, Delorier's mules were faster than the oxen, and eager to investigate, he slapped them with the strap and pulled out ahead toward Chatillon.

The dots had multiplied and become figures on horseback. Delorier knew what they were. Chatillon did too, though his attitude had not changed perceptibly. He stepped up his pace. It was a troop of soldiers from Fort Leavenworth, a large group, riding swiftly and with purpose.

They were still a long way off, and even though Chatillon was way ahead, it looked like it would take a while before he would reach them.

Delorier, of course, could not hope to catch Chatillon, but he moved on, hoping that when Chatillon met the soldiers, he might be close enough to get the news first. He knew about "war" with Mexico, and "pacification" of Indians, and that Colonel Kearney, commanding at Fort Leavenworth, had been ordered to protect freight caravans on the way to Santa Fe, as well as the emigrant trains when it was convenient. But this movement of cavalry was more than that. A major push against the Dakota? He didn't think so.

Behind him the oxen plodded along. He hadn't

been able to speak to Liz alone since the events of the night—a few exchanged words during breakfast, an unsuccessful attempt to catch her eye—that was all. When he passed her wagon, being driven by Shaw, she wasn't on the seat. Her place had been taken by Jeremiah. So there was Shaw, driving the Standfords' wagon instead of the Fleshners', and he still hadn't escaped the boy. Parkman, on the other wagon, had better luck. Lucy sat by him with Beckie on the other side.

As the distance between Delorier and the wagons behind him lengthened, so did that between him and Chatillon, riding ahead. Then, far ahead, he saw that a small group of the soldiers, a couple of junior officers and perhaps a sergeant, had peeled off and were riding toward Chatillon. Chatillon put Five-Hundred-Dollar into a gallop and soon met the men.

Delorier tried to get the mules to move faster, caressing them with curses and the flat side of the strap. The cart rocked under him. He hoped to reach them while the conversation was still going on, but soon he saw that that was impossible. Three men were conferring with Chatillon, in front and on both sides of him. He pointed with his rifle toward the wagons. The soldiers conferred amongst themselves, then talked to him again. Before Delorier could get close enough to hear what was being said, the three soldiers saluted, turned and rode back to the main body of troops, which had not halted or slowed down.

Chatillon stood a while and watched them. Then he turned and started slowly back toward the wagons.

When they met they were still a distance from the wagons. "I'm glad you came out, Jean," Chatillon said. "I want to talk to you first."

Delorier nodded. "That is most of the garrison at the fort."

"That is almost the whole regiment," Chatillon corrected. "The First Missouri. Who will be left?"

"A few, to man the fort. What is it? The war with Mexico?" Delorier surmised.

Chatillon nodded. "It's serious now. They want me to scout."

The word struck Delorier like a cold wind. "Did you say yes?"

"I told them I had responsibility for the wagons and had to get to Fort Laramie." They were both silent a moment. "Jean," Chatillon said. "How would it be at Leavenworth? Could we leave these wagons there? Are trains coming through?"

"There are always trains, but they're filled with people busy with their own lives. They set out without really knowing what to do. Not enough planning, not enough guides. Like the other train."

The wagons were moving toward them, apparently assuming that the main trail went where the leader did. Chatillon and Delorier turned to meet them, but Chatillon kept looking toward Fort Leavenworth. "Jean. Can we leave these innocents there?"

Delorier thought a while. He was balancing his feelings about the alternatives. It would certainly be easier for him if he left Liz behind, but would she be all right? And did he really want to leave her? "You mean, will they be safe?" Delorier finally asked. "I think they would be safe from Indians, and from outlaws." But he couldn't be certain even of that. Without the pacifying influence of the soldiers, Fort Leavenworth was still a frontier community.

"Yes. But more than that," Chatillon insisted.

"What more?" Delorier kept hedging.

Chatillon sighed. They were close to the wagons now and Delorier hoped his friend would say what he had to say before they got there. "Jean, how will they arrange for more supplies? For a guide? For the right train? And who's going to do it? That old man? Those women and children? This isn't even Westport." Chatillon pulled back on his bridle. The first wagon would soon be within hearing distance. "They will stay there, not knowing what to do. With the colonel and the soldiers gone, who will protect them from . . . another Beckwith? They'll be robbed at the very least."

Delorier kept his eyes down. "Others come through like that."

"And we know what happens to them," Chatillon added. "Sometimes a fortunate man is one who does not know, and so does not have choices."

Delorier did not answer.

The Standford wagon was almost up to them. Shaw was looking at him, waiting for the news. Instead, Chatillon waved a greeting and took the lead again. Delorier slapped the mules and kept pace with him.

"Jean," Chatillon said, "what about your wife, Colette?"

"What about her?"

"She takes in boarders, I think. Yes? If we asked, couldn't she help? Advise, maybe take care of the sick, tell them where to go?"

This time Delorier only pretended to hesitate, as though he were thinking. Then he said, "No."

"Why not?"

"She couldn't do it. She doesn't know how. And anyway, she wouldn't."

Once more Chatillon seemed to study the horizon. He said, "We move slowly. You could take a horse, go in to see your wife once more, and still catch up. I'll lend you Five-Hundred-Dollar."

Delorier shook his head.

"Why not? It could be months. That's a long time for both of you."

"I'm fine. And she will have company. Even with most of the soldiers gone, she'll have enough company."

They rode in silence. Then Chatillon said, "We will not go to Fort Leavenworth. We'll head for the Platte. If you can get Mr. Parkman or Mr. Shaw alone, you can tell them. They are our employers and we owe them an explanation. When we stop I can tell them the reasons. If they don't approve . . . we can discuss it." He shrugged. "We don't need to tell the others anything."

He pressed his heels into his horse and trotted ahead once more. They began to turn in a wide, slow arc, to the west.

Chapter 14

"Yet man is born unto trouble, as the sparks fly upward." Quincy Shaw's voice was naturally low and resonant. But when he read the Bible in the evenings it sounded as though he had been ordered by the Lord personally to pull out all the stops on the organ, and his voice assumed what Parkman privately called his cathedral quality.

It was getting to be too much for Parkman. Why were they reading the Bible in the evening after a long day in the saddle when he would much rather be resting, or telling stories with Chatillon, or even bathing when that was possible in the shallow Platte? Why? Because they were now bound to travel with these slow, lurching wagons. Because the majority of the party consisted of women and children, who needed to be exposed to the "proper upbringing." Because somehow they were losing sight of the reasons for which he and Shaw were making the trip. And, Parkman thought grimly, because Quincy was learning to enjoy sounding like the organ at Chartres during high mass. Yet he couldn't complain openly—not with the women and girls sitting so attentively, telling Shaw that it was as good as going to any church. Even his natural allies, Jeremiah and Delorier, were no help, each being so devoted to the major participants—the boy to Shaw, the muleteer to Miss Standford—that they were willing to sit through anything.

"Really, Quincy," Parkman protested, "do you think we need the trials of Job now, on top of our own trials?" Liz Standford turned her eyes to the ground, but the other females, including little Beckie, looked at him with such surprise that he quickly added an explanation. "I mean, among all the available texts, do you think such a gloomy one is good for the children?"

"Well, Frank, if all here would prefer another—" Quincy began.

Parkman excused himself, feeling guilty and angry at the same time, and walked over to where Chatillon was rubbing some kind of fat into his worn saddlebags to keep the leather supple. He kept his voice low, not to interfere with Job's comforter. "Henry, shouldn't we be seeing buffalo soon, somewhere around here?"

Chatillon sighed. Wood for fires was scarce on the prairie and for the past two days they had been using dried, odorless buffalo droppings, proof that there had once been immense herds in the area. "I thought I saw some, far off, today."

"Did you? Why didn't you say something?"

"I couldn't be sure. They were very far off. Could have been antelope." It could also have been Indians. That explained why Chatillon had left them for a time in the afternoon to ride ahead alone after warning everybody to stay close to the wagons. "We'll look tomorrow. It would be nice." Parkman thought that fresh meat would be nice, but Chatillon meant the activity and the hunting.

Parkman prepared for the night. Instead of spreading his blankets in the tent he usually occupied with Shaw, he slept in the open, a little distance off. He wanted to be up early and he didn't want the complaints of Job keeping him awake. Besides, as he noted in his journal, "Shaw had a propensity for luxurious indulgence." He would spread his blanket "with the utmost accuracy on the ground," pick up all sticks and stones, carefully adjust his saddle for a pillow and so on. Parkman meant to sleep, not be kept awake during Shaw's rituals. He fell asleep, lulled by Shaw's voice, still reading from the good book.

In the morning, Parkman rode Pontiac out ahead of the wagons alongside Chatillon. Chatillon carried his rifle, but he insisted Parkman leave his behind, though he thought it proper that Parkman take pistols. Chatillon didn't say it, but it was obvious he thought that both Parkman and he would be safer if the Bostonian did not use a rifle in a close encounter.

They were not far ahead when they heard a shout behind them and Shaw came up galloping on his sorrel. "Did you see any buffalo?" He looked around in all directions. "Is that why you're riding out here?"

Chatillon rode back to tell Delorier to take the lead and to fire warning shots should there be any trouble. He returned and announced, "It's time to hunt buffalo."

They rode for a few miles. Occasionally Chatillon rode off to one side or the other, looking for both buffalo and Indians.

Shaw's sorrel stepped into a prairie dog hole and tripped and Shaw fell onto the soft ground. They were in the middle of a prairie dog city, each householder standing at the entrance to his burrow, holding his hands up like a beggar expecting alms and yelping.

There were long checkered snakes sunning themselves
and little grey owls with white-ringed wide eyes. The
yelping rose to a new crescendo as Shaw landed among
them. He quickly got to his feet and helped pull his
horse upright. Neither was hurt. "This won't do,"
he muttered. "There's no wood around."

"Why do you need wood?"

"Somebody will need to make a stretcher before
this day is over."

The Platte lay to their right, a wide, chocolate-
brown ribbon. Streams feeding into it long ago had
formed ravines, now hidden by the tall grass, which
sometimes caught them by surprise. They passed a
small herd of antelope. The animals turned large, mild
eyes on the horsemen as they approached, regarding
them with curiosity, but not fear.

"Look sharp," Chatillon said. "The buffalo are
likely to be close when the antelope are tame like
that."

They mounted a hill and there they were, a herd
of bulls coming over the edge of the next ravine,
scarcely a quarter mile away, and disappearing behind
the slope.

They dismounted, tightened their saddle girths,
checked the pistols and remounted.

The bulls on the ridge raised their shaggy heads,
looked toward them, then began to shoulder one another, trying to get down into the ravine. The panic
had not yet spread. The large mass, moving like a
river of humps down the side of the hill and along
the bottom had not seen or smelled them yet. Chatillon
raised his arm and the three of them broke into a canter and, heads low over the horses' necks, started down
the slope.

Instantly the alarm spread. The bulls on the hill

rolled their red eyes, snorted and fought to get down. Those below jammed briefly into a mass, then, shouldering and butting one another, began a clumsy gallop toward a break in the hills. The men descended, spurring their horses on. The herd rushed, crowding and trampling, throwing up a choking cloud of dust.

As they drew closer, the frenzy of the fleeing buffalo increased. Parkman reached the rim of the stampeding herd. He tried to force Pontiac to enter, to run alongside the bigger bulls in the rear, but Pontiac bounded violently aside, almost throwing Parkman off.

Only Five-Hundred-Dollar, who had been trained for buffalo hunting, ran alongside a bull at his master's bidding. The bull, red eyes rolling, tongue lolling, foam dripping from his mouth and his sides heaving, slowed down and lowered that heavy head to charge. Five-Hundred-Dollar sidestepped neatly, remaining parallel as the dust rose higher. Chatillon gave the horse his head and, with both hands on his rifle, Indian style, prepared to shoot. Parkman thought he heard the shot, but in the uproar individual sounds were indistinguishable.

Shaw, though he hadn't gone into the mass of the buffalo, was able to run within a few strides of a straggler, despite the terror of his sorrel, and raised his pistol to fire. The bulls, the tattered remnants of last year's hair flying off in pieces, were disappearing over the crest of the next hill.

Parkman spurred Pontiac. The horse, not seeing the buffalo directly in front, charged forward, and then, on rounding the crest, found to his dismay that they were right in front and there was no way to avoid them. Pontiac jerked violently aside just as Parkman was taking aim at the bull, only to find himself close to another.

But if Pontiac could not escape the buffalo, Parkman could not get him to run close enough to one to hit a vital spot. Blows and spurs didn't work. Finally, when he seemed to be close enough to one, Parkman fired. Whether the shot hit the bull, Parkman didn't know, because the shaggy beast kept on. But the explosion caused Pontiac to swerve so violently that he stumbled, sending Parkman flying through the air.

He hit the ground clean, his feet clear of the stirrups. Pontiac struggled to stand upright and was off, at last free of his tormentor. But it seemed to Parkman that there were plenty of other hooves thundering around him. He remembered, before something struck and stunned him, that he had been told never to leave his horse when surrounded by buffalo.

He must have been out for a few minutes, because his next sensation was of a heavy head against his chest. Then strong arms lifted him up.

"All right, old man?" Shaw asked. And then a broad palm whacked Parkman's back, almost sending him down again. "That's a stout fellow!"

"You're bad as the buffalo," Chatillon said mildly.

Parkman gasped and struggled for breath. The blow had knocked out what little he'd had. He wanted to reply, but still felt weak. That head on his chest had been Shaw being the doctor again. He wondered if he would survive such treatment.

"Pontiac—" he said, but was unable to complete the sentence. "Pontiac—"

"I caught him," Chatillon said. "Don't worry."

"Yes," Shaw said reproachfully. "Saw him come busting out and left his buffalo to catch him."

Parkman moved his lips again, trying to make

apologetic noises, but once more no sounds came out. Shaw and Chatillon walked him around. He saw Chatillon's Wyandot standing obediently and placidly, tied to a wild-eyed and still trembling Pontiac.

In a moment Parkman indicated that he wanted to sit down again. They let him. His head was spinning, but when he cleared his throat, he found he could make sounds. "Sorry," he managed.

Chatillon sounded puzzled. "For what?"

"Buff—"

"I got a buffalo."

"Missed the second to get Pontiac," Shaw added. "And I didn't get to follow after my first shot."

Chatillon laughed. "Fine for a first hunt. Just fine," he said.

It took a while for Parkman to feel steady enough to walk around and then to ride, and it took Pontiac some time to settle down, but once he did he started to graze as peacefully as if he'd never thrown a rider. Shaw washed the bruise on Parkman's head and a cut on his shoulder, then gave him water to drink. Parkman sipped it slowly, watching while Chatillon rode up to where his buffalo had fallen. Chatillon skinned the bull and loaded as much of the meat as he could onto his horse.

At some distance he could see the slowly moving brown stream of the herd, its members once more peacefully grazing, covering the top of a hill. One of the animals may have been carrying Parkman's bullet in him, but none seemed to be much troubled. They were in no further danger from him.

When Chatillon returned, Parkman was walking around again, slowly. Shaw offered to exchange horses for the trip back, but Parkman refused. Pontiac gave him no trouble, and he had to admit that, the way his head was swimming, that was a blessing. He was grateful to be able to ride him.

"Quincy," he said, breathing a little harder than the effort warranted, "one small mercy."

Shaw yanked his rein so that the horse almost jumped across the distance between them. "You have only to name it, Frank."

"Let's . . . set Job aside . . . just for tonight. Shall we?"

The little caravan proceeded so slowly that the children could walk alongside and even stop to play games or examine the prairie dog villages and still catch up without slowing the wagons. The men, on horseback, could go pretty much where they wanted, and would occasionally go off to hunt, leaving the wagons behind entirely.

It was different for the women. Sometimes Lucy got out and ran and even played games with the children, her hair loose and flying, forgetting for a few moments that she was supposed to be a child no longer. But her mother usually reminded her before very long, calling fretfully from the wagon. Mrs. Fleshner seldom got out unless the wagon was stopped. The frequent jolts on rocks and in animal holes made her ache and the rocking often nauseated her. Sitting up front on the seat instead of inside the wagon sometimes refreshed her for a while, but her back grew tired. She would reprove Lucy softly, almost gently, but to Lucy it was a scolding nonetheless. "I wanted you to watch the children closely. Are there any snakes? Don't let them get too close to the wheels! Oh my Lord, Lucy, just look at those nasty insect bites all over your ankles! Oh Lord, I don't know what to do!" Sometimes when they rode on the seat together she would talk slowly, in a low voice but at great length, about the farm they'd left and household matters. She knew as well as Lucy that they were long behind. On some occasions she would weep because she couldn't visit her husband's grave, and would never see him again, but this so distressed Lucy and the children that she made herself stop. She needed another woman in these difficult times. But Lucy was still half a child, and Liz Standford was in the other wagon, with her own problems. Besides, she was beginning to act so strange . . .

With the other men gone on the buffalo hunt, Delorier took it on himself to call a noon break. There was a concentration of trees at a bend in the Platte, indicating a freshwater spring. That would be much better than the churning, muddy waters of the river itself.

After they'd pulled up under the trees, Delorier automatically started to lay out the spoons and mugs. "We can do that," Mrs. Fleshner said quickly, slightly irritated.

He nodded and smiled. "I forgot."

Liz appeared at the back of her wagon, bringing the old man out. Delorier went over to help. He could see that Mr. Standford's breeches were already damp. "You go sit with the ladies," he said to Liz. "It's all right. Take a little rest. I'll have him over"—he snapped his fingers—"like that!"

When he came back and delivered the old man, the women were chatting. They had found a small, clear pool behind some rocks and were sitting close by, the food spread out. The children, munching on dried biscuits, were walking in the cool water while Mrs. Fleshner alternately fussed and smiled at them.

Liz had been keeping busy, first with preparing the food and then with feeding her father. She wiped his chin and talked to him in a low voice, telling him to try this bit or that of food.

Delorier made sure the animals could graze freely, then came back and ate briefly. He really didn't like any cooking but his own, and he'd had little appetite since the women had taken over the cooking. Had they never heard of garlic?

Jeremiah waded out of the pool and demanded that Delorier join them. Delorier took off his shoes and went in. The boy splashed him with the cold water and he made such ferocious faces and slapped the water so vigorously that the children ran shrieking toward the opposite side of the pool. The muleteer gave one final leer and splash and came out of the water as Liz was trying to get her father to his feet and to the wagon. "I'll take him back," Delorier volunteered. "You stay with the ladies. Talk about lace for hats."

She shook her head and they led the old man together. "They can't do without you," Delorier said. "Who else can clean up the lunch?"

She turned back and he got Standford into the wagon. He helped the sick man lie down on his pallet, then shut the flaps at both ends of the wagon. "There, old papa. Some people have it easy, eh? No job but sleep. Now get to work, eh?"

"You always was a good boy, Sam," the old man mumbled. "Yes, a good boy. Never had the trouble with you I had with your brother."

So, there had been brothers, a family. All gone somewhere? And nothing left but the hope of California.

The old man slept. Delorier sat in the wagon and rested himself a moment. The sounds from the pool were muffled. Then he heard what sounded like cries of entreaty and then of delight from childish voices, followed by a woman's shriek of "Oh, it's cold!"

"Come on, Ma!"

So Mrs. Fleshner was now wading in the pool and they had a party going. Well, he really ought to break this up quickly and get them moving. Chatillon would be angry. But it was nice to relax. Let the children play.

He felt a tremor as someone mounted the front hub. A light foot, not a man's. The flap opened and of course he knew it would be Liz.

"He rests well. The papa did not need you to sleep. See?"

She sat down across from Delorier.

"Do you always work just for others? Don't you think sometimes of yourself?" he asked her.

For the first time that day she looked directly at him, questioningly. She'd understood the question, but she seemed to think it a strange one.

"Miss Liz . . . Miss Liz, believe me, I wouldn't hurt you . . ." As he came closer, he saw the pupils of her eyes expanding, growing darker. His own hands trembled.

She didn't resist. Or maybe he just didn't notice. He felt as though he were being swept by that river again, headlong. It was much later, thinking back with a little cold, tight shiver in his loins, that he realized that he didn't know if she'd really responded at all.

He did remember—an image brought back from the edge of his mind—that she'd turned her head to see if her father was still asleep. And he also remem-

bered, though it was muffled by the sound of the blood
pounding through his temples, hearing childish chatter
and light laughter from the direction of the pool.

They ate exceptionally well that night on liver,
hump meat, and buffalo ribs as tall as Jeremiah. Delorier outdid himself, racing around, roasting and sea-
soning the ribs. He was planning all the time what to
do with the rest. He wasn't an Indian dealing with
squaws, but there was no reason why the women
couldn't pound and dry the meat in the sun outside
the wagons as they moved the next day. There were
also casks, half empty, that still had brine in them,
for some of the meat.

He kept busy also because he didn't want to give
an accounting for the lunchtime delay to Chatillon.
He had rehearsed his justifications. "Eh, it was only
two, three miles we lost, Henry! For this the women
had privacy for calls of nature, they rested and relaxed. That is important. And the children had their
picnic—and washed their feet! Now we can go much
farther and be happier tomorrow!"

But he didn't bring the subject up. Nor did Chatillon, though Delorier could tell, from the reserve in
his manner, that he was displeased. Two or three miles
could not mean much. Except for a man who chafed
because he couldn't gallop ahead, because he had to
stay with them at all. For a man pulled by duty in
two different directions. And who had gone hunting
at least partly to work off his own inquietude.

Parkman had a bruise and matted blood on his
temple that Delorier had cleaned and dressed. He
was stiff and sore from his fall. After eating he had
gone to his tent early to lie down. Mr. Standford had
been brought out, refreshed from his nap and, for the

first time since the crossing of the Kansas River, had shown some appetite. Chatillon too had eaten well, if silently, then gone about his business of cleaning his rifle and the pistols, and preparing for the next day. Then, when the women and children had settled down alongside Shaw for the evening Bible reading, it was Delorier's own inquietude that caused him to bring up the subject he had been carefully avoiding.

"The women, the children, needed the relaxation, and . . . you know. We didn't lose much time."

Chatillon was examining the leg of Shaw's sorrel, to see if the fall had done any long term harm. Delorier remembered then that he thought the horse had favored that leg, and he got down on his knees to examine it closely. "Only the skin is scraped a little, and bruised. It will be all right." He got up, dusting his knees.

Chatillon nodded and patted the horse. "Jean, these are not the kind of women you are used to," he said.

Delorier looked up. What did he mean by that? That Jean Delorier only went with bad women? He couldn't fight Henry Chatillon, but when he had married Colette—

"These are Protestant, American farm women," Chatillon began.

Why did everybody say American like it was something different, and men like him and Chatillon were outsiders? True, he'd been born in Canada, but that wasn't far, and there were people of English stock there too.

"These are women of puritan training. These are not French or Indian women like Colette, or the others men like us usually know."

"I have met them before. I have known them." He could hardly speak.

"Not so close, so long." Henry too was having trouble speaking, trying not to hurt or to say the wrong thing, but wanting to be understood. "And not when we have the responsibility to lead them and protect them."

He hadn't meant to hurt. Delorier knew his Chatillon. But it was all changed between them. The hunter stood and watched him awhile to see what his reaction would be. He said nothing. Then Chatillon returned to examining a horse that didn't need examining and Delorier turned and went back to the coals.

Fuel had been added to make a fire bright enough for Shaw to read the Bible by. Jeremiah, who stuck to Shaw's side like a tick, was poking it enthusiastically, making the sparks fly up. Shaw had skipped ahead and was beyond Job.

From the journal of Francis Parkman: June 8, 1846:

> Four men are missing from an emigrant party camped across the North Platte. They set out this morning to try to find some strayed cattle and some horses stolen by Indians and have not yet made their appearance; whether killed or lost we cannot tell.

On the evening of June 7 they reached the south fork of the Platte, at what Chatillon told them was the usual fording place. The river seemed on a level with the flat plain they had traversed and appeared to be one broad sandbed, half a mile wide. Chatillon said, "There is nothing to fear. Nowhere I know is it more than two feet high. We will have no trouble crossing, as long as we stay out of the quicksand."

They made a fire and had a meal of buffalo meat. They decided to put off the crossing until the next day, though it was still light. They settled down. Chatillon poured lead into bullet-shaped molds, Delorier rubbed his mules down with grass and leaves and the children dipped toes into the shallow but muddy stream. On the other side was green meadow and the white tents and wagons of an emigrant camp. Its presence was one reason they hadn't crossed. They didn't want to be crowded, to have to meet and contend with strangers.

But this was not to be. A group of men and animals came to the water's edge. Four or five horsemen, seeing the party on the other side, entered the river and in ten minutes were clambering up the loose, sandy bank.

They were thin, sunburned men, worry etched into the lines of their faces. They got off their horses and stood an awkward moment around the fire. The leader first stared at Chatillon and Delorier, then his eyes moved to the rest of the party. When they reached the women, he took off his stained and tattered hat. He said, "Howdy," and shifted from one bandy leg to the other.

They nodded and returned the greeting, everyone except for Chatillon who kept working.

"Did you folks see four men? Riding horses like these?" the leader asked.

The horses were in deplorable shape. Four men could not have gone very far on horses the likes of those horses. Parkman said, "No, sorry, we didn't see anyone today till we came here."

The leader took a deep breath, then stood a moment with his lips working, as if he were chewing something. "Well, I guess you didn't see any stray cattle or horses?"

Now Chatillon answered, without looking up from his work. "No. I guess we wouldn't, if the Indians took them, would we?"

The visitors looked at him suspiciously. "How'd you know Indians took 'em?" one asked.

Chatillon set his molds down. "Because Indians get most horses in this country now by raiding camps. Maybe not cattle. If you don't watch, wolves get those."

The leader sighed and admitted he was right. The cattle—thirty head of their finest, which they were counting on to help them get started in California—had been chased into the night by wolves when the guard had fallen asleep. He was one of the men now missing.

Then, that morning, they had all been wakened by a tremendous yelling from the tops of the low row of hills surrounding the meadow. The ridges were alive with Indians, screaming, waving lances. They poured down toward the camp while the women screamed and the children hid, and the men who weren't asleep tried to get their guns. Their oxen were out grazing and their horses and mules were in a bunch close to the camp. Just before the Indians reached the line of wagons, they suddenly swerved, swept around the horses and were gone.

Chatillon sighed. "What kind of Indians?"

"What you mean?"

"Pawnee? Crow? Dakota? What?"

"I don't know. All look like devils to me. Dakota, I guess. Pawnee killed one of our men a week ago and they looked different. A big fella out front, almost naked, scarred—Satan hisself!"

Chatillon sighed again. "And you sent four men —like you—out to get them back?"

"They volunteered. Got to have them cattle and horses."

He watched Chatillon awhile. Chatillon had gone back to his work.

"Can't lose the men, either. Said if nothing else, they'd bring back some meat. Where would you think they'd be?" the man asked.

He shrugged. "Maybe they're following game, or trying to follow Indians too far. Maybe Indians have killed them. Maybe they got lost. I can't tell."

The man kept watching him. "Don't seem to bother you much."

Chatillon looked at him levelly. "If they'd been my men, I would have said, 'Don't go,' or at least I'd have told them to go with someone with experience. Like me. Now—who knows?"

The bandy-legged leader was about to say something else when one of the other men took his arm and they conferred. He came back. "Well, you're the guide here, I reckon. Mebbe you know the country. Would you help us look?"

Chatillon collected the bullets that had cooled. He said, "It's almost dark. You can't look today. And I have my own people."

"Well, tomorrow morning. We got to help neighbors."

Chatillon turned, began to gather his equipment. The sun had just set. The clouds to the west still retained their glory, but to the east they were turning grey. "I have my own people."

The men left soon after, splashing back across the river. One stepped into a hole about half way out, and they could see the surprised horse flounder. But mostly the water did not go much above the hocks.

Chatillon, to everybody's surprise, suddenly threw down his tools and exclaimed, "Damn!" He went to the sandy bank and called out, "All right! Tomorrow!" But the tattered grey men had already faded into the grey evening, toward the wagons.

It was barely dawn when they made their crossing of the Platte. The current was surprisingly swift and curled up around the wheel spokes and the legs of the animals. The children, remembering the crossing of the Kansas River, were nervous, and Beckie cried, biting her lip to keep from sobbing. But Chatillon had scouted the ford, and except that Delorier's cart got caught briefly in quicksand and some of its load got wet, there was no mishap.

The ford they chose was a little downstream from the emigrant camp, with a patch of woods and a small hill ending in a bluff between them and the camp. The sun was just coming up, casting long shadows ahead of the trees and the knoll. Chatillon waited impatiently for the rest to come across the river. With temper rare for him, he told Delorier, Parkman and Shaw that the men in charge of the emigrant camp were children and idiots. Then he rode on ahead to help them.

Parkman and Shaw stayed behind to help Delorier dry out his cart as the wagons went ahead behind Chatillon. Suddenly they heard a shot, followed by Lucy screaming. They ran forward on foot, past the Fleshner wagon.

"She waved her petticoat," Mrs. Fleshner called to them. Her eyes were wide and her face pale.

"What the devil does that mean?" Shaw shouted. Parkman drew his pistol and moved forward rapidly, running from tree to tree.

He saw a man holding a rifle erect at the edge of the encampment, dark figures running behind him. He ducked behind an ancient oak, holding his pistol up. The man was arguing with a woman, who answered in a querulous voice. Quincy Shaw came crashing up, attracting attention and making himself the perfect target. The man with the rifle was not aiming it. He appeared to have taken it from the woman. Parkman stepped out, his pistol still ready. The man, bearded, with grey hair flying in all directions, saw him and gripped his own rifle. They stared at one another briefly, then Parkman lowered his pistol and the man relaxed.

Parkman then saw Five-Hundred-Dollar grazing not far away. Chatillon lay in the grass, held by Lucy. His head rested against her breasts, his eyes closed. Strands of her hair had broken loose from her bun, her face was contorted and damp, and she was crooning to him. Some kind of trimmed, colored cloth lay thrown to the ground next to her. As Parkman approached, she raised tear-streaked eyes beseechingly.

Chatillon opened one of his own eyes and winked.

She said with a catch in her voice, "Can't you help him?"

Parkman could see a group of men in various stages of undress hurrying toward them. He said to Chatillon, "You all right, old man?"

Chatillon sighed heavily and straightened up. "How's Five-Hundred-Dollar?"

As he rose, Lucy's mouth fell open. "You're . . . all right?" she gasped.

He glanced at his horse, then crouched down again by her. "Much better. So soft, like heaven," he sighed.

"I saw you shot and fall!" She stared at him, bewildered.

"I'm very sorry. When somebody shoots, it's wise to fall down and make a small target." To Parkman, he said, "I didn't know she saw. She screams, runs, waves this." He held up the cloth. It was a petticoat that Lucy had apparently been working on.

The men were around him now. The first man said, "After them Indians, she got scared. Didn't know who you was," he explained, referring to the woman who had fired the shot. But it was not exactly an apology. He and the other men glared suspiciously at them. "Why didn't you say something?"

"While she was shooting?" Chatillon picked up his hat. "I see, with that guard, how the Indians got your horses." He picked up his rifle and faced them. "If we leave soon, I'll help you find your men."

"Well," the leader said, abashed, "she couldn'a hit a barn anyhow." They milled around a moment, conferring.

Lucy had come to realize that she had been tricked. "Oh!" she cried, and tried to slap Chatillon, first with one hand and then the other, so that Chatillon had to seize both her wrists while she struggled.

"Really, Miss Lucy," he said. "It was lovely. The nicest moment on this trip. I do not lie."

She broke away from him, snatched the petticoat out of his hand and ran crying back to the wagon. "She is still half child," Chatillon sighed.

Shaw voiced the opinion that helping the emigrants find the lost men was a very Christian thing to do.

"We'll lose the day," was Chatillon's terse remark.

"Never mind that. Will one day be enough?" Shaw asked.

"That is all I will take. They are either lost or have found Indians and wish they had not."

"Well, it's the Christian thing," Shaw repeated.

Chatillon merely walked over and took the bridle of his horse.

Shaw insisted on going with Chatillon and the search party. The others stayed behind, Delorier to spend more time mending gear and Parkman because of a return of his old complaint.

By evening Parkman felt better, but he began to grow anxious for the search party. He saddled Pontiac and rode in the direction the searchers had taken, looking for high ground from which he could watch for them.

He had to look into the setting sun, since they had ridden west where the Indians and the lost men were most likely to be. Far off, against the blinding red orb, he thought he saw black dots dancing. He watched. Yes, they were probably horsemen. The dancing was to a steady rise and fall. They disappeared then reappeared growing steadily more distinct. He took the chance that they were not Indians and rode toward them. Soon enough he recognized the peculiar figure Shaw made on his little sorrel.

The party was larger than the one that had set out. They had with them four ragamuffin specimens, one with an arm in a makeshift sling. "Hello, Frank," Shaw said. "Just lost, that's all they were. Might have kept riding around until kingdom come—or more likely until the Pawnee scalped them—if Henry hadn't been able to find some kind of trail."

"Any adventures?" Parkman sounded envious.

"Well, we did scare a party of maybe ten Pawnee. We whooped and hollered like we were a whole cavalry and they took off. Maybe we did save the buggers from scalping after all."

"They were just lost, like strayed children," Chatillon said later that evening. He was chewing on a long rib bone, his third. He and Shaw were both ravenous, and the women and Delorier had had time to outdo themselves in preparing the meal. Chatillon wiped one greasy hand on his fringed breeches without lowering the rib. When he finally finished he wiped both hands on the deerskin and told Shaw, "I will now finish the Christian thing."

There were scattered campfires and the shadows of wagons over the meadow. Somewhere, someone was plucking a stringed instrument and singing a nasal lament. Chatillon, followed by Parkman and Shaw, went up to the fire where the bandy-legged man, who seemed to be the acknowledged, if informal, leader, was eating. As they approached, he rose, apparently still a little stiff from the saddle. "Howdy." He sucked his teeth and seemed at a loss as to what to say for a moment. "Sit with us a while and have somethin'?"

"No. Thank you," Chatillon refused. "I thought we might talk."

"Why, sure." He sat down, gingerly. "Go on. Set."

Chatillon crouched. A woman ladled something out of the pot on the tripod and said, "You'll have something, won't you?" but he shook his head.

The leader said, "I guess we ain't thanked you enough, told you how grateful we are . . . an' sorry . . ."

"Mr. Stubbs," Chatillon said, "I will lead your wagons, along with mine, to Laramie. You must follow my orders, and must be ready to leave at dawn."

There was silence. Mr. Stubbs looked at the faces around his fire. No one spoke. The men kept smoking their pipes or eating. He turned back. "Well, I don't think we kin rightly do that yet—"

"Mr. Stubbs, you will not get your horses and cattle back if you stay here. And you may lose more, and more time. I promise I will find out what I can at Laramie. But we must leave tomorrow."

Again there was silence. "Well," the leader said, "can't you stay over?"

"No."

"Well, I don't see how I rightly can—"

Chatillon nodded and stood up. "Well, good luck to you, sir." As they returned he said to Shaw, "The Christian duty is finished."

At dawn they left, before most of the rest of the people seemed to be fully awake. Before mounting his horse, Chatillon said to Lucy, who was passing, carrying water, "I would like to be shot again, if it could be as it was this morning."

She turned away. But after he had moved off, she smiled, touching her free hand to her bosom.

Chapter 15

When they were only a few hours from Fort Laramie, Chatillon called a halt for the night. He wanted to come in by daylight. "Indians camp around the fort and they get whiskey from the trains, and, I think, from the *bourgeois* there, who thinks it stops wars. But the Snake and the Crow, they come there and they insult the Dakota chiefs in their resting places and shout at the Dakota in the fort, and there is always trouble. We will come in by daylight."

In the morning, when breakfast was ready and the tents and other gear were being packed, Liz went to the wagon to get Mr. Standford, who'd become less restless of late. She came back with her face stiff and expressionless. "Would you come with me a minute, please?" she said to Shaw. "I think he's dead."

The old man had died peacefully in his sleep.

"I wish he could have lived to see Fort Laramie," Liz said later. She was sitting on the ground with Parkman and Shaw. Chatillon and Delorier were getting the body ready for burial.

"It wouldn't have made any difference," Shaw said. "He didn't really know what was happening."

She looked at him.

"God decides these things," he added.

She nodded, but was unappeased. "He could've got a Christian burial."

"He can get that here. I'll see to it."

They found soft earth and dug a grave four feet deep, with smooth sides. The coyotes and wolves could not get to it, they told her.

What of the Indians?

They looked at her in surprise. Chatillon just said, "The Indians cannot either." She nodded.

They put planks on the bottom of the grave and laid the body, freshly washed, in its best clothes, on that. They put a plank on top.

Delorier had made a cross. But Liz was afraid that if they used it to mark the grave the Indians might dig it up for the scalp. Delorier started to argue, but Chatillon stopped him and put the cross on the plank above the body. He said, "Now God will know but not the Indians."

"How will *I* know," she asked, "if I come back?"

"We'll put a headstone there," Shaw said. "A beautiful stone, but plain. One of those lying close by." She nodded once more.

"I don't want to make too much trouble," she said.

Shaw read the service. The men took their hats off and the women bowed their heads. Jeremiah looked around restlessly, but Beckie gave him a poke and he took off his hat and bowed his head too.

Shaw began, "Man that is born of a woman is of few days, and full of trouble."

Liz was trembling, and Parkman shot his cousin a "make it short" look. Shaw went on, ". . . for the trumpet shall sound, and the dead shall be raised incorruptible, and we shall be changed . . ." And he finished with the pedal notes of the organ which Parkman thought he could tolerate this time, "O grave, where *is* thy victory?"

Parkman glanced at Liz Standford. She seemed, if not entirely at peace, calm at last.

The Dakota warrior lay in the trampled damp earth next to the fire that, on Beckwith's orders, was being built up until it seemed to light up the whole disordered village. The Dakota had been wounded and his horse shot out from under him by the most experienced of the Crow buffalo hunters. That was how they had been able to catch him and haul him back, fighting and striking savagely at his captors the whole time, and the blood from those wounds still dripped onto the ground. But new stains were spreading from his head, where he had been scalped while still alive, and the fire lit up the bare white bone, laced with red streaks. Beckwith was afraid that he might die too soon. He had tried to get the braves to hold off on the scalping, but they had been too worked up.

He couldn't really blame them. The Dakota—the whole war party—needed scalping, and if his Crow could have caught more he would have enjoyed doing it himself, making it last while the others were forced to watch. But he had to blame somebody. Fury pounded at him. He said to Two Ravens, his voice bitter and sarcastic, "Before you let them scalp, shouldn't you at least find out if it is the son of a chief? Not like last time?"

"They attacked *us*," Two Ravens insisted. "And I know who it is."

"And if it had been Bull Bear?" Beckwith asked.

"They attacked us. And it's an ordinary brave,

not Bull Bear." Two Ravens raised his eyes. "I wish it had been."

Most of the Crow had the idea that the Dakota war party had been under the command of Bull Bear because it had been so swift, ruthless and clever, and also because they feared him—and the incarnate spirit of his father—so much that every defeat had to be ascribed to them. But Beckwith wasn't so sure. He didn't think that a party led by Bull Bear would have been so neat and surgical, leaving quickly when the goals had been accomplished—the guards killed, the horses stolen—before retaliation could be organized. Bull Bear would have wanted to twist the knife a little before leaving. To some extent, Beckwith felt, he understood Bull Bear.

Beckwith couldn't understand how the party could have gotten into the village without anyone noticing and giving the alarm. After it was over they found the guards dead, strangled with buckskin thongs and stabbed. But there had been no sound, not so much as a horse neighing. They must have crept up before the moon rose, the horses' hooves muffled with cloth or deerskin, the animals held in check, perhaps with cloth over their noses, until the forward scouts saw all was clear, signaled them to come quickly, and then sprang on their own mounts as they passed.

Suddenly they'd been inside the village, a tornado, counting coup, throwing lighted brands inside the lodge of the chief and cutting down any who ran out. The horses were rounded up in one lightning maneuver and they were gone. If the one horse had not stumbled and Man Afraid of Thunder had not been close by with his bow already in hand, all would have escaped.

All the good Crow horses were gone. Three, released in a contemptuous gesture by the Dakota, deliberately slashed so that they could not be used, limped back into the corral later. Squaws screamed and mourned and tore their garments. And all they had gotten was this one cripple bleeding on the ground, almost dead.

They'd cut the tendons of their captive's ankles and wrists, but it had hardly been necessary. The man could barely have moved anyway, and if he'd felt much pain, he hadn't shown it.

"I'll do it," Beckwith told Two Ravens. "I want information. Your revenge can come later."

He took two wooden rods shaped for arrow shafts, and using them as tongs pulled a white-hot coal from the fire. He touched it to the captive's tender upper lip, then pulled it away. The lip turned red and a touch of smoke came from it. The warrior came alive. He grimaced and turned his face. The blazing fire threw red and yellow light on the dead white skull where the scalp had been torn and cut.

"Where is your village?"

Beckwith brought the coal back to the lip and kept it there. The Dakota shivered.

"Where is your village?" No answer. "Are Whirlwind's warriors ready?"

No answer. He dropped the coal. Any more on the lip and the warrior wouldn't be able to talk in any case.

Two Ravens spoke up. "You said they wouldn't be able to strike."

Beckwith had to hold himself in check. He answered between clenched teeth. "I did not say there would never be a war party. Where were your guards? Where were your warriors?" He glared at Two Ravens, then added, "If the Dakota at La Bonte's Creek hadn't been drunk and fighting each other, they would have wiped you out." He gritted his teeth, the silver flashing in the firelight. "We have to stop Whirlwind before he joins them. And that's all."

"I sent back the scalp of the son. I asked for peace, sent presents," Two Ravens said heavily.

Beckwith turned on him. "Sure—"

A low sound, a crooning, came from the Dakota. Beckwith whirled. "What's he saying?"

"It's a song, his death chant."

Beckwith listened carefully. Sometimes, half out of their heads, on the edge of death, men said things.

"Grass dies, men die. Only the land and the hills remain. The Grandfathers have already told us . . ."

Beckwith picked up another, larger coal and thrust it against the warrior's side. He said through clenched teeth, "Where is Whirlwind?"

No answer. He held the coal against the smoking flesh. "Are the warriors ready?" he demanded. Except for a slight quiver at the beginning, the wounded man showed no reaction. Maybe he was almost gone. Or that damned Bull Bear had taught them to be like himself. Beckwith removed the coal and grumbled, "All right, he's yours."

Several braves picked up the captive and swung him onto the fire. The hair and the breechcloth flamed. Two men held the body down with lodgepoles until it quit writhing. A burning stench filled the air.

Beckwith walked off, back to his lodge. "Savages!" he muttered.

Whirlwind stood at the edge of the meadow near his village and looked down at the body before him.

One arrow had entered the lower back just to the right of the spine and had started to come out the front. There was another arrow in the side, but the first had been enough. The dead brave had gotten most of the other wounds after he had fallen. Everybody, apparently, had wanted to take a hack at him, including the women.

"How many?" Whirlwind said to Bull Bear.

"They saw two. This one and the one who got away." He pointed at the bluff rising above them. They had climbed down. They'd been trying to climb back up when Mad Wolf's arrow had caught this one, and he'd come crashing down. The other scout had been clever enough to dodge behind a rock, which turned Mad Wolf's next arrow. When Mad Wolf had reached the rock, the scout had disappeared.

"Mad Wolf and Jumping Horse are after him now," Bull Bear reported. "I think they could catch him."

Whirlwind agreed. "Mad Wolf doesn't give up easily." But he also lacked good judgment. For the time being, Whirlwind thought, I will have to believe that the other scout learned where our village is, how big, how many warriors, and that he got away.

He'd been studying the broken body before him. The man's feather and deerskin quiver and bow were Crow.

"Could there be more?" Whirlwind asked.

"Mad Wolf and Jumping Horse could find out. If any more are up there"—he motioned again toward the bluff—"they should know by now."

That meant if there was a raiding party up there, waiting to hear from the scouts, Mad Wolf and Jumping Horse might already be dead. But they would have heard some commotion, at least some singing. Mad

Wolf wouldn't fight without singing his war song. And, no matter what the circumstances, Whirlwind thought, Mad Wolf would hold off dying until he had given his death song, too.

Whirlwind knew that a raiding party would not have sent its scouts so far in advance. It was too great a risk for too little gain. These were spies, sent out far ahead to pick up information for a war party. He reached the same conclusion as he had before: the spy had learned what he needed and had gotten safely away. "Where we are," he said to Bull Bear, "could not be kept a secret. Perhaps we may expect visitors soon."

The chief examined the bluff again, measuring what it might mean to a war party, and the defense against one. From the top, invaders had the advantage of height, and would be able to pour arrows down on the village, but with his own scouts and guards, they would be detected before they got there. They could come charging down on horseback, building up momentum, and be on the village in a rush, but they could not do it quietly.

Since surprise was important, they could come along the banks of Laramie Creek, around the bluff, from upstream or down. They would have to come single file from the upstream side because the bluffs came down close to the creek. That left advance from the downstream side the most desirable for stealth, which was why Whirlwind had outposts and guards there. It still worried him a little, however, because the Crow could move silently between the broad trees. But he had people among the trees too.

He said, "You think the warriors are ready?"

The sullen eyes of Bull Bear lit up. If he could not yet fight himself, he could fight through his warriors. All the hours of practice with the bow, behind the village and on the hunt, the exercises with the lance, the riding, the wrestling—Bull Bear was sure his side would be victorious. "They will die if they try to attack us. But I would rather we attacked them."

"We have a war party out now. When it returns, we will send another." He didn't say anything about Bull Bear leading that one, either. He would have to decide. "We now can decide who to attack and where and when."

Whirlwind did not add that they in the village were now the only ones he could count on for the fighting. His old dream that the Teton Dakota, gathered at La Bonte's Creek, could, as a single force, sweep other tribes from the territory was fading fast. Chiefs quarreled and, in a huff, pulled away from the others, or even took their men and departed for home. Idle warriors quarreled over horses and squaws. An old, sad story: jealous chiefs who would not work together. And now whiskey, deliberately brought in by white men and their Indian allies to weaken and eventually destroy the greatest Indian nation on the Plains. Had he been wrong to keep his village out of La Bonte's until they were ready? They were ready now, the most deadly and efficient warriors on the Plains.

Bull Bear turned over the body with the toe of his moccasin. "Deal with him," Whirlwind ordered, and after another glance at the bluffs, he walked away. The enemy would be scalped, probably by Mad Wolf, who had killed him. During the next week, some daring young brave, eager for reputation, perhaps selected by Bull Bear, would travel by night through Crow territory and leave some unmistakable part of the dead man's clothing or weapons—or his body—where the people who had sent him out would be sure to find it, perhaps even in the village itself.

Whirlwind called back to Bull Bear, "I go to see your sister now."

Bull Bear looked at him, but said nothing. Was Bull Bear becoming reconciled to staying in the village, to be close to his increasingly ill sister? Probably not. It would probably be a great relief to Bull Bear to face enemies that could be defeated by arrow or lance.

Whirlwind saw Blue Eagle Speaks almost every day. Yet he went through the same ritual each time, first getting his eyes accustomed to the dim light and his skin used to the heat. They always kept a fire going in the lodge because, though swathed in blankets, she was always cold. He made sure that his shock at the way she looked did not appear on his face. In the eerie glow of the fire, the flesh of her face seemed almost to be falling away. He thought he could see the skull.

He glanced at Many Flowers, sitting close by. She lowered her eyes as he looked at her. But she was not submissive. If the spirit of the dead came for her sister, it might have to fight her first.

He knelt down alongside Blue Eagle Speaks. Her eyes, even larger now that the flesh had retreated from them and ever alive, fixed on him. He said, "I have word that he was delayed, but he is now at the lodge the whites call Fort Laramie." He paused. "I do not know why he was delayed. I think he led some wagons out. He would have come earlier if we had told him about you. You yourself told us not to."

She opened the dried, cracked lips. "He can come now?"

"I will send Horse tonight."

She said, "Now . . . he can come fast. As fast as he can."

"He will have the message."

Her eyes grew dull and she closed them. They seemed to sink into their sockets. She was silent a moment, then said, "I want to go out to meet him. It is my will."

Whirlwind stood up, his brow furrowed. "Go out? As you are?"

It took her a long time to gather breath to speak, yet her words seemed without breath. "I will not live longer here. After we talk . . . will be a good time to die."

"The Snake—the Crow chiefs—they will have war parties out, looking for the helpless—"

"Mahto Tatonka can take me. Each . . . has his work. Him to fight . . . me . . ." But her breath could no longer sustain speech.

Chapter 16

"There's a cannon in that front blockhouse," Chatillon said. He motioned toward a rectangular structure with round holes punched in its sides, held up by pillars and overhanging the main entrance to Fort Laramie. "The Indians are afraid of what they call the loud voice of the big gun. They say it is just sleeping when it is quiet and they're afraid that it will wake. So they behave and do what they're told when they're here. And come in to trade only when he allows them."

Laramie Creek was low there, so they had crossed it without much difficulty, passed over a little plain and up a steep bank to the gateway of the fort. The tepees of Indians waiting to trade were scattered across the plain and some of the young men, carrying lances as they expected imminent combat, rode up and down. Children came running out of the tepees, or from where they had been playing in the grass to watch the small procession of two wagons and a cart, although they must have seen many more in the past.

Parkman had not expected a king's welcome, but he had thought he would be greeted by fur company and fort officials with some interest and consideration. Chatillon carried a letter from Carlin, the director of the office at Westport, and should have been known in his own right. Parkman and Shaw had even put on their most presentable breeches, and had gone so far as to trim beards and shave necks, putting up small mirrors on the trees and using muddy water from Laramie Creek. A short, fat man named Bordeaux, who was acting boss in Papin's absence, regarded them suspiciously from the gate, and at first acted as though he would not let them enter at all. Chatillon had to assure him that they weren't traders and then gave him Carlin's letter. Bordeaux squinted at the letter and finally called a clerk to read it to him. Then he relaxed a little, but was still not friendly. Without speaking, he ushered them toward the sheds and dwellings built along the high wall.

The walls of sun-dried brick were about fifteen feet high, with a catwalk and railings where there were firing slots. In addition to the elevated blockhouse in front, there were two other blockhouses, in a diagonal arrangement: "So," Shaw instructed authoritatively, "as to give them a field of fire on all sides." But it was not primarily a military fort. There were few soldiers there. It was a trading post set up by the fur company. The Indians outside, it developed, were part of an Oglala village there to trade, bringing furs for beads, cloth, tobacco, coffee and whiskey.

Bordeaux would not allow the wagons inside, though he let Delorier bring in the cart. But he did give the women an apartment and let them bring their belongings in. Mrs. Fleshner looked dubiously at the wagons and at the Indians. Chatillon tried to assure her that they were safe. Some curious Indians, mostly children, had gathered close to them, and one adventurous boy was climbing a wheel. Loud enough so that all nearby could hear, Chatillon said in the Oglala dialect, "I am the one who makes the big gun make its loud talk." The boy climbed down from the wagon and some of the children drew back.

Inside, a small group of Indians was trading and several white men were lounging around. There were no white women visible. Parkman suspected that if there were any, they would be prostitutes. A few of the men had squaws with them. To the left was a corral, surrounded by high clay walls, empty now, apparently waiting for the establishment horses and mules to be brought back at sundown.

Bordeaux showed the men a railing at which to tie their horses, walked up the steps, tramped along a rude balcony and kicked open a door. The room had coarse plank floors, two chairs, a chest of drawers, a tin pail for water and a board to cut tobacco on. On the bare wall was a brass crucifix to show that God had not abandoned them.

But there was something else as well and Parkman and Shaw stopped and stared at it when they could see clearly in the dim light what it was. It was a dried scalp, hanging on a nail, with hair dangling from it almost a yard long.

"Good God!" Shaw cried. "What is that?"

Chatillon and Delorier had been unpacking and putting out the blankets. Bordeaux, who didn't understand English very well, called out through the door for buffalo robes. Chatillon did not answer Shaw's question. Instead he explained that, contrary to appearances, this was the finest apartment in the fort, usually occupied by Papin, or visiting dignitaries, and they were being treated well. The buffalo robes being brought, they were made up into beds better than those to which the men had been accustomed for weeks. Chatillon thanked Bordeaux, who grunted, lowered his head in a brief nod and left.

Then Chatillon turned to Shaw. "That is the scalp of the son of Whirlwind."

"Well, who's he?"

"A well-known Oglala chief. It is his village I was going to take you to visit to live in for a while."

"What's it doing here?"

"It was taken when an Oglala war party was surrounded by a bigger party of Snake and Crow Indians and all were killed. But when the Snake and Crow found out that one of the scalps was from the son of Whirlwind, they were afraid, because there are more Oglala, more Dakota, than Crow and Snake. They did not want war. So they sent a peace message to Whirlwind with the scalp, some tobacco and other presents. It was carried by old Vasquez, a trader."

"Good Lord," Shaw said. "What a bizarre and horrifying custom!"

"Did he accept it? And the apology?" Parkman asked.

Chatillon shook his head. "No. He has determined on war. I don't think he likes it, but feels it must be done."

"Seems a little stiff to kill a man's son, then ask for peace. And send back the scalp."

"All tribes take scalps. The Oglala have taken Snake and Crow. It's more than that. The Dakota have had their war parties beaten, their braves killed. The Snake and Crow invade their territory, steal horses, take squaws. There is mourning and cries for revenge in the villages. Whirlwind is a chief."

"Haven't the Dakota done the same?" Parkman persisted.

"But their losses have been great. And their territory is invaded. They feel if they do not stop it, it will get worse. It's what happens when war is a way of life. And killing the chief's son makes it personal. A man cannot live or be respected if his brother or son has been unavenged."

Despite his tattered deerskin dress, Shaw looked as indignant as he ever had in a Boston parlor. "We have wars too," Parkman said mildly, "even more bloody."

"But taking scalps! It's barbaric!" Shaw protested.

Chatillon said, "I have seen hunters and trappers —white, half-white—take scalps off Indians, count coup, and even make the victory dance when they win. I know that some soldiers cut off scalps and worse than scalps. I've heard stories from old soldiers about ambushes of the British during the revolution."

Parkman found himself getting angry. In a casual conversation, about hypothetical cases, he might agree. But a descendant of Frenchmen—who was he to throw stones? What of the French in the so-called French and Indian wars? Who taught Indians and fought alongside them?

"I'm sorry," Chatillon said. "It isn't up to me to judge. I know what I think, but I am an ignorant man and nobody wants me to judge." He stood, groping for the right words. "You don't understand. Indians fight their own way. Mostly swift raids. Counting coup, proving manhood, winning honors. These can count as much as what whites call victory. What do you call it? Strategy." He turned to Shaw. "You say barbaric. But it usually balances. Some win, some lose, each tribe stays on his own land.

"Now white men change the balance. They bring

in guns and whiskey. Now Jim Beckwith is with the Crow. He was a pony soldier, kicked out because he steals, because he fights senior officers. He teaches the Indians new things—not to count coup but to attack and ambush like whites, to trick into traps, to kill everybody in raids, in villages, to use guns better, to terrorize women, children."

He turned and faced them. "Whirlwind has asked me to help. He says the Crow and Snake have white help. He doesn't know Beckwith, but I do. That was why I tried to hurry. But I couldn't with the wagons. And I couldn't leave those people. But now I will leave soon for the village." He paused and stood watching them.

Parkman forgot his anger, forgot his fatigue, forgot the physical pains. The way Shaw turned and stared at Chatillon he could see he felt the same. Finally! A real Indian village! And in time of war!

Chatillon continued, "I agreed to take you to live, for a time, in an Indian village. I didn't know then that there might be war. I couldn't tell you the rest until now. You didn't agree to risk your lives, and I cannot ask you to do that, or lie. But I must go. It is up to you."

"When do we leave?" Parkman answered immediately.

Shaw spoke in almost the same moment. "Let's go, let's go! Good Lord! Will I have time to take a bath first?"

For the first time that day, Chatillon smiled. "Yes. By all means, be clean."

"Can't let them take dirty scalps, eh, Quincy?" Parkman nudged his cousin. "Spread nits through the village?"

"Oh, as if I ever—" Shaw began to retort.

"When, Henry?" Parkman asked again.

"I'll try to wind up our business here and do something for the others. If it can be done, we'll leave tomorrow. Is that agreeable?"

"Not only a bath, but a decent bed and maybe a decent meal!" Shaw was almost exultant. "Yes, yes, it's agreeable! Early in the morning?"

"We'll see. We have business to take care of before we can leave."

Delorier had been silently unpacking things, making beds, hanging objects on nails on the wall. When Chatillon started to speak he listened attentively. At one point, he stopped working for a moment and raised his eyes to watch Chatillon, but then he went back to work. At no time did he speak.

Toward the end of the conversation, Chatillon had been watching the muleskinner from the corner of his eye. Now he addressed him. "Jean, we can do what is necessary here first. But when we travel, we'll move fast, on horseback, and we won't need the cart or a muleteer. You can come now if you please, or you can come later. One of us will come back or we'll send a messenger. You can decide for yourself."

"Will you need me?" Delorier asked.

"You are of the party," Chatillon responded. "You too work for these two gentlemen." He paused. Delorier didn't answer. Finally Chatillon added, "I am of two minds. I want you to go. You would go if we hadn't gotten involved with these families. Maybe you owe it to Messieurs Parkman and Shaw, and I think you would enjoy it with the Indians. But it would be helpful if someone stayed here for the women and children. Yes. I don't think we can trust Bordeaux to do it."

Delorier thought. He kept his head down. "How long would you be gone?"

"I don't know. But sometimes we would come back for a while even if we stayed long. And messages can be sent."

"Then . . . I think I will stay, for a little while. Until our business here is finished, as you say."

"Then, if you stay, I think you can help to see that the women and children, if they insist on going on, join up with a good train, led by a good guide."

Delorier nodded.

Chatillon started to say something else to him, then turned his head to include Parkman and Shaw. "I don't think that Miss Standford can go on by herself. Maybe she can sell the wagon and go with the Fleshners." By the end of the conversation, his words were once more primarily directed to the muleteer. "Or," Chatillon continued, "she might want to go back. Back to the farm, or Missouri, wherever home was to her. Maybe the papa was the one who wanted someplace new. In that case, we could take her when we guide the gentlemen back and then you go back to Fort Leavenworth, Jean."

Delorier's eyes stayed on him. "I'm only thinking," Chatillon said. "We can talk to them. And when Papin returns, if you stay, you can talk to him. He has better sense than Bordeaux. But Miss Standford cannot go on alone through Snake and Ute country, through the mountains."

"As you wish," Delorier acceded. "I'll try to be helpful."

Chapter 17

The evening meal was something of a celebration. They had gotten through to Fort Laramie safely. They could rest from the road. Parkman was happy that he could now get to his Indian village and that they would be free of the encumbrance of the women and children, however fond he had grown of them. Shaw had his bath and his bed and was happily anticipating the next adventure. The women arrived fresh, clean and with heightened color. They had access at last to what passed for a real kitchen, real dining tables and the chance to do themselves proud, which they did.

Delorier didn't interfere in this meal, nor did he turn up in the kitchen. He sat silently, very unusual for him. He ate little, which might have been expected since he never approved of anyone else's cooking. But he didn't complain, shake his head, mutter *sacre* curses or talk about spices. He simply picked at his food.

Liz Standford was also quiet, but then she always was. She moved like a ghost around the table, serving, bringing seconds, trying to be of use. When she reached Delorier to refill his plate and found that little had been touched, she looked at him inquiringly. He lifted his hand to indicate she could take it away.

Jeremiah whooped and ran around the table with little regard for his mother's scolding. It finally took Lucy's palm on the seat of his dusty breeches to get him to sit down.

Later, when the main course was over, Jeremiah slipped quietly from his seat and went to force a space on the coarsely carved bench between Shaw and Parkman. There he sat sedately, as though he had finally achieved his natural place.

Chatillon decided not to make his announcement that he was leaving until after the festivities, when they would all gather around in Mrs. Fleshner's words, "to visit a spell." He went to the brick alcove that served as the kitchen. The smell of the women's cooking had attracted a bedraggled squaw and her children and some others who crowded around or stepped inside. The women passed food to them. Chatillon smiled. Liz was doing most of the serving to the outsiders. He noticed that she worked apart from Mrs. Fleshner and the girls and that they hardly spoke. He knew that much of that food must have been bought from Bordeaux at inflated prices. He was quite sure, too, that some of that money had come from Liz.

"Mrs. Fleshner, I must compliment the chef. Better than a St. Louis restaurant. Much better." Generally, he preferred buffalo meat over an open fire, prepared by Delorier, but for a change, in civilized surroundings, this could not be surpassed.

Her face reddened. She smiled, wiped her hands on her apron and took his hand. "I am so pleased. And so thankful." Her eyes searched his. Disheveled as she was in the steamy kitchen, her hair matted on her forehead in damp tendrils, she looked young again —young in a land in which women often became worn and broken with childbearing and work by forty. The hand pressed and shook a little. "We'll talk about the future soon."

"Soon. When you women can come and sit down. Then I'll have an announcement to make and we can talk."

"One small thing," Mrs. Fleshner said. Her eyes were now on Liz's retreating back. She frowned. "Well, I wonder if you would be so kind, if it's possible . . ." She paused. "I think it would be nice for her if Miss Standford had a little room of her own. You know, if she could."

He looked at her. "But, I don't know. I know there isn't much space. Women often are put—stay—together. Company . . . safety. . . . Why?"

She was distraught. "I don't want to be unkind. But I have young children . . ."

He squeezed her hand gently and let it go. "We'll talk. I have many things to discuss with the *bourgeois*, Monsieur Bordeaux."

The festivities had been held partly in the quadrangle, under a shed roof where horses were usually tethered, with walls on three sides but open to the curious and the greedy on the fourth. People walking around the quadrangle, Indians and trappers trading by the storerooms, stopped to watch. Some of the mountain men, bearded, fur-hatted, chewing freshly acquired tobacco, greeted Chatillon with smiles or yells. The squaw and her children stood stolidly, watching without expression. She caught Liz's arm and pointed to the coffeepot, saying something unintelligible. Coffee was a particular delicacy, available only from the white man. Liz brought her a mug and she stood there again as stolidly, sipping slowly. Her children didn't move at all, except occasionally to steal glances at the Fleshner children, especially Jeremiah, who made faces at them. Bordeaux stopped by once and sat for a few minutes, delaying Chatillon's plans to speak. He brought a bottle of sour wine, which the men sipped and the women did not. He took what was left away with him when he returned to his own quarters.

Chatillon had managed to clean up, trim his beard and tie a new piece of red yarn around his rudimentary pigtail.

"Speech!" Parkman called.

"Hear, hear!" Shaw followed and applauded loudly, throwing Chatillon into such confusion that he held up speaking until most of the giggling had settled down.

"We have come the long way—" Chatillon began.

"Hear, hear!"

"Oh, shut up, Quincy," Parkman said.

Jeremiah echoed, "Hear, hear!" and pounded on the table.

Chatillon addressed the women. "We didn't catch your train. I didn't think we would. But you will be safe here until you can make arrangements with another train, with a good guide. I have talked to the *bourgeois*. Many trains and other travelers stop here."

The women and children suddenly quit smiling; large eyes trained on him. Mrs. Fleshner said, "You're not going on?"

His answer was mild. "I'm very sorry. I have my business around here. I am working for Messieurs Parkman and Shaw, and this is where they want to go. But don't worry. You will be taken care of and safe. And we will stop by sometimes until you can go."

"Then we cannot leave soon?"

"There is no train." He looked at the sky, as though it were a great clock or calendar. "There are great mountains. I think you would have to go fast to get through them all before snow. I don't know, but I don't think you can, with oxen, without a good guide and train."

"But how can we join up with the Donner party?" Mrs. Fleshner asked.

"Donner party? I thought—the Colby train?"

"Well, I guess we should've explained. We was just to go with the train to someplace—not far I think, up the North Platte River. Is there someplace called the Sweetwater?"

"The Sweetwater River."

Mrs. Fleshner gestured vaguely in a westward direction. "Well, we was to break around there. The rest of the train, I think, to go to Oregon. And the Donner party to go more south on the trail to California. We was bound for California. We heard the weather was better there. Stacy, my husband, had the lung trouble—" She glanced quickly at the children and stopped abruptly.

"You would go by South Pass. That's the best way. But if your guide didn't go with you, he went to Oregon. . . ." He stopped. "It's wild, no road, hard and slow with oxen. You must get through the passes before snow. You should have time and a good guide. Even if you had stayed with the Donner party, I wonder . . ." Female eyes, all around the axe-smoothed table, were on him. "Even with the Donner party, I wouldn't be sure. But now they're gone. I think you must stay here, or this side of the mountains, anyway, at least until a good train comes along and the weather changes. I'll help you find what you need."

After the more formal session, he approached Mrs. Fleshner. She had remained at the table while

Lucy and Liz had put away the dishes. Chatillon glanced at Liz. He would have liked to talk to her too, but she seemed lost in her own world.

He sat down opposite Mrs. Fleshner. "I told you —all would be safe here," he said. "Even work, maybe, if you need it. Bordeaux knows good cooking. But if you don't want to stay here—men are rough, people steal—there are Christian missionaries at the Popo Agie River. It's not far from the Sweetwater, not even far from South Pass, where you want to go. I could take you there later maybe, when I come back."

She said, "Mr. Chatillon. Let's talk straight, all right? We 'preciate all you did. We know what it cost you. And we'd like to pay something."

He shook his head. "I work for Messieurs Parkman and Shaw. They pay me."

"Could we pay you now?"

"For what?"

She brought her hands, tightly gripped, up on the table before her and leaned forward. "We don't want to wait. Stacy, my husband, he talked about gittin' to California and the new farm and warm weather before snow falls much. The winters in Illinois, they killed him. The way you talk, we'd be here in this place for months."

"Don't have to be this place. I told you about the missionaries."

"California. California! Mr. Chatillon, couldn't you find a way to take us there? You been there, haven't you?"

"Once."

"We'd pay you. In your mind and in your heart you know how we need you. And it's beautiful out there, I mean, if you wanted to stay . . ." She sighed and glanced at Lucy. "But even if you wanted to come back . . ."

He shook his head, slowly but definitely. "I am sorry, very sorry. But around here is where I work, where I live. And I have made my contract."

"Well, I could talk to Mr. Parkman and Mr. Shaw. They are nice gentlemen. I don't believe they'd argue—"

The head shake was just as slow, just as definite. "I am very sorry, Mrs. Fleshner. Besides, I think you want a guide who is a guide. I'm a hunter. I've only been to California once."

"Mr. Chatillon, we are women alone. With children—and two of them girls. We are out in the middle of . . . almost nowhere. And mountains and I guess . . . Indians ahead. Couldn't you find it in your heart—"

"Tomorrow I must leave for my Indian village. I have great duties there." In his ears it sounded pompous, and a little petulant. For a moment he almost reminded her that if it hadn't been for the wagons, he would have been at the village days earlier.

But of course she had a point. Women alone—with children—in this wilderness.

"I worry about the children," she said. "But 'specially 'bout Lucy. A girl that young and that pretty without a man to protect her. And these rough men, and these Indians." She looked up at Chatillon intently. When he remained silent, Mrs. Fleshner added, "You want us to wait. We would wait till you came back." In the face of continued silence, her voice faltered. "You will come back? And you'll think about it?"

"We will be back. Two weeks maybe. But—yes."

Maybe he should emphasize, again, that he couldn't lead them. He considered it with growing irritation. But he had said it enough times already to make it clear. There was no point in pounding away. "I have said I would help, Mrs. Fleshner, but only in ways that I can."

He envisioned long, exhausting days over hills and rocks with blue and white mountains all around; Henry Chatillon, celibate, lonely, riding or sitting always close to those bright eyes, bright smile, those lovely, unrestrained breasts against which his head had already softly pressed and rested. Then the chilly nights on which, sooner or later, he would be fulfilled and comforted in a way he had almost forgotten —soft, sweet sounds next to his ear, gentle shudderings against his reborn flesh. And then the realization that the discreet noninterference by Lucy's mother hadn't been because of ignorance; the realization that the formalities of marriage were no longer necessary. The weeks would wear on . . . Henry Chatillon, arriving in California, beyond returning; Henry Chatillon, staking out and settling down on a farm, Henry Chatillon, deserting his responsibilities for some young flesh—

He put his palms on the table, preparatory to pushing himself upright. "A wonderful meal, Mrs. Fleshner. I haven't enjoyed such a meal in a long, long time." As he got up, he faced her squarely and told her bluntly, "You have help. Miss Standford is strong and experienced in driving oxen. Besides, she can't travel alone. You could sell one wagon. They'd be glad to buy 'em here. Keep the best one and travel and work together."

She looked distressed. "I don't understand," Chatillon said in answer to her look of consternation. "Why not?"

"You know."

"No."

A moment's silence. "I have young children. Miss Standford is a very nice woman, but I simply can't travel with young children in the company of . . . of a fallen woman."

Chatillon was dumbfounded. Offer Lucy, condemn Liz. What kind of morality was that? Did she know what could happen to Liz here, left alone? He said, "Mrs. Fleshner, I won't be leaving till after dawn. I'll see you all once before we go."

He wasn't sure exactly where Whirlwind's village was. But he would find it.

Before going inside, Chatillon stopped at the corral. He'd gotten permission for their horses and mules to be kept there with the fort's animals, and wanted to see that none limped, that the mounts that would be taken out tomorrow for the trip to the village were ready, and that there had been no last minute "accidental" disappearances in the final round-up. They were all there and looked to be in good shape. Five-Hundred-Dollar, Pontiac and Shaw's sorrel were probably the only ones worth stealing.

Darkness had settled around them, but not such darkness as they had known on the trail. Lights had appeared in some of the rooms, a torch on a pole was close to the gate, and the moon was starting to rise over the wall. He could see Shaw with the children beside him confronting the squaw and her children and trying to communicate with them by some kind of Boston sign language.

"Mr. Chatillon."

He turned. Lucy was at his side. How could he, who had trained himself to detect the footfall of an Indian or an antelope in the wild, not have heard her come up? Possibly because he was not in the wild. The horses snorted and stamped. And he had been lost in his thoughts.

"Well, Lucy. Not working?"

Had her mother sent her? But Mrs. Fleshner was at the opposite end of the quadrangle, hurrying toward her children.

"I guess we're finished in that kitchen," she said. She was obviously tired, but she sounded happy. He couldn't see her clearly. The torch sent flickering lights and shadows across her face. "Are you really leaving tomorrow?" Her voice shook slightly.

He nodded. "But I'll be back." Then he made it a point to add, "Though not to stay."

"Well then, should we be saying good-bye?"

The Dakota believed that man lives in a false world, with masks, props and illusions, a kind of exile. The real world could only be approached in dreams and visions. In those visions, as in his, the animals, the light, the women, shimmered and danced in sheer beauty.

He put his hands on her shoulders. "Little Lucy, is there ever good-bye?"

She slid into his arms and he held her against him. She was sobbing. He looked around for her mother, but she was now by Shaw, talking to him and to the squaw. He and Lucy were in shadow. They were undetected so far. Was there someplace he could take her? Bordeaux or one of the mountain men roistering in a shack against the far wall would be happy to give him a place.

He pushed her gently away. She didn't understand.

She started to come into his arms again. "Little Lucy, I will see you again. Tomorrow, maybe in two weeks. Tonight we both have work and duties." He kissed her gently.

The large eyes, black and flickering in the fitful light from the torch, stayed on him. He smiled, put on his hat, touched his hand to it and walked rigidly away.

He waited near the corral, hidden in the shadows, for Delorier. He knew the little man wouldn't neglect their horses, not the day before a long ride, and Chatillon wanted to see him alone.

Delorier arrived and began examining a shoe on Pontiac. He put the horse's foot down and turned slowly when Chatillon approached.

"I waited for you," Chatillon said.

Delorier nodded. "I see." He had a tattered dignity, this little man with the absurd mustaches and hat. He stood erect, his eyes watchful and unwavering.

"I've talked to Mrs. Fleshner. I told her that now that Mr. Standford is dead and Liz is alone, they should travel together. Liz can't go on alone. I said they should sell one wagon and go together in the other. They would have more hands, more company." He waited for a response. Delorier looked at him steadily. "She says she will not."

"Will not? Why?"

"You know why. She says she must think of her small children and can't keep company with a woman like Miss Liz."

Delorier slowly stiffened. "I think in the beginning, the Standfords—did they not stay behind, to help Mrs. Fleshner?"

"I am telling you what she says. I cannot judge

or argue with a woman left alone with three children."

They watched one another. Then Delorier said, "You tell me this for your reasons."

"Miss Liz has nothing to go back to. She cannot travel the mountains alone. You know what happens to women alone here with no place to go . . . women in despair."

Delorier turned his head a little and his eyes, under the thick brows and behind that big nose, were deep in shadow, as though hollowed out. "I must handle my own problems."

"They are not only your problems." And what finally could Chatillon do, except scold him and condemn him, which was cheap and easy? Delorier had responsibilities now in two directions. Could Chatillon order him to care for one woman and desert the other? Jean Delorier, you head of cabbage, why the hell couldn't you keep—Chatillon shook his head, exasperated. "I'll see you before I go tomorrow, and when I return we'll have more time to talk of this. Let me know if the horses aren't ready."

Who am I, Chatillon thought, to judge anybody? But my God! He turned and walked off.

His instincts served him better that night than they had when Lucy had surprised him. He was awake in an instant and silently threw his blankets aside. Something was amiss. It must have been after midnight. He couldn't be sure because under a roof he couldn't see the moon or stars. He couldn't hear anything outside the room except the creaks and echoes of the building. He crept across the room to where his rifle was.

Parkman and Shaw were snoring away, and though Delorier didn't snore, he did breathe heavily and sometimes made strange whining or muttering noises. Chatillon could separate the noises outside the room from those inside, as he had been able to distinguish on the trail the night sounds of the prairie from those around the fire. He cocked the rifle, made sure it was loaded and dry and balanced it lightly in his hands.

The door began to creak open very slowly. He raised the rifle. A dark figure started to enter. Chatillon could see in the reflected moonlight a face, with two feathers upright above it. Dark enough to begin with, it had been blackened with dye to celebrate the killing of a Pawnee warrior. It was Horse.

Speaking in Dakota, Chatillon whispered, "I am happy to see you, Horse. We will talk outside."

Horse's eyes opened wide to see Chatillon facing him, holding the rifle. But he stepped back in acknowledgment. Chatillon slipped on his moccasins and came out the door. The sounds of snoring and deep breathing behind him in the room had not changed.

They went outside and stood in the shadow under the shed roof.

"Why have you been so late coming?" Horse asked. "Whirlwind expected you many days ago."

"I am very sorry. I had to help women and children stranded on the prairie."

Horse showed signs of impatience. A few white women and children out on the prairie did not balance the urgencies and needs of their own band and village. His eyes looked hostile. A white man, of course, would put whites first. Very likely, Chatillon thought, he's already told Whirlwind that. The hunter knew that Whirlwind's desire to consult with him would not be popular with the younger warriors. Was there something else?

"Again, I have said I am sorry. But why have you come here now? You knew I was here. And if you trust me, you know I will leave with daylight to travel."

"Things are not as they were."

"What has happened? Has Whirlwind changed his mind? Aren't the warriors ready and trained?"

"Our brothers, our allies," Horse almost spat the words, "no longer want to fight. Except fight each other. They are soaked in white men's whiskey and white men's ways."

That had happened since he'd left. He'd known of the gathering at La Bonte's Creek, had been nervous about it, but he had hoped that the presence of so many warriors, and more on the way, might have cooled off the Snake and Crow and brought about suits for peace. The Crow *had* sent the scalp of Whirlwind's son back, the Snake and Crow *had* sued for peace. Whirlwind mourned his son, but gifts, a few victorious raids, then treaties and sacrifice of territory might have prevented a large scale war of attrition.

How had they gotten the whiskey? Beckwith was back and had been at work. Chatillon cursed his delay. "Isn't Whirlwind's village at the gathering at the creek?" he asked with concern. "The warriors aren't drunk and quarreling, are they?"

Horse spoke with scorn. "No! *Our* war parties strike! *Our* people are ready! Mahto Tatonka is like a blazing fire! Why should we wait for white men—"

Chatillon couldn't help smiling. So the old rivalries with the Bull Bear faction were still alive. As for the "white men" part, the Indians might consider him white, but to the emigrants, Chatillon was a "French Indian," and Beckwith was a mulatto. Though he certainly thought and acted like the worst of the whites.

Of course, he wasn't much concerned with the opinions of Horse, who was a poseur and talker rather than much of a warrior. "That's up to Whirlwind to decide," he said. "Beckwith was once a pony soldier, and he cares for nothing except his will and desires. Whirlwind believes I can advise about how he will think and act." He frowned. There was something else behind all this. Was the village hidden in so remote a place that Whirlwind had thought it desirable to send Horse to guide him in? Something else? "How are my people?" he asked.

"That is also why I come," Horse began. "Whirlwind says to tell you that Blue Eagle Speaks asks for you. She is very weak and you must come to her."

Chatillon straightened up as though he had been struck. Blue Eagle Speaks had been a little ill when he had left, but she often caught colds, and he had been sure that he would finish his business and be back soon to find her well again. He was a hunter. He often left for months to hunt, to guide, to travel to the rendezvous or to trading posts. "Weak? She is very ill? How ill? Speak up!"

Horse had his own priorities about what was important. He saw no need for tact. "She is very thin and weak. I don't know how long she'll live. Mahto Tatonka is riding with her. They're coming this way. Whirlwind says I am to bring you to her before we go to the village."

Chatillon knew that Whirlwind would not have sent a messenger if she were not extremely ill. They wouldn't be carrying her toward him if she were not near death.

Horse went on in his casual way. "Your children

stay with Many Flowers, who will take care of them. I think they have sung their songs and said their farewells. When can we go?"

"A small group, with squaws, with few warriors except Bull Bear, carrying a very sick woman and moving slow? With Snake and Crow war parties out, looking for revenge?"

"It is what she willed and told Whirlwind. She said she would see you before she died."

Leaving Horse outside, Chatillon returned to the room, quietly shook Delorier and whispered to him for a moment. Silently, the muleteer put on his moccasins and they slipped out together. They took the material and supplies he would need from the cart and loaded them onto small saddlebags for Five-Hundred-Dollar and onto a pack for a horse that Chatillon would lead. Chatillon went back to the room to get his rifle and clothing ready, to tell Parkman and Shaw he was leaving, and to get together his gifts.

He didn't have to wake them. Parkman rose to his elbow when the door opened. "What's up?" he asked.

"I am very sorry. Something important has happened. I have been sent for. I must leave at first light."

Parkman's voice was fuzzy. "When is that? Now?"

"Hour and a half, maybe. It will be hard riding. I don't expect you to come."

"Then why are you waking us now? Of course we'll come! Wake us in an hour." He pulled the blanket back over his head and settled to sleep.

Chapter 18

When Chatillon said first light, that was what he meant. A dim greyish pink was just starting to relieve the darkness to the east as they started out, heading west into darkness. Horse had left before them, to take advantage of darkness, but not before he'd told Chatillon that the village was straight ahead on Laramie Creek, less than two days' riding.

The world became brighter as they rode. Though they were generally following the stream, there were mountains all around and often the creek passed between high, white limestone bluffs, along the tops of which they sometimes had to ride. The sun at their backs lit the hills like a stage set. The mists from the valleys and forests around them lifted and the sun on their backs took the morning chill away. Parkman felt a surge of joy, as if they were off on a picnic, but then, when Chatillon glanced back to see how they were, Parkman caught sight of the hunter's drawn face.

They climbed a hill and had a clear view over the creek valley to their left and the marching hills to the right. Far ahead to the right one peak rose above the rest. Parkman spurred Pontiac ahead and pointed toward the summit.

"Laramie Peak," Chatillon called out. He did not slow down.

Parkman made mental notes about the scenery so they could be entered quickly into his journal when they stopped. "Cacti were hanging like reptiles at the edge of every ravine," he muttered aloud. Late in the morning they descended to a meadow for their first rest and watering stop of the day. He spent much of the short time sitting cross-legged and making rapid notes. "We looked down on the wild bottoms of Laramie Creek, which far below us wound like a writhing snake. . . . Lines of tall cliffs, white as chalk, shut in this green strip of woods and meadow land, into which we descended. . . ." He had to chew on his dried beef while he rode after they remounted because he hadn't taken time to eat.

They rode along the creek when they could, but much of the time had to climb and descend what seemed an endless succession of hills. ". . . our horses treading upon pebbles of flint, agate, and rough jasper." Once he thought he saw Horse far ahead and went forward to show Chatillon, but Chatillon had already seen the figure and was watching it steadily. "I don't think it's Horse," Chatillon said. The figure disappeared in a ravine, and they did not see it again. Another time, what looked like two horsemen appeared on a bluff somewhat closer. Chatillon quickly turned onto the slope leading down to the creek and they scrabbled through a shower of dust and stones out of sight. Once when they stopped for a few moments to rest the horses and to make adjustments in girth straps and packs, Parkman remarked on how isolated they were to Chatillon, and the hunter, without bothering to study the ground, pointed out a partially obscured hoofprint, without shoes, a dried and almost invisible ball of manure and a broken twig that meant something to him but not to Parkman.

Chatillon would not waste a moment, it seemed. They kept pressing forward faster than they had ever ridden before. Yet it was not quite dark when he called a sudden halt. He had seen or sensed something. They descended to a small grassy bank alongside the creek, protected from a clear view from above by a curved and hollowed bluff. Chatillon rode up and down, studying the ridge, then announced they would camp there. The place was damp. The creek spread out into a wide, curved pool which narrowed and picked up speed farther down. It appeared to Parkman that he could already see mist rising from the water. But this was the place Chatillon had chosen, and Parkman and Shaw settled down with the best grace they could muster.

During the night, the mist rose and covered them and Parkman and Shaw huddled, chilled, under their waterproof cover. When Chatillon woke them, the morning was grey through the mist. While they prepared, chilled and grumpy, for the day, Chatillon reconnoitered a little, then built a small fire under the rising mist and they ate breakfast. Mounted, they found that bluffs pressed close to the bank would keep them from following the stream at this level and they had to climb to the ridge. Chatillon pointed to signs that both of them could see. A large party of Crow Indians, Chatillon said about thirty, had passed there sometime during the night. The mist had saved them.

Hours later Chatillon pointed out some sagging branch platforms built into trees alongside the trail and broken bones on the ground. It was a Dakota holy place for the dead. The relatives had reverently placed the wrapped bodies on these platforms, above the prowling nocturnal animals, and performed their rituals. That same Crow party had happened on it and knocked the skeletons down and in an orgy of fury smashed them, desecrating the burial ground.

"They are very angry," Chatillon concluded. "They won't take prisoners." He moved around, examining the ground, and then straightened up to look in the direction the party seemed to have taken. It was away from the creek, and therefore, Parkman thought, away from their own route.

"I don't think this is the only party," Chatillon frowned and studied the path. He pulled on his reins and they rode on. Chatillon put his horse into a trot and the others bounced over the uneven ground after him.

Apprehensively, Parkman began to imagine what a raid on the village might be like—the sweeping attack out of the forest without warning, the defending warriors leaping to their horses. Magnificent! An Indian battle! He kicked Pontiac into stepping up his pace.

They found the Dakota group a good hour before sunset. The band had already set up five lodges in a clear space at a bend in the winding creek. It was a good place for the night, with clear water and some protection from the surrounding hills. There were only five men, four of whom came tumbling out of the lodges carrying bows and lances when the watch sounded the warning that horsemen had been sighted. They looked ferocious enough, one in particular, but they seemed lonely and a little frightened, this small band in that immense wild territory, with women and girls clustered behind them.

The muscles of Chatillon's jaw tensed above his stiff beard. "It's Bull Bear!" he cried. He waved the rifle over his head and the three started to gallop down toward the tepees. As they came into clearer view, the fiercest looking brave said something and the others lowered their bows and arrows.

Chatillon rode directly to the assembled warriors, and then stopped so abruptly that Five-Hundred-Dollar reared. He was off the horse and had thrown himself on the apparent leader of the braves so fiercely that Parkman, astonished, thought for an instant they were going to fall to the ground in some kind of combat to the death. Instead they stood, face to face, legs braced, holding each other's arms in what was some kind of intimate greeting and embrace. A woman had caught the bridle of Five-Hundred-Dollar who, excited by the run and the smell of the other horses, kept pawing the ground and tossing his head, nostrils quivering and flickering like the wings of a butterfly.

Parkman and Shaw pulled up, still watching to see what was going on between the two men. The Indian, half naked, was not quite as tall as Chatillon. He had scars on his cheekbone and the bridge of his nose. His physique was matchless. Parkman and Shaw got off their horses cautiously, watching the braves and the two men. Though a squaw reached for it, Parkman held on to his own bridle. Chatillon and the warrior were talking to each in the Oglala dialect. The Indian's words came out more emphatically, his face contorted with emphasis and passion. Chatillon suddenly turned to Parkman and Shaw. There were tears in his eyes. "He is my dear brother-in-law," Chatillon told them. "Mahto Tatonka, Bull Bear in English."

Shaw came over, stood awkwardly a moment,

then held out his hand. The Oglala looked at it, then inquiringly back to Chatillon. The hunter grinned, took the Indian's hand and brought it down until it touched, palm to palm, with Shaw's.

"Pleased, I'm sure," Shaw said. "Glad to meet you."

The Indian, still looking puzzled, nodded several times, and when he realized what was expected of him, clutched Shaw's palm like a vise. Shaw winced, smiled and nodded several times himself. Then it was Parkman's turn, an honor he could not refuse, because it was always possible that Bull Bear might consider refusal a rejection or an insult. Parkman stared into the dark, hard eyes. He endured the viselike grip.

They heard another sound, a crooning, like a breathless song. Chatillon broke away, ran into the lodge from which the sound came with his dark brother-in-law right behind him. The women outside the lodge now took up a cry in counterpoint, a general lamentation.

Evidently, Parkman and Shaw had been accepted. The other braves no longer looked at them warily or with hostility. Parkman felt a hand exploring his trousers and looked down quickly. A young girl, about thirteen, was curious about the structure and function of the waistband and the deerskin fringes, and was satisfying that curiosity directly. He removed her hands and shook his head. She laughed.

The entrance to the lodge into which Bull Bear and Chatillon had disappeared was not guarded and hadn't been closed. Shaw circled over toward it and stuck his head inside. The Indians watched, but didn't seem to disapprove. Parkman joined him.

It was dim inside, but there was a glow from live coals close to the center of the lodge and some light filtered down through the crossed lodgepoles at the top, open to allow smoke to escape. A squaw, wearing a beaded white gown, partly covered by a rich buffalo robe, lay on a kind of stretcher of hides attached to lodgepoles.

Parkman, when he could see her face clearly, was shocked at her appearance. She seemed little more than a living skeleton. Chatillon's presence, though, had revived her so that her eyes in their dark sockets were open. She was speaking, though Parkman couldn't make out what she was saying. The sounds were soothing, consoling, and expressed a weak but deep joy.

Chatillon, speaking Oglala most of the time but occasionally lapsing into rapid French or English exclamations, could be more easily understood. Why hadn't they let him know? He would have understood and rushed back. At one point Parkman thought he saw the mighty hunter, in the vague light, lower his head and weep.

A skeleton hand came out of the robe, wavered a little and rested on his head. Chatillon kissed it and held it against his cheek. She crooned again—a voice almost without breath. The dying woman was trying to console the desolate, guilt-ridden Chatillon.

Hovering above them was Bull Bear, the woman's brother, standing perfectly still except for the muscles occasionally playing along the back of his thick neck. Sometimes he looked like a thundercloud ready to shoot out lightning. He glared at the faces in the entrance.

"The Oglala, the Brulé and other western bands of the Dakota are thorough savages," Parkman had written in his journal back in Fort Laramie, a day before they had started on the trip. Then, by explanation he added, "Not one of them can speak an European tongue, or has ever visited an American settlement." Parkman remembered his harsh judgment and mentally took back his words. The Indians at great risk had come away from their safe and comfortable village because a dying woman wanted to see her husband. The husband, the white man, was breaking down, and the Indians, including the dying one, were supporting and consoling him.

Parkman motioned Shaw to step back. Then he closed the flaps.

Chapter 19

Parkman slept fitfully that night, not because he wasn't tired or the beds weren't comfortable. He and Shaw had been accepted into the band and made honored members. They had, of course, come away without their tent, but they had brought their blankets and could have slept in the open. But their hosts wouldn't hear of it and so they'd been ushered into one of the lodges and given the softest buffalo robes.

But the lodge was crowded. Privacy was not as highly valued in Indian villages as in Boston, so the sleeping arrangements were a little snug to begin with. And, of course, sleep had to be put off until all of the rituals of hospitality had been exhausted. Moreover, as he noted in his journal, "The Oglala are inordinately fond of children," and the children had the run of the packed place. The children, in fact, took a special liking to him and to Shaw. Indian children, Parkman wrote, are shamelessly indulged. "They eat too much and have too few duties." When he finally lay down to rest, he found children snuggling up to him in irritating and occasionally embarrassing ways. "I had to punch some savage heads," he wrote later.

But he was unusually restless anyhow. Occasion-

ally, even above the sounds of the sleepers, he believed
he could hear soft murmurs or whispers. After a while,
when snuggling children had awakened him for the
third time, he rose and took the latest aggressor, now
fast asleep, to a different part of the lodge. And as
long as he was up, he went outside.

He couldn't see the familiar figure of Chatillon,
wrapped in his blankets with his gun by his side, anywhere. But he could hear murmuring coming from the
lodge of Chatillon's wife, Blue Eagle Speaks. He drew
closer. This time he didn't draw the flaps. He could
hear Chatillon's low tones and, very occasionally, her
answers, so faint as to be almost inaudible. Where
had she got the strength? Chatillon, quoting Bull Bear,
had told them that she had hardly been able to speak
or move on the way out. Now they had been together
for hours, reliving years, sometimes embracing gently.
They must still have the faint bed of coals—Parkman
could see a dim reddish light in the cracks in the
hides covering the poles—but that would be their only
light. He didn't know what time it was, but the night
must be at least half through. Perhaps she might finally fall asleep. But then, he expected, Chatillon
would sit up with her—or perhaps keep up his end
of the conversation even though her ears were temporarily deafened, unburdening his heart before the opportunity might be lost forever. Finally Parkman went
back to his bed.

In the morning Chatillon woke him. The guide's
eyes looked tired and a little red, but probably no
worse than his own, Parkman thought. While they were
talking, the hides were already being stripped off the
lodge and the women were starting to move about,
getting ready to travel. Chatillon had discussed it with

Bull Bear and decided that the mission of the trip from the village had been accomplished—he and Blue Eagle Speaks had been able to meet and talk—so there was no point in the Indians continuing on to Fort Laramie, particularly in view of the danger. They were going back to the village.

Bull Bear was particularly eager to return to his warriors, and Chatillon had urged that the Indian go on ahead and they would follow. But in this respect, at least, the younger Bull Bear was not like his father. He would not sacrifice everybody—at least not his sister—to get what he wanted. They would go on together.

That was good news to Parkman. With those two riding up ahead, he felt safe for the first time that trip. "What happens if we meet that Crow party?" Parkman asked.

"We will not *meet* them. They will find us or they will not."

"Well, if they find out we are here?"

"They will kill all without mercy," Chatillon disclosed matter-of-factly.

"Women and children too?" Parkman's mind reeled.

"Yes." Chatillon rose and went off a few steps, then stopped and looked back. "I am very sorry to have gotten you in this. I . . . had to break my word. But I tried to get you to stay at Fort Laramie."

"Wouldn't miss it for the world." Parkman gave him the broadest smile he could manage, then swallowed hard as soon as Chatillon had turned away.

They started shortly after, without, as Shaw pointed out, "proper ablutions." And without proper breakfast either, Parkman thought, chewing on pemmican as he rode along. He was still a little stiff from yesterday's hard ride. Soft from the layover at Fort Laramie, he decided.

But he did loosen up and enjoyed the warmth of the early morning sun in the brisk fresh air. He stayed with the main party. They went along slowly, generally moving along the creek banks when they could. They rode over the hills only when they could not follow the stream, or when the creek doubled back on itself so much that they could save miles by moving through whatever passes were available. The lodges, the equipment and the smaller children had been tied to travois, dragged behind horses and mules. Blue Eagle Speaks had also been lifted onto a travois and secured on it. It was partly because of her that they moved so slowly. She looked like a mummy, her eyes closed, her cheeks sunken. Two of the squaws walked alongside her, watching her anxiously.

Parkman kept his eye on the broad backs of Chatillon and Bull Bear. Despite the coolness of the morning, the Indian was naked from the waist up as he had been on the evening before. The buffalo skin that covered him only in bad weather hung loose around his waist, secured by a belt. His head was bare, his hair gathered loosely in a clump behind with no decoration except the mystic whistle, made from an eagle's wing bone, tied on top. His horse had no bridle, but was controlled by a cord of hair lashed around its jaw. He rode the typical Oglala saddle, wood covered with rawhide, and pommel and cantle rising at least a foot and a half on both sides straight up. Bull Bear was wedged so tightly in it that nothing could get him out, except the bursting of the girths.

Chatillon's saddle, though old and worn, was of course more comfortable, and he wore a shirt and jacket. Still, the men looked remarkably alike from the back. They functioned like teammates, communicating and coordinating their efforts without words, each covering overlapping territory in front to seek out the best path.

Once more the rising mist on the river, the sun coming over the limestone bluffs, the green meadow and the bunched buffalo grass on the slopes so entranced Parkman that he paid little attention to physical discomfort or danger. The clearer the air, the brighter and more beautiful the hills, the easier the band could be seen, but what could hurt them on a morning like this? He could see the remaining four braves, riding along the perimeter of the band, looking toward the hills and exchanging anxious glances. He could watch the women, on foot or on the mules pulling the travois, whispering nervously to one another and telling the children sternly to be quiet. But the day was too glorious for worry.

They had been traveling for less than an hour when a signal from Bull Bear brought them to a halt. Far off on the horizon was the silhouette of a single horseman. The squaws uttered little cries and clustered together. If that horseman was a spy for the Crow party and he spotted them, they were all dead. Pontiac, sensing the tension, snorted and stamped a hoof. Parkman dug a heel into him and told him in a furious whisper to be quiet.

Chatillon and Bull Bear dismounted and crouched low, watching the distant figure. They waited. The squaws and children, who could not see clearly from their position, watched the men, waiting for news. Only Blue Eagle Speaks seemed unaffected. She opened her eyes when a young squaw spoke to her, but she soon closed them again. Death did not frighten her.

Parkman looked once more at the spot on the horizon, his eyes dazzled by the contrast between mountain and sky. It seemed to him the horseman had disappeared. Shaw was more confident in his opinions. The horseman was no longer there, he said. Gone off and good riddance.

Chatillon came back to confer with the other men. They hadn't seen the horseman clearly enough to identify him. If he, or others, did not reappear in a few minutes, they would go on. But it was close to an hour before they did go on. The squaws were afraid and didn't want to budge. In a while, Bull Bear came charging back, glared at the squaws and the braves, barked two harsh words and returned to Chatillon. The band moved forward.

They traveled most of the day, dragging the travois painfully over rocks and roots. On one particularly rough passage, Parkman winced as he watched Blue Eagle Speaks jolt in her basket. Occasionally Bull Bear or Chatillon rode back to see her or talk to her. Late in the day Bull Bear dropped back to be with her, and Parkman and Shaw, glad to be forward, took his place with Chatillon. Ahead was a distant valley, green and brown, with what looked like a herd of grazing buffalo, still as in a painting. Behind them blue mountains formed a jagged horizon.

They heard Bull Bear call. Chatillon yanked up his horse's head and they turned and galloped back. The whole band was gathered around the now stationary travois of Blue Eagle Speaks. Chatillon leapt from his horse, pushed through the group and knelt at her side. Parkman and Shaw followed and also dismounted. They couldn't get close to the stricken woman, but they heard the death rattle in her throat.

There was silence for a long moment. Then a

wail arose, a heart-stopping lamentation, started by
the women and taken up by the children and men.
As he listened to the cries, he remembered the legend
that the Indians were descended from the ten lost
tribes of Israel.

But if, to Protestant eyes, the tribulations of Blue
Eagle Speaks were finished, that did not accord with
Oglala customs. Whether the Crow war party was in
the area or not, the proper rituals had to be performed.
Chatillon informed Parkman and Shaw that he, like
other relatives of his wife, had to give valuable presents to be placed alongside the body in its last resting place.

Chatillon went to the extra load that he had put
on the pack horse. Parkman had wondered at the
time what extra items Chatillon was taking on the
trip. Now he knew, though he didn't pay particular
attention to the ornaments and objects that the hunter
took out. Chatillon had known when he packed the
presents that they were for his wife's funeral.

They carried the body to a deep hollow surrounded by dreary, flattened hills in the gathering night.

While the lodges were being set up, Chatillon,
Parkman and Shaw got back on their horses and reconnoitered the area, riding along the ridges. Bull Bear,
as younger brother and closest male relative, stayed
with the body. Chatillon, as husband, would have liked
to stay too, but someone had to look for signs of possible danger, and it was obvious he didn't trust Parkman and Shaw to do it alone. They looked for sil-
houettes or signs of movement or light from possible
campfires. They also listened for strange-sounding bird-
calls or wolf howls that might be signal calls. They
noticed nothing unusual.

They returned from a different direction. They

could hardly see four of the lodges though their eyes
had become accustomed to the darkness, but the fifth,
the largest, was illuminated by a red fire inside, shining through the translucent covering of rawhide. Other
than that there were no signs of life. The city of the
dead, Parkman thought, and felt chilled.

They rode to the largest lodge. A squaw came
out and took charge of the animals, but did not speak
or greet them. They entered. The lodge was crowded.
There were three rows of silent Indians in a circle
with a large fire burning in their midst. A place was
made for them at the head of the lodge, robes spread
for them to sit on, a pipe lighted and handed to them.

Hours passed. Parkman nodded off several times.
Once he fell against the Indian next to him. Other
times Shaw elbowed him awake. The fire died down
and the lodge grew dark, the silent figures fading like
wraiths into the gloom. When only embers were left,
a squaw would reach out and throw a piece of buffalo
fat on them from time to time and a bright flame
suddenly would spring up, casting the motionless
bronze faces in stark relief.

At dawn they were able to escape. Even the grey
light outside dazzled them. They walked stiffly toward
the next lodge, following Chatillon, who carried the
presents. Inside was the corpse in lonely and opulent
grandeur and peace. The robes and wrappings that had
bound her tightly in the hope of holding in life a
little longer were off now. The hollow-cheeked figure
was seated rigidly, propped as on a throne against the
lodge wall. Her body was dressed in blue-beaded and
figured deerskin, a white buffalo robe, intricately
worked beaded and colored moccasins and a chain of
small copper plates hanging in her hair like large
earrings.

The presents were laid, reverently, close to her. They were objects that Chatillon, from his life with her, knew that she might have found useful, or simply would have liked. Food and household implements had already been placed near for her use and sustenance "over the dismal prairies to the villages of the dead," as Parkman wrote later in his notebook.

When they came out, the best Indian horse, a mare as multicolored and beautiful as a calico cat, was staked close to the lodge that held the corpse. The mare stood with its head raised to smell the grass on the nearby hills. Parkman said, "What will they do with that horse?"

"Blue Eagle Speaks was made lame in a fight with the Pawnee," Chatillon answered obliquely. "It is a very long trail and she cannot walk far."

"You mean they're going to kill it?" Shaw was incredulous. Chatillon did not answer.

"It's their custom," Parkman confirmed.

Chatillon had an intense conference with Bull Bear. It sounded strange to Parkman, listening to the white man expostulating at length and with some passion in Oglala, while the Indian grunted, occasionally responding with monosyllables.

Later Chatillon summarized what had been decided. "I must go on to the village. I don't see what I can do here. Whirlwind has been waiting and I am needed. I wanted Bull Bear to hurry ahead with me or come soon. He is needed too, but he is her brother, and what is all right for a *meneaska* is not all right for him."

"Won't there be some sort of—uh—funeral?" Shaw asked.

"They will build a platform according to their custom." Chatillon paused. "To me . . . she is no longer . . . here." Another pause. "I have to go. You must come with me."

Parkman asked, "What does Bull Bear intend to do?"

"He will lead the band back, at least part way."

"What do you mean part way?" Parkman grew concerned.

"I think he has his own plans. I think he thinks if he goes back, Whirlwind will keep him busy training and he cannot fight. There are now two war parties out and he knows where one is. Maybe both. He didn't tell me. He doesn't want me to know. That way, I won't have to lie. He goes his own way." Chatillon had been crouching, watching the sand sift through his fingers as he'd talked. Now he straightened, beat the dust off his palm against the long fringes on his breeches. "We must leave."

The same squaw who had taken their mounts the night before brought them their horses. Parkman and Shaw mounted, but Chatillon went back into the lodge to his wife's body. He was gone for several minutes. But when he came out, he got on his horse without a word or a backward glance and started. The lodges were being struck, the travois loaded. Some of the band at least was getting ready to leave. They performed a final service for the Indians by riding a circuit of the surrounding hills, surveying them and a distant valley for any sign of Crow. Then they moved ahead swiftly, following Chatillon's pace.

In a few hours, while passing through a patch of trees overlooking the winding Laramie Creek, two Indians, lances in their hands and striped for battle, rose up silently out of nowhere on both sides of them. Chatillon exchanged a few words with them. Then he,

Parkman and Shaw passed on. In a few minutes their horses were half sliding, half trotting down a bluff. They rounded a bend and Whirlwind's village lay on the meadows on both sides of the bank before them.

Chapter 20

"He didn't come with you," Whirlwind said.

"No." Chatillon's speech was as clipped as the chief's.

"He will come with the rest."

Chatillon sighed. "The band, the women and children, should be here soon. I had to come first, as you requested."

Whirlwind watched him closely. He sensed the evasion. "He must come soon. He is commander in the field of our warriors."

Chatillon had noticed that a large proportion, probably a majority, of Whirlwind's most experienced and able warriors was gone. What remained were the hot-blooded youths, willing to throw their lives away, too anxious to prove themselves and earn reputations. They were not reliable unless under the control of experienced commanders. There were also the older men, some approaching middle age, who had experience and wise counsel to offer, but who were growing fat and out of practice.

"We cannot wait long," Whirlwind said. "There have been spies. He will come tomorrow."

"I cannot speak for Bull Bear," Chatillon said.

"As you know, he follows his will. I have an opinion."

Whirlwind did not answer or ask. He waited.

"Your best warriors are already moving in war parties."

"Yes. I didn't want to send the second so soon or make it so large. But Bull Bear had followed my will in all else and I gave him that," Whirlwind explained.

"I think he'll bring the band to where the pickets can escort it in. Then I think he and maybe the warriors with him will go to join a strike party. He told me he knows where one is." Chatillon's implication was obvious. If Bull Bear was sure about where the warriors were, it probably meant that he had given them instructions to be there. The father reappeared in the son. He had disobeyed orders and the decisions of the council, had followed his own will and was out in the field. "I cannot know," Chatillon went on rather lamely. "I give you my opinion." It was more than opinion. There were things that Bull Bear had told him that made his intention clear without putting it into words, but Chatillon didn't want to say more.

Whirlwind stood still, his face immobile. He was still chief and his orders had been disobeyed. He would have to do something. But, facing crisis, simple punishment of Bull Bear might not be the best thing to do. On the other hand, he had to keep discipline. He had to do what would be best for the village. Until he had decided, he would not speak of the matter unless he had to. The old nightmare haunted him. There was fighting within the village.

Chatillon helped him. "I don't think he wanted to disobey. He has wanted to fight. He thought it was his time. Didn't you tell him that he could go soon?"

"I had told him he could head a war party."

Whirlwind was resigned. What was done was done. It was time to set it aside, at least for now. "I sent for you because I want to know how to fight like Medicine Calf. I know he is honored by the Crow and tries to teach them new ways to fight that he learned in Two Star's army."

Whirlwind had the too simple belief that the Crow successes, sometimes under Beckwith's leadership, were due to some military magic he had picked up before being kicked out of the American army. But most of it was just due to better preparation and more ruthless leadership, which the Oglala, whether Whirlwind realized it or not, now were matching. At least that was true of this village, of the leadership, training and planning done by Whirlwind and Bull Bear. Perhaps, though, coordination was faulty. And there was the other problem. With the chaos and fighting now reported from the camp at La Bonte's Creek, the advantage of numbers might be going.

"How many warriors do you have still left in the village that you can rely on?" Chatillon asked.

"What you see. Most are still here," the chief gestured toward the lodges.

What Chatillon could see were untrained braves deprived of leadership. Where, he wondered, were the war parties that Bull Bear surely had trained? "Where are your war parties?" he asked.

"They attack the Snake and Crow where they find them. They have raided Medicine Calf's village, killed warriors, taken horses, counted coup." Whirlwind sounded proud. "They are like lightning, striking without warning, spreading terror. Our women sing again of heroes."

Chatillon ignored the boasting and tried to pin

down the facts. "Have any of their villages been destroyed?"

Whirlwind looked puzzled for a moment. He repeated, "We kill the Snake and Crow where we can. We destroy lodges." Then it occurred to him that Chatillon was thinking of something broader. "We don't let our enemy rest. They don't know when or where we will strike. We make them keep their parties closer to the villages to defend them, so they cannot raid."

"Beckwith also knows that way."

It wasn't just a matter of destroying villages. Indian war parties did that when they could. It was a matter of a broader strategy, covering large areas, that would knock an enemy out of the war. What was the white man's secret? That is, apart from more guns and the big guns that spoke thunder. A white commander, if he was worth anything, would plan a campaign as a whole. He would know his enemy's strengths and weaknesses, and prey upon those weaknesses, paying no heed to counting coup or gaining honor. Whirlwind would not comprehend. He couldn't use a strategy that killed buffalo to starve Indians.

"We saw a Crow war party. They are out too. I told you. We barely escaped," Chatillon reminded him.

"How does Medicine Calf tell the Crow to fight?" Whirlwind asked, seeking a simple, magic technique.

Beckwith not only fought like a white man, he fought like an Indian, too. Bull Bear and his cousin White Shield, operating independently, would spread anger and terror among warriors. Beckwith would coordinate his forces and look for the weak spot, to destroy the heart and let the limbs die. Being Beckwith also, he would not hesitate to wipe out the women and children, or take them captive if he thought it helpful. He did not believe in heroics, only in victory.

Chatillon was distracted by Whirlwind's youngest squaw who, sitting comfortably alongside the chief while he toyed with her braids, kept staring at the hunter. Bull Bear was gone, most of the young braves were gone, and Chatillon was young and new. He was going to have trouble with that one, the hunter thought. "I can only tell you what I would do." He paused to think that over a moment. "If I were Beckwith, I would first make a treaty with the Snake. Let them send out warriors. I would move my villages, maybe in the night. I would send out spies and scouts."

Whirlwind nodded.

"When your war parties were away, busy, thinking the Snake meant real war, I would wipe out this village."

Whirlwind straightened. "You know this?"

"I know nothing. I don't know if the Snake would agree to a treaty with so many Dakota at La Bonte's. I'm just telling you the way I might think if I were Beckwith."

Whirlwind nodded again.

"Can you get in touch with Bull Bear or White Shield? Can you get some of the warriors back if you have to?" Chatillon asked.

"I'll send out messengers with first light."

That meant that Whirlwind didn't know exactly where they were. It could take days to locate them. Bull Bear, in any case, would be difficult to find.

The young squaw smiled at Chatillon. He started to smile, but caught himself. To Whirlwind he said, "Don't waste your warriors. You may need them. Take two foolish youths too young to fight well, but who

want to prove themselves, and tell them you will punish them if they are reckless or do not do as told.
Then send one to La Bonte's Creek to see if we can
get help, and the other quickly on the trail to Fort
Laramie. Perhaps Bull Bear has not yet left." He
knew that the last mission was almost hopeless, and
the mission to La Bonte's Creek was almost as bad.
But they had to try. Even if they did meet Bull Bear
he might not listen, and even if he did, they wouldn't
gain many warriors. But Bull Bear himself, leading
those in camp, might make a big difference. "Have
the one messenger tell Bull Bear if he finds him, that
the fight will be here. A fight worthy of him." Chatillon sighed. "Now I want leave to see my children
and Many Flowers."

Whirlwind's squaw snuggled closer to the chief.

Chapter 21

Chatillon watched a vision of his late wife. Blue Eagle Speaks was standing before him, her back to him, leaning over and talking to little Sparrow Hawk, their daughter. He knew it wasn't really Blue Eagle Speaks, but he clung to the image—Blue Eagle Speaks in their early marriage, before the Pawnee raid that had crippled her, before the illnesses that had weakened her, and this last, that killed her. Blue Eagle Speaks tending their children, preparing the meat, the bed, for him coming home from a hunting expedition.

Sparrow Hawk shouldn't be that tall, look quite that much like an Indian, the big black eyes staring at him from the light copper face, and only the brown, curling hair un-Indian.

The woman turned to him. It was not, of course, Blue Eagle Speaks, but her sister, Many Flowers. He saw the slight scar on the upper lip and the bitter pride in the eyes that had probably kept her virgin. She had been younger, a mere girl, when he had left.

He bent to his daughter. "Celestine," he whispered the white name he had given her that he'd hoped one day they'd use. Why didn't she come to him? Had she forgotten? Indian children were seldom shy.

She put a thumb in her mouth, like a white child. He smiled and held out his hands. Still she didn't come. Many Flowers whispered something to her, her own black, harder eyes on him, and then took the girl to him. Sparrow Hawk didn't resist, but she didn't come of her own accord. He had disappeared, had left her for months that must have seemed like forever to a child. And now the mother, who had never left her, had also disappeared. So what was to be believed?

He took her head in his hands and kissed her on both cheeks, then on cool, dry lips. He said, feeling foolish, "I am Papa."

She answered in Dakota. "I know." Then, because it was expected of her, and because Many Flowers had given her a slight push, she dutifully kissed his cheek, then returned to cling to her aunt, the large eyes watching him once more.

He straightened. It would take time. He asked Many Flowers in a low voice, "Has she been told?"

"We know nothing. No one has told us."

Did Many Flowers mean to reproach him? He could tell nothing from her expression, neither approval nor disapproval. He had always been a little uncomfortable around her, a silent, watchful presence. She waited and the child waited. Of course she knew, but he should have told her. Still, she must understand that when a chief calls. . . . "Sparrow Hawk," he said, putting his hand on the little girl's head, "could you go see where your brother is, and tell him to come? Tell him Papa is here."

Now she broke into a smile and ran outside. He was left alone with Many Flowers. "She died," he said, "yesterday. After we had turned the band around and were coming back to the village. She was on the travois." He took a deep breath. "We talked long.

Almost the whole night before." Many Flowers looked hard at him at that.

"I know Bull Bear said she had been almost too weak to talk. But she tried. I'd hoped we could get back to the village," Chatillon added.

"My sister died, and I couldn't sit with her. I couldn't lament, or sing her death song, or sit with the wake and leave presents and dress her for the long trip."

"I know, but I didn't ask you to stay. Whirlwind thought it better that you stayed to take care of her children. That was also Blue Eagle Speaks' wish, so that the children wouldn't be killed too if the Crow found them."

"I will not see her until I join her again in the villages of the dead. And I could not help prepare the body, or cry to the Great Spirit."

"She was beautiful. She was washed and prepared by the squaws, and the beaded deerskin, whitened with clay, was put on her, and she was given food and implements and a multicolored mare to go with her. We talked together long hours. She was content." Many Flowers appeared unappeased. "We must care now for the living," Chatillon pursued. "The children will be here in a moment. I'll tell them about Blue Eagle Speaks."

"You are their father."

"I thought I would talk to you first."

"If you wish, I can tell them first, to make it softer and clearer, so they can understand. You don't know all our customs of the dead."

He knew them. What she meant was that he didn't really feel them, not being Dakota. So his Indian children had to be taught the legends of their people, by one of their own—to be told that the world they saw around them wasn't the real world but a cold and shallow distortion, like a reflection in muddy water, of that shimmering glory in which the animals and Dakota were brothers and sisters, where they danced like enchanted beings and the dead could come and speak to them.

And where would he be in such a world? Farther and farther away, hunting most of the time, while Sparrow Hawk and Laughing Elk settled more firmly into the tribe with their new mother. Could he really believe anything else was better for them?

Now they came. A wild cry outside and they burst through the flaps. The boy was in and around his father's legs, laughing and yelling and climbing up on him as if he were a bobcat. Laughing Elk's actions broke Sparrow Hawk's reserve, and she, too, was soon laughing, and grasping his other leg, so that he was like a tree, with his offspring hanging from him. The contagion did not spread to Many Flowers. If anything, she seemed stiffer and colder.

Chatillon laughed and lifted them both up. He looked at the boy. Again, the lighter skin and curlier hair with the laughing Indian face. And the size for his age! The bones, the muscles developing like Bull Bear's!

They didn't have to grow up as Indians. He was their father. He had the right to take them away. Maybe a hunter couldn't raise children alone, but he was also a guide. There was California. And they could have another mother.

Chatillon glanced at Many Flowers. He didn't need to discuss plans for the future before her—if there was a future. She had helped raise the children, she would still be with them, for a while. Besides, war was coming and they had to be protected while he

fought. He would still be in debt to her, perhaps for
their lives. He really couldn't imagine anyone, even
Beckwith and his Crow, hurting them while she was
on guard.

"Now, we will sit down together, all of us," Chatillon said looking at Many Flowers meaningfully, "and
roast buffalo meat on the coals and eat. I've come a
long way and I'm hungry. We have much to say, to
make up for the time I've been gone. And I—and
Many Flowers—will tell you about your mother. Many
Flowers will tell about the real world where so many
live."

He had gotten through to Sparrow Hawk now.
She grew quiet on his arm and he put her down. She
didn't cry. Perhaps, while she remained in this village,
she would never cry, but her hurt eyes darted. Laughing Elk kept kicking and shouting. He was a boy and
a future warrior.

Chatillon let him down and sat with them on
the ground. Many Flowers started for the meat drying
outside to put on the coals, but he motioned for her
too to wait. He wanted to say that they would sit in
love and sadness together for this little time, whatever happened later, but he didn't know quite how
to phrase it in Dakota.

Chapter 22

Parkman and Shaw had wanted nothing more than to rest for a while. But, when Chatillon had gone into his huddle with Whirlwind, the Indians had gathered around them as though they were specimens on display. Although most of these Indians had seen trappers, who could hardly count as white men, and some had spent time in Fort Laramie or Bent's Fort, ordinary whites were something exotic.

So there they were, separated from their guide still, on display. There was the usual fingering of garments and of person, which Parkman had to stop. This went on for some time. Then there was a shout. Some of the women and children stepped back and an immensely fat Indian on a large white horse rode up. He must have weighed three hundred pounds. Parkman nicknamed him *Le Cochon,* the pig, and Shaw agreed that it was fitting.

Le Cochon kept pointing to Pontiac. He rode up to the animal and examined its teeth. Chatillon, attracted by the crowd, came over and explained to Parkman that the fat gentleman was the richest man in the village, being the possessor of a herd of thirty horses, and he wanted to add Pontiac to his herd.

Le Cochon broke out into a rapid mixture of English, French and Dakota enhanced with waving arms. Parkman opened his mouth to say no, but he stopped at Chatillon's sudden grin.

"He says that U.S. money is not so easy to get, so he will offer a daughter for that horse. He has plenty of daughters," Chatillon translated.

"Inform the gentleman that I cannot accept his kind offer," Parkman said.

Le Cochon was not put out. He laughed, waved the arm again, and said that there would be another day to bargain. He kicked his overburdened horse into a shambling trot, waving good-bye.

"Go visit Big Crow," Chatillon suggested, and pointed toward a nearby lodge. "He likes white men. I'll come and call you as soon as I finish some business."

"Could I just intrude like that?" Parkman hesitated.

"He'll consider it a great honor that you chose him. He'll insist that you sleep there." That sounded good to Parkman. "So would most of the other Indians in the village."

Big Crow's squaw silently took and tethered their horses. Big Crow greeted them effusively as the squaw, working swiftly, removed saddles from the horses and took them inside the lodge for seats. She spread buffalo robes and brought in boiled buffalo meat. They were hungry and began to eat. But feathered and painted heads kept appearing in the entrance and they were invited to other feasts being set up throughout the village. They were not mere visiting white men, but friends of Henry Chatillon, who had married into the family of the great Bull Bear. They must be honored. It would have been impolite, as well as impolitic, to refuse, and so they began to go from lodge to lodge to eat and smoke.

By the time Parkman did get to lie down briefly, before the ultimate feast and the council in Whirlwind's lodge, he was too stuffed to be able to nap comfortably.

The council that night in Whirlwind's lodge was, as Shaw pointed out, the high point of the social season, and they had to attend. But Parkman, stuffed and sleepy, did not appreciate it as he should. Still, it had its moments.

Whirlwind seemed to be in a particularly expansive mood, and those who attended were mostly patient elders and men friendly to the whites. There were few warriors. It was obvious that the council was intended mostly to honor the guests and to show pleasure at the return of Chatillon. So good fellowship, stories and the pipe filled up most of the time.

Chatillon was uneasy. He was the guest of honor and the translator. Nevertheless, occasionally he would get up from the council and go outside, leaving the Bostonians and the Indians to stare at one another, pass the pipe and swear regard and eternal friendship in mutually unintelligible languages. Then Chatillon would return, and he and Whirlwind would whisper for a moment. Then, turning toward Parkman or Shaw, whoever had spoken before he had left, he would say, "Pardon, my *bourgeois,* what were you saying?"

Old Mene Seela, the gentlest of the elders, told Chatillon after one such trip outside the lodge that he worried too much about the Crow and Snake. The white men were the friends of the Oglala, and all would be well now that they were here. Chatillon translated.

"Ask him where he got the idea that we could be of much help," Parkman requested. He suspected that Chatillon exercised mild censorship in his translations, but still the answer surprised him.

"Because, he says," Chatillon replied, "he knows that the whites and the beaver are the wisest people on earth. In fact, he knows they are the same people."

"Beaver and whites? How did he arrive at that?" Parkman hadn't a clue.

"It's a story of a vision he had one day, before he had seen any whites, while he was hunting beaver and got caught in their tunnel and thought he was going to die. But I've already told you too much. I cannot tell his stories, especially his visions, unless he gives permission," Chatillon backed off.

"Well, ask him," Parkman pursued.

But Mene Seela, with great but quiet dignity, refused. As Chatillon translated, he said, "It's a bad thing to tell the tales in summer. Stay with us till next winter, and I will tell you everything I know. But now our war parties are going out and our young men will be killed if I sit down to tell stories before the frost begins."

"I can explain it, Frank," Shaw said. "These Indians have no beards. And if we don't get a civilized haircut and shave soon, the resemblance will grow."

Whirlwind caught some of the tone behind the English words and he smiled lightly. The chief seemed to be a religious man, Parkman decided, but not as superstitious as many of the others, who drew no fine line between higher beliefs and everyday superstitions. There was Big Crow, for instance, Parkman thought with exasperation, who was convinced that he could ward off misfortune by breaking into a monotonous dirge every few hours.

Whirlwind's eyes became lively. "Perhaps the thunder will help us. There are some who say they can control the thunder. Others say they do not know what the thunder is."

Mene Seela, Red Water in English, had been warming his withered hands over the pan of coals. "I have always known what the thunder is," he intoned. "It is a giant, a huge black bird. In a dream I have seen it, swooping down from the high peaks, with loud roaring wings. It flapped down over a lake and beat the lake, and lightning sprang up."

The medicine man had been sitting silently, muffled in his buffalo robe. He spoke for the first time. "The thunder is bad. He killed my brother last summer."

"Ask him how," Parkman said. But the medicine man simply shook his head, and in a while, without asking permission from Whirlwind, he rose and went out.

Whirlwind showed little sympathy. "He's a fool. And his brother, if that is possible, was a bigger fool."

"Why do you say that? What happened?" Parkman figured he was bound to get a whole story sooner or later.

"I will tell you, and you can judge for yourself." With Chatillon's help as translator, he explained that the brother had belonged to a mystic society whose members claimed that they were the only ones who could control and tame the thunder. "When the thundercloud would approach with its broad, black wings, they took bows, arrows, magic drums and eagle-bone whistles, and other things like guns, and ran out to shoot at the clouds, and shout and threaten and beat the drums. They thought they would frighten the thundercloud.

"One afternoon a big cloud rose, like a bad spirit, and they went up on the hill and threatened it, but it came ahead anyhow. When it got right above the medicine man's brother, who was shaking his lance at it, it just threw a lightning bolt at the lance and killed the brother!" Whirlwind looked both contemptuous and self-satisfied. "Now, wasn't he a fool?"

"Was that an iron-tipped lance?" Parkman asked.

After the translation, Whirlwind's lip curled. "Yes. But it did not frighten the thunder. Now, wasn't he a fool?"

It wouldn't do to say that a white man who did that was a fool, but an Indian was not, Parkman thought. "Well, why do *you* think he was a fool to shake his lance at the thunder?" Parkman asked.

Whirlwind brought his hand down on his thigh hard. "Because anybody but a fool would know that the thunder is too powerful and bad tempered to be scared by a bunch of fools jumping up and down and shaking guns and lances at it! What does the thunder care about curses and drums when it can shake the earth and frighten the buffalo and the bear? He should have known the thunder would punish him!" Whirlwind crossed his arms with a smug finality, his point proven and documented. "Now, wasn't he a fool?"

Late that night, Chatillon rode out along the bluffs east and west of the village. He could look down at the lodges and see the glow of fires still burning despite his orders. He wanted to check the positions of the sentries. The moon was nearly full. From the bluffs west of the sleeping village, he could see, despite the darkness, great distances along the plateau before the mountains rose. There were, he knew, ravines and hillocks where warriors could hide, but he also knew that sooner or later they would have to come onto level ground, with horses that could seldom be kept silent. An Indian picket, one who had been careful not to look in fire so that his eyes were accustomed to the dark, would be able to see them a long distance off.

He scrambled down the bluff into the meadow on which the village had been pitched. His trip to the eastern bluffs was brief. He had come that way from Blue Eagle Speaks' funeral and he knew what to expect. He decided that it was unlikely the Crow would come that way. Their lands were to the west. If they decided to attack from the east, they would have to cross Laramie Creek to the north or south of the village without being detected, and then circle around through land that was poor for grouping and maneuvering. And if they managed that, they would still have the stream to cross before they could get to the main village and Whirlwind's lodge.

To the south and north, bluffs crowded the stream. Attacks from either of these directions would have to come through narrow passes through which the warriors would have to slip only two or three abreast, or they would have to come on the creek itself, by canoe. Unlikely.

How well the north passage was guarded was revealed dramatically when, in almost complete dark in the trees, he was surrounded suddenly by armed men with bows drawn.

"We almost killed you," said Mad Wolf gruffly.

"Will you stand up and talk to the next man who intrudes without a password or will you shoot?" Chatillon answered, just as gruffly.

Mad Wolf lowered his bow. He was still angry. But then he always was. "We know you. And we saw that you came from the village."

Chatillon nodded and turned back. His fault was as great as theirs, and he had no desire to die for such a foolish reason.

The lay of the land was such that even if an attacking force decided to try to be clever and attack from some other direction than the west, they would still have to come from the Crow or Snake lands, and and unless they wanted to travel many miles out of the way, they would have to cross that broken plateau to the west somewhere. Alert patrols or pickets ought to be able to detect some sign of them. The attack would come from the west, and probably not at night, not down that steep slope in darkness, with the defenders, on flat ground, alerted and waiting for them.

He rode back. He debated for a moment the merits of tethering Five-Hundred-Dollar close to his lodge versus turning him loose for one last night with the other horses on their enclosed grazing grounds. He decided the Wyandot deserved at least one more good night with friends and good food.

Finally he got to his blankets and robes to rest. The two children were now fast asleep, their arms around one another. He snuggled against them, as he had once with Blue Eagle Speaks in this same lodge, and threw a blanket over all. The children did not stir, their gentle breathing remaining constant.

A few feet away Many Flowers lay wrapped in her blanket, her face toward the lodge wall. Her breathing did not change either.

Chapter 23

Close to midday, the funeral group reached the village. The messenger whom Whirlwind had sent to find Bull Bear preceded them by a few minutes. A cry rose up and a crowd gathered around the new arrivals. Those women who had tended Blue Eagle Speaks told the story of her dying and her death. Lamentations and songs started once more.

Chatillon had been playing with his children. He heard the cries and stood up. Sparrow Hawk looked from her father to Many Flowers and began to weep. She understood the cries. Laughing Elk wanted to keep playing. He pulled at his father's hand.

"I'll be back soon." Chatillon told him. "Take care of the squaws." He ducked out.

The messenger, a teen-age boy, was surrounded by a small, admiring group, mostly young girls, and was relating what sounded like great deeds. Of the five warriors who had gone out with the original party, including Bull Bear, only two remained. Chatillon ordered them out of the crowd. He accompanied them across the creek to Whirlwind's lodge.

When they were alone, facing Whirlwind's frowning authority, Chatillon asked, "Where is Bull Bear?

And the others? There were five warriors. I see only two."

The two men remained silent. The young messenger began to explain, volubly, that these were the only two men he'd found with the party. The others had gone.

"They wouldn't have gone far. Bull Bear wouldn't have left the band to be rubbed out by any wandering war party. He and the others were probably in sight the whole time. They wouldn't have left completely until they could see the village. Didn't you check?"

"I didn't see them. And they wouldn't tell me anything." The boy indicated the two warriors.

Chatillon turned to them. "Where is Bull Bear?" They gave no answer. Chatillon had asked the question deliberately, rather than have Whirlwind do it, because he didn't want them to defy their chief directly. "While Bull Bear and the others are out looking for Crow and Snake to attack, a large Crow war party is on its way to attack here. I know this as I know the sun rises tomorrow." Chatillon did not really know but he believed that he would see major fighting before Bull Bear did.

Chatillon surveyed the three before him. The teen-ager was trying to look defiant, but wasn't succeeding. He wouldn't know where Bull Bear was and he was too inexperienced to send on any important mission.

The other two sat on the ground as though cast of stone. Had the chief they faced and disobeyed been the elder Bull Bear, they would be fighting for their lives now. But they didn't move, and Whirlwind, having given the field command authority to Chatillon, waited. One was heavy, strongly muscled, a famous hunter. He would probably be the better for hand to hand combat. The other, Tall Bear, though famous for his endurance and horsemanship, was thinner and more wiry, with hollowed cheeks and a thrusting nose.

"All of you go and have meat and be ready for duty. You, Tall Bear, when you have eaten, take three days' dried meat, your weapons and the best horse in the corral. Go out and find Bull Bear and his band. Go the shortest way you can think of." Chatillon suspected that Tall Bear had a good idea where Bull Bear was.

"Tell Bull Bear that if he wants to fight Crow, they will be here to attack the village before the moon wanes." The two warriors stirred for the first time and their glances hardened. "Ask him if he wants to hear that another sister died, tortured and killed. And other members of his family." He paused and his voice grew lower. "We need his help. There will be no punishment. He must come back as soon as he can."

The three rose, the teen-ager taking his cue from the older men, made their salutations to Chatillon and then to Whirlwind, and left. Tall Bear didn't take long to eat, greet his family and collect his supplies. He took no time to rest. Chatillon hadn't thought he would. Chatillon watched him run into the corral, carrying his rough saddle, and throw it on the horse he chose, a small, but strong and spirited bay. A few minutes later Chatillon saw him climbing the bluff north of the village. He didn't look to left or right or hesitate. Chatillon smiled.

Chatillon spent the rest of the day in preparation. First he lined up all the able-bodied men to see what he had. They would not be enough, but they might be able to hold out until Bull Bear and perhaps White Shield returned with their parties.

He ordered all noncombatants, the old, young and crippled, to get over the creek onto the east bank. Their lodges would be occupied by his best bowmen, hidden and waiting for targets on the bluff. One old man kept waving his lance, even thrusting it toward Chatillon, and announced that he had never retreated before enemies and would battle to glorious death. Chatillon told him that he would need his wise counsel in designing strategy, and got him out. He also had a little trouble with his own family, including Many Flowers, but he finally ordered them peremptorily to gather their belongings and get across the stream. Many Flowers didn't like that, but he didn't care.

The attacking forces would be spotted by sentries along the bluff who could notify the defending forces below, giving the bowmen easy targets on the descent. As soon as the Crow were on the meadow in any force, the warriors on the west bank would be ordered to retreat across Laramie Creek under cover of fire from behind fortifications on the east bank. Once they'd gotten into the village, the Crow would find empty lodges and warriors attacking them from across the stream.

They spent most of the afternoon building fortifications, barricades of logs, dirt and brush forming a flattened half circle around a deep indentation into one of the highest sections of the bluff. Chatillon walked around the busy fort and wondered, What will Beckwith do when he sees this? But the question didn't keep him from sleeping well that night.

Chapter 24

The Crow struck in the late afternoon, the second day after the fortifications had been built. The village was relaxed, with some of the men stretched out on the grass and some in their lodges. A sizable number of noncombatants had drifted back across the creek to their regular lodges.

During most of the fighting, the sun was in the eyes of the defenders. On top of that, they hadn't gotten as much warning as Chatillon had expected. The scout farthest out was killed. When the Crow reached the edge of the bluff they threw his body, scalped and mutilated, over it. Chatillon realized that the attackers had moved across most of the plateau in the night and hidden in ravines until Beckwith had given the signal.

The Dakota first heard the cries of their sentries close in to the top of the bluff, a cry taken up by other sentries along the line so that Whirlwind and Chatillon, running out of their lodges, could tell where the main thrust would be. Brush fires were lit along the edge of the bluff to warn the people below, and to outline where the bowmen should concentrate their attack. They could shoot over the rim so that arrows would fall among the Crow before they appeared.

Two of the sentries had rifles, three others bows. They set up a skirmish line at the top of the bluff and Chatillon could see them firing as fast as they could. He shouted at them. They turned and plunged down the slope. One fell part way down and the other braves rushed forward and pulled him to his feet. Feathered heads appeared along the top. Arrows flew down.

Chatillon ran through the shadow village, ordering the noncombatants who had returned and the braves who were not needed back across the creek. This time they didn't argue. Some rode, some took canoes, a few of the younger ones swam.

Whirlwind told his bowmen not to waste arrows, shoot only when they saw their targets clearly. The Crow could not win the battle from up on the cliff. They would have to come down sooner or later.

But the Crow didn't attack immediately. They were dancing the war dance, mostly out of sight, on that bluff. The sound of the chanting, backed up by drums, rose and fell. To the Dakota below it seemed to come from a multitude, perhaps hundreds, of warriors. No doubt the sounds were exaggerated by echoes, but it was a fearsome noise nonetheless. Chatillon could see the effects on the faces of the braves around him. Then the war chant passed into a victory chant, as though they had already won and nothing remained but the mop-up.

Whirlwind, naked to the waist, wearing his chief's war headdress with the feathers of three war eagles and his panther skin quiver with the hanging yellow claws, stood out in the open, visible to the archers above. He ordered his strongest and best bowmen to shoot over the cliff in the direction of the loudest chants. The archers got the range and fired as rapidly as they could. There were a few shouts and cries from above, and the rhythm of the chanting was disturbed. Boys ran out, dodging swiftly, and picked up the arrows that had been shot down. There was a certain relish in firing Crow arrows back at Crow warriors.

Chatillon tried to imagine what Beckwith was doing up there. He thought Beckwith and perhaps Two Ravens would be riding up and down the rim looking for a better place to descend and attack. But there was none. The fires had moved along the rim and out onto the plateau, leaving smoke that made seeing difficult and dancing flames that would cause horses to balk and rear. Upstream and down, the banks narrowed and the bluffs became steeper. The distances to the barricades and the final battle would be greater.

Beckwith could spread out his charge and try to outflank the defenders. Whirlwind and Chatillon watched for a diversion, but they couldn't spread their forces too far. The main thrust would have to come where they were.

A sudden shower of flaming arrows with burning straw attached fell onto the lodges like meteors. The grass was green; those that landed on the ground were soon extinguished. Some, more carefully aimed, stuck into the tepee walls, leaving smoking, stinking holes in the old, dried skins. More and more fell. Tepees began to burn. The smoke and smell drifted over the area.

Suddenly the Crow came over the rim and down the slope. Some were on foot, some on horseback. The horses plunged and some fell on the steep slope. The attackers whooped and yelled, firing as they came.

Some carried burning torches to finish off the con-
flagration they had begun.

The defenders were partially hidden by smoke.
Showers of arrows hit the bluff. Men fell. Other defenders rushed from the protection of the lodges and
the smoke and finished off the fallen Crow with lance
or tomahawk. A horse, screaming, arrows in its belly,
fell off the slope, its legs jerking. Its agonies cata-
pulted the rider out over the other fallen Crow and
into the crowd of bowmen. Still alive, he managed to
get part way to his feet before he was killed. His
scalp was taken by the men who had grabbed him
before he was allowed to fall.

A new shower of Crow arrows, some fire-tipped,
came down from the bluff to drive the defenders back.
A few Dakota were wounded. They were dragged
to the creek bank, where squaws and young boys fer-
ried them across. Others had to retreat.

A running hand-to-hand battle started along the
bottom of the bluff. Bowmen from both sides were
forced to withhold shooting because of the danger of
hitting their own men. The Dakota bowmen shot above
the fighting onto the Crow coming down the bluff in
a steady stream. Some fell onto rocks with arrows
and lances in them, but most were able to get through
and swell the ranks of those fighting below. Gradually they pushed the defenders back.

Chatillon and Whirlwind saw, far to the right,
a thin, twisting stream of horsemen with torches coming down the bluff by another route that they'd found.
There were no defenders there. They got to the bottom and charged for the closest lodges, hacking them
down, lighting those that would burn.

Whirlwind was standing among his braves. Part
of his headdress was chopped off. The tip of his lance

was bloody as was his neck. His chest was heaving. He was not a young man. Neither he nor the outnumbered defenders could hold out much longer.

Chatillon shouted to Whirlwind and pointed toward Crow horsemen on the flank attacking the lodges. Whirlwind shouted an order, also pointing. With a wild cry most of the Dakota warriors, leaving a small rear guard to fight its way back to the bank, rushed to the defense of the lodges, the Crow on their heels. Some Oglala braves raced into lodges and out slits they had prepared in the back. They called family names. The Crow, singing victory songs, rushed after them to drag out squaws and children and, seeing their comrades destroying tepees as they came in from the right flank, went into an ecstasy of destruction, hacking and setting fire.

While the enemy was chanting and chopping at what they were slow to realize were empty lodges, most of the defenders made the creek and plunged in. They could not take all the wounded and Chatillon, as he swam across, could hear the terrified screams of those few left on the bank as they were hacked and scalped. There was one teen-ager who, faster and more agile than the others, was racing along the bluff, hacking with his tomahawk at the enemy and running away before he could be harmed. Over his shoulder Chatillon could see the boy, naked except for a breechcloth, dodging the enemy who began to close in on him. He finally plunged into the creek, but the water slowed him down. The attackers caught him and chopped away, leaving him bloody and headless on the bank.

Most of the Crow had come down the bluffs in a widening stream that had spread out and deepened along the bank like a flood temporarily blocked. A trickle still came, without opposition. There were fewer than Chatillon had thought there would be, but they were well trained and there were enough to overwhelm the Dakota. Beckwith and Two Ravens had stripped their villages for this battle.

While the west bank defenders were still in the water fighting the current, many of them wounded and exhausted, arrows and bullets began to fall around them. Crow horsemen urged their animals into the stream after them. The Oglala archers behind the breastworks held off responding as long as their own fighters were in the line of fire. But they couldn't wait until the rescuers on the east bank, pulling the swimmers out of the water, were entirely out of the way. From the large store of arrows accumulated and stocked in the fort, they now began to fire volley after heavy volley into the massed Crow on the opposite bank and some of those already in the water.

Parkman and Shaw crouched with the defenders behind the fortifications. "Really bully. Like Horatius at the bridge!" Shaw cried.

"My favorite childhood story, Quincy," Parkman remarked. "But there never was a bridge, and this creek is no Tiber to hold them back." Nothing like a little sarcasm to distract one from mortal danger, he thought.

"We're here now, Frank. Can't change it. Might as well make the most of the opportunity."

He was right, of course. Chatillon had warned them, and as recently as the night before had urged them to leave, offering them a boy for a guide. They had refused. They had wanted to see an Indian war, and they were seeing one. If they could only survive to tell about it!

The laments, threats and bragging inside the fort, shouted to the Crow, had now given way to a half ferocious, half desperate rage. The archers fired over the wall. Squaws and children brought them more arrows and lances, while other squaws and old men tried to throw up some kind of cover to protect the more helpless from the arrows starting to fall inside. But there were still threats and shouts of defiance. Whoever said Indians were stoic! Parkman thought.

"We really ought to join the fight, Quincy," Parkman said. "Great opportunity. They won't spare us, anyhow."

"Besides," Shaw added in a more pragmatic vein, "we seem to be the only ones with rifles who could hit anything."

The abrupt realization that he was actually about to shoot at human beings made Parkman queasy. "Look!" he shouted suddenly. "That's Henry out there!"

The fighting on the other bank, among the tepees and on the bluff beyond, had been confused and indeterminate. Everywhere were men running, dust, shouting, fire and smoke, and tepees falling. When the battle had moved to the bank it had become clearer to Parkman and Shaw, but still so confused that they couldn't distinguish much detail or discern many individuals. They could see Whirlwind because he had mounted a horse and was swimming it across, erect in the saddle despite the arrows flying around him. And not far behind him they could see among the bare Indian shoulders Chatillon's fringed arms swimming with a kind of clumsy breast stroke, and that black head, sleek as an otter's, in the water.

Parkman and Shaw elbowed their way to the barricade, their rifles at the ready. Parkman was suddenly grabbed from behind and spun around. He was surprised to find himself looking into the intense eyes of Many Flowers. She was as strong as a man, Parkman realized. Imperiously, she thrust her hand, finger pointed, toward the stream. He recognized that she was asking a question. She didn't speak English, but it was clear she was saying the name "Henry" and was demanding that Parkman show her where he was. But Chatillon, for the moment, was out of sight. Suddenly Whirlwind pulled ahead, revealing the fringed, soaked jacket. Parkman pointed silently.

Many Flowers shouted something in Dakota and motioned behind her. Then, despite arrows going in both directions, she vaulted the breastwork and, head lowered and dodging back and forth, ran for the bank.

Behind, above all the noise, they heard a young girl crying in fright and a younger boy, a small child, shouting confused things as though trying to keep from crying.

"My job I guess," Shaw said, handing Parkman his rifle. "Hold this for me a moment or so, old fellow." Shaw went back to soothe Chatillon's children, without knowing a word of Dakota. In a few minutes, the crying ceased.

The Crow temporarily abandoned the attempt to ford the creek directly before the breastworks. Scouts moved upstream and down looking for a more protected crossing. Others were chanting victory songs and shouting taunts, waving their lances and dodging arrows. The village had not been able to get all its horses inside the fort, and had hidden some in what they had hoped was a carefully concealed corral on the west bank. But the Dakota stallions called to the Crow mares and so the attackers found them. Now they paraded them along the bank to more howls of rage and frustration from those behind the breastworks. Parkman wondered how many daughters *Le Cochon* had left. He hadn't seen the fat man once since the fighting had started.

The rescue operation at the creek was proceeding. Some of the men had been swept downstream and rescuers had had to go after them. The creek wasn't deep there, enabling some of the squaws and older men to wade across. Whirlwind had come ashore, still sitting magnificently and foolishly erect behind the horse's dripping mane, shouting orders. Parkman caught sight of a shadowy figure on the other side of the bank close to the bluff. He was wearing a full buckskin suit and didn't look like an Indian. That scoundrel Beckwith, he was sure. He tried to take careful aim with his rifle, but just as he was about to pull the trigger, the head of one of the Indians directly before him rose in his sights. He lowered his rifle.

Many Flowers was in the stream up to her waist, the current tugging at her. She had Chatillon by an arm and was pulling him out of the shallows. Whirlwind rode up to the breastworks and called to a squaw to take his horse. He jumped from his saddle, scrambled over the barricade and once more started shouting orders.

Chatillon came ashore, leaning on Many Flowers. Most of the men and horses were across. Parkman let loose a shot over their heads, hoping that it might strike something on the other side or at least scare somebody.

The last of the rear guard stumbled up from the bank, reached the breastworks and were helped over the logs and earth to safety. Arrows rained down. A squaw fell, struck in the back. Her young daughter screamed, jumped over the barrier and tugged at her. But the child didn't have the strength to lift her over, and stared beseechingly at Parkman. Parkman reached over to try to help, knowing that he couldn't lift her over either, but one of the men got a shoulder under her and hoisted her over. She and Parkman fell inside, and some one hundred and sixty pounds of panting and wounded squaw had to be lifted off him. It took him a little while to get back on his feet.

New, repeated volleys from the Dakota side flew across the stream, and another attempt by the Crow to cross was driven back. A wounded and dying horse lay in the shallows, kicking in agony. Parkman could see the Crow, in their turn, pulling their wounded out of the water and toward the rear.

Chatillon reached the breastworks, still supported by Many Flowers. Except that he was panting from the swim, he seemed sound. At the breastworks she released him and bent down so that he could use her back for a step. He refused and told her to go over. Parkman had seen none of the braves act that way, wounded or not. Most would have used the back. That's what squaws were for. She argued with him and he shouted some kind of order in Dakota back at her. Arrows hit close by. Chatillon climbed onto the barrier, reached back and practically yanked her across by main force, and both fell inside.

The Crow still could have managed the crossing in spite of the arrows and casualties and reached the fort without great losses. But they seemed in no hurry. The sun was beginning to sink. They went back into their victory dance and the shouting of insults and taunts. Parkman relaxed. As he saw the shadows lengthening across the creek, he felt a sudden chill. They must be waiting for darkness. How could they be stopped from crossing at night? From breaching the wall and killing everybody inside?

Shaw, relieved from duty with the children, came up. "All right here, Frank? Breezing along, eh? I tell you, if those Crow get hold of those children of Henry's, this fight's going to be over right there!"

Parkman picked up his rifle with a sigh and let it rest once more on the barrier. Shaw, at least, wasn't worried about things not coming out all right. "Remember that snowball fight with those St. Francis-in-the-Fields' boys? Really set them back, didn't we?" Shaw grinned.

Whirlwind was shouting. They looked around. He was pointing toward the far right. The Crow had found another ford. While the main body was holding its victory chants and dances directly across, a thin stream of horsemen and a few others, some swimming and some clinging to straps along the horses' sides, were moving across the stream. They were out of range of the braves in the fort. There was nothing to stop their charge until they came into range again, and by that time they would have numbers and momentum. With increasing horror, Parkman saw movement to the south as well. He could see warriors entering the water there, though he couldn't follow their progress because of a bend in the stream. So they were crossing, and would be closing in, from both sides.

They couldn't understand Whirlwind's words, but his gestures began to order a party to meet the few attackers who had reached the bank before they became too numerous, but Chatillon caught his arm and they had a rapid exchange. The strategy Chatillon wanted followed, Parkman realized, was basically still what had been outlined days ago: the warriors had to stay in, or be able to retreat to, the fort. If they let themselves be split up into little bands there was no hope. Parkman showed Chatillon the crossing to the south, Chatillon showed it to Whirlwind and the discussion was over. He could not send out two parties in opposite directions and still defend the fort.

Many Flowers, still wet herself, came up silently with a dry buckskin shirt, the children just behind her. Chatillon had been standing in the breeze, his pigtail and fringes dripping like melting icicles. While the hunter took off the wet shirt, the children, yelling, tackled him, one to a leg. He ordered the woman sharply to take the children away and bring his rifle. She said nothing. The rifle was there. She had been guarding it, keeping anyone from using it, however badly needed, until he returned. She pulled the children from him. The girl started to cry and the boy knotted his fists. Chatillon, as though aping Delorier, said three rapid *Sacres,* squatted down, gave each child a swift, bone-crushing hug and pushed them away. He grabbed his rifle, took careful aim and then fired at the warriors on the far edge of the darkening meadow.

Now creeping in shadow, the Crow warriors came toward them from both left and right. On the opposite bank the dancers were melting away, drifting toward the crossings. The Dakota now had three fronts to watch, and Whirlwind kept running back and forth, to see which posed the greatest menace. Distracted in this manner, they couldn't keep those in front entirely pinned down and some came plunging across.

"If they rush us all at once," Parkman pondered, "we wouldn't stand much chance, would we?"

"Wouldn't say that," Shaw answered.

Parkman addressed the question to Chatillon.

"They're Indians," Chatillon answered enigmatically.

But that did not satisfy Parkman. In fact, he didn't understand at all and kept looking at Chatillon questioningly. He asked again.

Chatillon, never taking his eyes off the warriors gathering on the right, whom he apparently considered the greatest menace, sighed. "They just won't charge. Each must show he is brave, maybe braver than the others. He'll jump back and forth, he may taunt us to try to shoot him. He might even run up and hit the logs with his hatchet singing out what a hero he is. And when he does, we'll shoot him."

Parkman remained silent. And how long would that last—especially with the leadership of Beckwith, if he was there? And what would happen after nightfall?

Chatillon answered Parkman's unspoken questions. "And I know Bull Bear is on his way."

Bull Bear is certainly on his way, Chatillon thought. But we could be dead in an hour. Except for those taken as slaves.

Many Flowers had left the children with an older squaw and had been quietly loading his rifle and pistol. He stopped shooting. He told Parkman and Shaw, "Let's leave it to the arrows for a little while and hold the rifles in case they rush. They take longer to load. We want to be ready." That was true. It was also true that they didn't have any ammunition to waste.

Just as Chatillon had predicted, the Crow began to jump from cover, shooting arrows and bullets and whooping and yelling, leaping from side to side "like devils incarnate," Shaw said with some indignation. Whirlwind ordered the defenders, including women and children, to stay behind and below the barrier, though he himself did not. The missiles landed in the

earth and in logs and some passed harmlessly over-
head. For a moment or two there seemed to be some
kind of commotion in the Crow ranks, orders being
given, retaliation threatened if they were not obeyed,
but blood was up, victory and revenge seemed assured,
and the warriors could not be restrained. Honor and
glory were better than life itself. Killer of Horses
jumped out, screamed his war song, shouted that he
had killed many Dakota, that he was the bravest and
ran closer and threw his lance at the breastworks.
Chatillon shot him down coolly.

With that example of valor before them, the
Crow became more frenzied. Three braves, one after
the other, each singing his war song, charged the barrier. Chatillon tensed. If the rest followed, they were
done. But the rest did not follow. Nor did these three
try to climb over and get inside. Each ran to the breastworks, hit the logs with a tomahawk or lance and
turned to race back to his comrades. All fell and died,
stopped by Dakota arrows. A fourth, trying to imitate
his heroes but hesitating just a little too long, didn't
get even that far.

Parkman was appalled. A squaw gives birth, she
nurtures the child for years, he grows strong, is trained,
practices for war, loves, and it ends in a silly, horri-
ble moment like this, he thought. His early enthusiasm
for hero tales was waning quickly. But of course the
Indians didn't see it that way. Those who died did so
gloriously and they would be remembered in village
legend.

The strange antics of the enemy went on for an
hour. Only one Dakota was wounded, but there were
many wounded Crow who had been pulled back by
their warriors, and several dead heroes lay sprawled
before the breastworks.

"You see, Frank?" Shaw reassured his cousin. "We can certainly hold out till morning. Bull Bear and White Shield on the way, and all the rest of it."

Parkman groaned. If Shaw could talk that convincingly to the Crow, they might indeed have a chance. But Parkman's arms were already tired from simply holding his Hawken, and that long, blind night that Shaw looked forward to so confidently still lay ahead.

He glanced at Chatillon. If anybody had a right to be tired, he did. Chatillon had left his rifle in the girl's hands to be reloaded and was looking up at the broken rock on the concave bluff behind them. Parkman followed his glance but could see nothing except darkening shadows. Of course, Chatillon had eyes like an Indian. Maybe he was resting them—maybe that was how he slept, on his feet like a horse, and probably then only between flickers of an eyelid.

What would Beckwith do? With his military training and recklessness, Chatillon thought, he won't stand for this much longer. He'll give orders, exert authority. Give them a little leeway to prove themselves, then organize a rush. He wondered if Beckwith could make them follow orders when their pride was at stake. But they would thrill to, and follow a heroic example, as Killer of Horses had proved.

His eyes moved carefully over the bluff behind. It was higher and rockier than the one the Crow had descended across the creek. But it was not a single granite face. Softer layers had worn away on the massive fault. Long lines slanted down, hidden by shadow and vines, indicating slender broken ledges. Could they be climbed, he wondered, silently, in the shadow, while the charging warriors on the ground kept the defenders busy? Climbed by some kind of madman and his followers?

He'd once watched a fight between mountain men at a trading rendezvous at Bent's Fort. Beckwith's side, composed of people more or less like himself, had been smaller and getting the worst of it. He'd kept shouting to his men to attack, to be more aggressive. Finally he'd lost patience. "You're all fools and old women! If you got guts in your meat bags, follow me!" And he'd jumped from a table with a newly sharpened knife into what had, until then, been little more than a boozy brawl with fists.

Chatillon looked back up at the bluff. If only a few jumped down from those ledges undetected, they could kill several of the defenders before they were themselves killed. They'd pull the defenders away from the barrier who would then be unable to react quickly. And in the midst of the fighting, the war cries, chants, and general confusion, the rest of the Crow could come streaming down to attack to certain victory.

The attacks from the main force to the right had stopped. There was some kind of powwow going on there. Chatillon could see the tips of raised lances catching the last light and hear some kind of guttural argument.

He passed his rifle to Many Flowers. He motioned toward the breastworks, as though his gesture alone were enough to explain everything, and pulled off the dry shirt she had given him only an hour before. In the shadows his dark skin looked like any other Indian's. He put the loaded pistol and his knife in his waistband and turned toward the bluff. One ledge, about fifteen feet up, slanted down and continued outside the limits of the fort. He wanted to go up and get a closer look.

Her hand caught his arm, a viselike grip, so unlike that of any other woman he had known. "Where do you go?" she asked.

He flicked his free hand again toward the barricade. "Stay here. Shoot straight if they charge."

She followed his eyes to the bluff and along the ledges. "You're needed here. I can climb better than you." She tried to pass him but he pulled her back. "Why do you go? Who sends you?" she demanded.

He said in a low voice, "You will do what you are told and you will not argue."

In a few steps he was close to the lodges and the shelters where the older squaws were taking care of the children. He heard children's cries. In a few more steps he was among the rocks and broken shale at the bottom of the bluff.

What would Beckwith do? A classic, simple maneuver for an old soldier—get behind and above the enemy. But white soldiers would not clamber among these rocks, and even if they tried, they couldn't do it quietly enough. Indians could.

He raised his eyes. It wasn't a friendly bluff—not much earth, broken rocks, some crevices. Some vines and bushes hung precariously from the surface, but they only served to make it more forbidding. Loose limestone and broken shale lay along the bottom as if the bluff were in the middle of construction, with debris all over the place.

Chatillon began to climb, reaching for handholds. He had to raise his knees high sometimes to get footholds and the pistol and knife kept jabbing his side. He could do little about the pistol, but he took the knife out and put it between his teeth.

A man climbing down would have a great advantage over one going up at the same time. He would see more clearly. Springing, he could break his fall on his victim and kill him at the same time. A man climbing up was at the mercy of whoever was above him.

Chatillon reached the first major ledge, the one he had aimed for, the knife still in his teeth. He crouched there, shoulders against the rock. The cold and fatigue made his back muscles start to cramp with tension. Above him he heard the sound of boots scrape on gravel and pebbles. A hoarse voice muttered a one-word curse in English and a two-word order in Crow. Chatillon knew it was Beckwith, probably leading a small group of braves.

Chatillon waited for Beckwith to reach the ledge. He crouched, gripping the knife in his right hand. He balanced his weight on his knuckles and toes so that when he was ready, he would shoot his entire weight like a coiled spring toward the man whose feet, even now, were reaching cautiously down for the ledge a few feet in front of Chatillon's eyes. This would not be a fight in which rules were observed. Chatillon tried to ignore the tremors in his tensed, tired thighs.

Beckwith's right foot found the ledge. He was wearing the fancy boots he'd picked up in Westport, even though they were more clumsy for climbing than moccasins. The left foot came down too, searching a moment for solidity. The boots kicked gravel down the bluff, narrowly avoiding Chatillon's eyes. But, though that was the widest part of the crumbling ledge, Beckwith was still not quite confident. His hands held on till he could be sure that his feet were steady. It was at that instant that Chatillon shouted his Dakota war cry and sprang.

His shoulder struck a projecting rock, throwing

him slightly off target and he missed Beckwith with the knife. Before he could recover his balance, arms like those of a bear were around him, squeezing his ribs, and Chatillon was slammed against the stone wall. His knife was pinned to his side with his right arm.

They struggled back and forth on the narrow ledge, loosening gravel and pebbles that cascaded down the bluff. Shouts came from below, the Dakota responding to what was going on on the bluff, the Crow shouting their war cries. Chatillon heard the bark of Bull Thrower, his rifle, and then there was a rain of arrows striking the bluff above them.

Chatillon got his arm free and struck again with the knife but it did little damage. And then he felt, like racing fire, Beckwith's knife slash his arm and rip along his side. Whether he had ever been as strong as Beckwith didn't matter. Because of fatigue, he had not been as strong when they first began to grapple. He was faster, and on level ground he might have been able to outmaneuver him and win. But he was not on level ground, and the strength he had left, and perhaps his life, was ebbing away, running down his side with his blood.

Before Beckwith could strike again, Chatillon fell backward onto a narrow part of the ledge. Sharp rocks struck his back like hatchets. He drew up his legs, braced for that last onslaught of Beckwith's. He was beyond thought. Thought was little good in a fight so swift and violent as this.

In a blind fury, Beckwith brought up the knife and dove at Chatillon. Chatillon kicked out as hard as he could. The left foot missed altogether and the jerk as it snapped straight almost threw him over the edge, but the right foot caught Beckwith in the chest, staggering him.

Beckwith wasn't hurt, but he seemed to have forgotten that he was on a narrow ledge. He stepped back for a new start. Chatillon heard him roar, saw his arms windmilling and the knife, still clutched, picking up the last of the dying light. Chatillon, with the last of his strength, kicked out as strongly as he could, with no thought that he, too, might go over. His feet struck solid flesh and the rebound pushed him back on the ledge. Beckwith fell off like an inexpert diver, head first with flailing arms and legs.

Beckwith wasn't killed by the fall, but he landed close to where the older squaws were—those who were taking care of frightened children, who had seen their sons, or cousins, or husbands die in the fighting across the stream—and they were on him in an instant. Chatillon, looking down, as in a dream, saw what looked like a pack of furious dogs slashing at a wounded and struggling bear. Once Beckwith humped up, lifting some of his attackers with him, a drowning beast in raging and unrelenting rapids, but he never reached his feet.

Chatillon tried to sit up, but he began to fall forward toward the edge, so he lay down, hoping his head would clear. The pain was mostly gone. It would have been lovely to just lie there, but he knew he would die. The blood flowed unchecked down his side and arm. He crawled to where he recognized the path by which he had climbed to the ledge. He saw two footholds, old, but now unreliable friends, by which he had climbed. "We must trust," he said aloud. The words echoed. Where had he heard them before?

One leg trusted. The foot moved around until it found that first foothold. The hands had little faith. They held on like grim death. He spoke to them to get them to let go, at least enough to allow the other foot a chance to search until it too could find a step. The hands, right before his eyes, still gripped desperately. The footholds for the moment appeared firm, though it seemed to him he could feel his body sway above them, and it was a little easier to convince the hands to take one more chance. Once a foot slipped, and the hands, betrayed, clutched desperately, but he kept up his persuasion. He floated as in a dream, getting weaker and weaker. Arrows and stones fell around him, and once something heavy, perhaps a body. He began to sing. Oglala war chants and appeals to the Great Spirit seemed appropriate. *Le bon Dieu* had always been good to him, though he had often tried His patience. Would asking for another chance strain that patience too much?

Perhaps heavenly arms did sustain him, because he floated away before he actually reached bottom. Perhaps he fell, but he didn't feel that he struck anything. And there were arms around him, carrying him. And there were sounds, war cries, galloping hooves, victory cries all fading in the distance.

Chapter 25

Time became a blur of half-formed images. Chatillon was aware that some preparation, from bark or mud or leaves, something astringent, was put on his wounds to slow the blood. It felt cool and restful. He wondered about many things, but his fevered mind supplied no answers. Had Bull Bear come back? And if so, when? When he had come down from the bluff? Or later when the Crow, confused by their losses and left practically leaderless, were starting to pull back or to reorganize for another attack? The question was not clearly understood by those around him because he could not speak clearly. There were other things to talk about, but Chatillon grew sleepy again and eventually gave up trying to find out other details.

Sometimes he woke and Sparrow Hawk and Laughing Elk were there, hugging him when they saw he was conscious. Once he was awakened by the boy pounding on him, demanding that he wake. Then Chatillon saw small kicking feet going out the lodge, and the strong back of Many Flowers hauling the child away.

She was always there, remote, efficient. He wondered later if she slept at all, because when he awak-

ened and called weakly for water or help in the middle of the night, she came within moments, always
dressed. She did everything: replacing what passed for
dressings, feeding him, turning him on his side and
cleaning him when in the first day or two he had
needed that. And she had also taken care of the children. When the men came—Whirlwind to find out
how he was, Bull Bear, or the others—she stood quietly apart, not the subservient squaw, never subservient,
but in a different world.

He had lost a lot of blood, Shaw told him. It
would have to be replaced. Someday men might be
able to give each other blood, or take it from animals
to put into sick people, Shaw told him. But right now
he would have to replace it himself and that would
take time. "How the devil did you lose so much and
still live?" Shaw asked him.

Shaw pointed out that he knew a little about
doctoring and labored mightily to keep the wounds
clean, in spite of a lot of trouble from Indian remedies. He scowled at Many Flowers, who was in her
usual place at Chatillon's side on the buffalo robes.
But he wasn't a surgeon. And Chatillon badly needed
a surgeon. Those wounds had to be sewn! He heard
Shaw talking to Parkman about it, and Parkman saying that the patient couldn't stand the trip to Fort
Laramie, and who said they had a surgeon there anyhow? And there were still war parties on the trail!
Then Shaw came back into the lodge, strode up and
down and said "Damn!" three times and told Many
Flowers to keep those wounds clean and exposed to
enough air and no nonsense! She always followed his
instructions carefully while he was in the lodge—white
medicine was very powerful, too—but went back to
her Indian poultices and remedies when he was gone.

They never wrangled no matter how he shouted, because she never answered.

So Chatillon's wounds weren't sewn. They healed, although not properly, or properly enough for Shaw. The scars were red and ragged, the skin over them thick and sometimes stiff. When he rode, or hunted with Bull Bear, they didn't stretch enough and became painful. They made it difficult to hold a gun steady with that arm. He tired more quickly. He told himself that that would pass. And he *could* ride. He *could* hunt.

He came back from a hunt one day earlier than the braves he had gone with, and sat down stiffly on the robes to catch his breath. Then he told Many Flowers that he had made a pledge with Parkman and Shaw to guide them in hunting and on the trip back to the great river called the Missouri from which they had come. He would leave in two days for Fort Laramie for the first stage of that trip. She who had been so faithful, so reliable, so strong in everything, if she would take care of Sparrow Hawk and Laughing Elk just a little longer. He couldn't take them this trip. He didn't know when he would be back, but it wouldn't be longer than three moons. Then he would take the children and she would be free at last.

As always she stood stiff and still, with no change in her expression.

Chapter 26

It seemed to Francis Parkman that the trip back was a kind of elegy, nothing to do directly with grim death or mourning, but a gentle melancholy that marked the ending of something he now thought wonderful that would be gone forever, never to be repeated except in memory.

It wasn't obvious. They all seemed happy enough, in fact more carefree now than they had been on the whole trip so far, freer to enjoy the riding, the hunting, the camping and each other's company. Perhaps nobody was even aware of it except himself and possibly Shaw, to judge from his occasional moody scowls. Chatillon and Delorier were more tranquil than they had been at Fort Laramie or in the Oglala village, and smiled a good deal, though Chatillon's content seemed to be balanced by a hint of rueful resignation.

That was partly, no doubt, because of his wounds. He could no longer spring onto his horse as he had in the old days. There was stiffness and pain, though he never talked about it. He often rested Bull Thrower on a rock or on his knee when he shot, rather than holding the heavy gun for long periods steadily in his hands to get the shot he wanted. He grew tired more readily and a few times he called an early halt, saying that, though they still had some time till sunset, they might not be able to find as good a campsite later. Shaw was the only one who mentioned the wounds to him. He kept insisting that, though he had avoided infection and had healed almost entirely, Chatillon still should see a surgeon. They could make a side trip to Fort Leavenworth for the army surgeon to look at the scars, or they could probably find some kind of surgeon at Westport or Independence. Shaw swore he would pay for it. "Why not go on to St. Louis?" Shaw persuaded. "You can see your mother. There are hospitals there."

Chatillon shook his head. "It's in the past."

"Damned superstition!" Shaw muttered, but he later admitted to Parkman that he couldn't see what a surgeon could do anyway, this late, short of cutting it all open again.

The normal travel time between Fort Laramie and Westport was about thirty-five days. They would make it faster, not being burdened with wagons, oxen, families and similar responsibilities. They didn't hurry. They took time to savor the clear bright days, the cool nights. Their last school holiday, Parkman thought. End of summer.

They seemed remote from their time. From the occasional traveler, they heard talk of the war with Mexico. The leader of one wagon train expressed fear and hatred of Mormons, who he said were out for revenge and to destroy Christianity. Later they met a small train of Mormons who were cautious until they found out that, despite their guns, the horsemen were friendly.

The four men had long conversations, some while riding, but more during the breaks and especially in the long evenings around the campfire. Chatillon and Delorier were as fascinated by descriptions of the lives of Shaw and Parkman in Boston and abroad as the Easterners were about *their* lives. So Parkman and Shaw tried to describe it in the face of raised eyebrows and significant glances back and forth, until Shaw began to embellish with gaudy details that surprised even Parkman, but gratified the frontiersmen.

They also talked about more immediate things, the futures that awaited them, particularly those of Chatillon and Delorier, and the dangling threads of lives that they had left behind. There were no secrets. They would be parting soon.

"And what of Lucy?" Parkman asked.

Chatillon puffed a few times on his short pipe and moved his scarred side a little closer to the fire. The sky to the west was still bright, with ruddy-rimmed, elongated clouds, though the sun was gone. Glancing at it, Parkman felt a sudden stab of terror. It reminded him of the sun gone beyond the bluffs in the battle of the village, the coming of night and the anticipated Crow attack. But the expression on Chatillon's face was mellow. He wasn't thinking of death. "She said she understands," Chatillon smiled.

"Understands what?"

"That I was married. I didn't tell her at first, until I was called for the death. I should have told her." He tapped the pipe to get it to draw more easily. He wasn't smoking pure tobacco, but the usual Indian mixture with chopped red willow bark. "It may be, well, things appear different to a man of thirty-one than to a seventeen-year-old virgin. I don't know. Maybe I should've said. But she understands and still . . . has affection."

"What will you do?" Parkman asked, then added

in Bostonian tact, "Of course, I understand it's really not my concern."

Chatillon seemed to go off on another tack. "Did you notice how many wagons around Laramie? And not so many tepees? And all the trains we meet?"

"Yes."

"That's the way I think it will be maybe, more and more. Not right away, but after a while. Plenty of trains. She would be safe. Not so many Indians." He paused. "Not so much buffalo and beaver. And there'll be many hunters, trappers, and more and more are becoming guides. It's a little harder for me to hunt now, but I could do that too—guide to California. Maybe I'll come back. She said she would wait. Did I tell you that?"

"No."

Shaw and Delorier, as well as Parkman, were listening. Delorier, in fact, was listening so hard that Parkman thought he might fall over.

"I could stay. It's a beautiful country with lots of space. A man should settle down. His children should be raised among his own people—Celestine and Charles." He savored the names for a moment, along with the smoke. He gave "Charles" the softer, French pronunciation.

"That seems sensible," Shaw said. "The right thing." But he didn't sound as cheerful as his words.

"His own people. That's right," Chatillon repeated.

"She's a beautiful little girl," Shaw said.

Chatillon nodded.

On other evenings around the campfire Chatillon discussed Delorier's situation with him. It was a convoluted conversation that had started back in Fort

Laramie. It had many twists and turns and took strange tacks when Parkman and Shaw weren't around, so that much of what they heard was fragmentary. What was worse, the interchanges were sprinkled with dialect or bastardized French, making it especially hard to follow. Perhaps Chatillon and Delorier didn't realize that Parkman knew French so well, though some of the expressions would have confused any Frenchman.

"We'll pass close to Fort Leavenworth, as you know, Jean. Will you go to see Colette?" Chatillon asked one evening. Delorier shook his head. "You won't even see her, to tell her anything?"

"I see no need. She has her soldiers."

"Jean, is this the way one behaves? Not even to say good-bye, and to explain?"

"Henry, she has told me more than once she doesn't care if I don't return. I always pretended she didn't mean it. Now I'll change. I'll pretend she does."

Chatillon's eyebrows went way up. Parkman listened carefully. He was often surprised by what shocked different kinds of people.

"And the vows taken before God? Nothing?"

"It's a most surprising and remarkable thing," Delorier said, "that Colette, and I, and a priest, could never quite get together in the same room at the same time. At least not for marriage."

Now Chatillon was totally speechless. Delorier continued, explaining, "When Colette was a thin girl, that is, years ago, and wanted to, and I was willing, we had trouble finding the priest. Not many came through. Later, when a priest would appear, she had her soldiers. Then she didn't care. She didn't want to go to confession. And I didn't care either." He looked at Chatillon steadily for a moment, with that almost ridiculous dignity. His voice was soft, but final. "Henry, it's finished."

Chatillon thought about it a while, puffing on that pipe. The corners of his eyes crinkled. "Well, Jean, you're used to fat women . . ."

Delorier shrugged. "You know, when one has been in the mountains a long time . . . a little relief . . ."

"Flat plains?"

"Foothills perhaps. Henry, you don't know everything."

"I've heard that, ah, older Protestant Anglo women who have never been married are cold." Delorier merely smiled. "Well," Chatillon said, "we're not being serious enough. Jean, what will you do? Where is Liz now?"

"She's with the missionaries at the Popo Agie River. I took her there while you were gone. I told you," Delorier answered.

"Pardon. It slipped my mind. What does she do there?"

"What did she do before? She helps others. She cooks, chops wood, prays, wipes the behinds of babies and the sick. And she waits. I will come."

"You will live there? Your work is at Leavenworth."

"I'm a muleteer and cook. There's a war, there are trains. There's plenty of work. We'll build a cabin, probably close to Laramie Creek."

"And while you are gone, she will wait?"

"She, I am sure, will wait. Or work for those who need it."

Chatillon sighed, though he sounded happier than he had when he'd started the conversation. "Jean, this isn't Colette, this isn't one of the ladies of the saloon in Westport. A religious woman. She wouldn't want a priest, but she would want a minister." He looked at Delorier. "She wouldn't force you, but she would suffer. And in simple decency——"

Delorier's voice had an angry edge. "She will be married by a minister. As she wants."

"Jean Delorier will be married before a Protestant minister?"

"In a manner of speaking, *le bon Dieu* and I have our understanding."

"He is very tolerant, *le bon Dieu,* of Jean Delorier!"

All things came to an end, or at least, like old clocks, wound down. They reached the edge of Westport. But they didn't actually go in that day. They felt a revulsion for those crowded, riotous streets, the dust and noise, perhaps the prospect of meeting some of Beckwith's old friends. But mostly they simply didn't want too abrupt a farewell. They pitched their tents in a meadow not far from the log bridge that led into the center of town and lingered over their campfire like the last party guests, loath to leave and go into the cold.

Next morning they rode into town. Chatillon and Delorier visited the fur company. Shaw and Parkman went to the landing and waited there to find out about possible steamboats. While waiting, Parkman wrote a description of the trip in his journal. "Westport had beheld strange scenes, but a rougher looking troop than ours, with our worn equipments and broken-down horses, was never seen even there. We passed the well-remembered tavern, Boone's grocery and old Vogel's dram shop. . . ." A small steamboat came in from

Leavenworth, but the captain said they were all booked up. Parkman felt they could probably have bribed their way aboard, but he hesitated and finally didn't try. Perhaps Shaw understood this, but he said nothing. Another steamboat was due in two or three days. They went back to town.

On the way they were accosted by horse dealers who weren't put off by the "broken-down" condition of their horses and offered them a good price and were delighted that they also had mules. The Conestoga wagons and the freights were coming through, and horses and mules were needed.

Parkman and Shaw said they would think about it. As they left, Shaw said that he didn't think they'd been offered enough. And there were things they wanted to talk about. He stamped on ahead, without realizing that Parkman was behind, that he was walking alone. After about twenty feet he stopped, looked around, and came back, smiling sheepishly. "Damn it all!" he said.

Each had his future. Shaw, in the afternoon, read part of the journal, objected to a few errors in grammar and some of interpretation—"Really didn't rain that hard, did it?"—then handed it back and said, stretching, "Frank, you're going to be a great man. Finish this and then get your histories started, will you?" So he had a book to write. Maybe the first of several.

Chatillon smoked his pipe. They talked of a separate world, a different planet. He couldn't even read, but he listened. He was still a young man yet Parkman suddenly thought, looking at him in profile, that he was an antique figure, the kind that appeared on medallions or tapestries. Like some of the Indians, like Whirlwind.

"You'll go back to Fort Laramie?"

They all knew that, but Chatillon didn't resent the question. He nodded.

"And California? And Lucy?"

Chatillon once more had trouble with a blocked pipe. "Well, I'll tell you." He tapped for a moment. "I'll help them get a good guide and a good train. They shouldn't leave till the passes are free from snow—"

The others sat up. "And Lucy?" Parkman repeated.

"You know, the white settlers, they spread out— California, Oregon, everywhere. They build up. The rest is pushed back. But Henry Chatillon—what would he do there? I live on the mountains, on the plains. I've lived with Indians. My children are Indians. Pull them up, like baby trees by the roots—pull me up, like a big oak—and say, 'I will take you to California, then stick you in the ground and you will grow there'?"

He went back to puffing the pipe. They waited. He said, in his own time, "I think I will go back, stay with my children with the Indian names. I think I will live with that ugly girl. I think she is pretty enough for me."

Shaw burst out, "Why, what do you mean ugly girl? Why, she's beautiful! You mean that silly little bit of nonsense about that tiny harelip? Why—"

"Well, that is what I say," Chatillon said. His smile was broad. "She is pretty enough for me! And maybe I won't travel so much after that."

But it still wasn't over. Shaw took Parkman aside in the morning. They had all told their plans to one another, but Shaw didn't want to tell the others his, yet. "Damn it all, Frank!"

"What is it, Quincy?"

He stamped on the ground, chewed on the corner of his mustache. "The fact is, Frank . . ." A long silence.

"Yes, Quincy!"

"Well . . . would you very much mind going on alone? I mean—this time?"

"What are you saying!" Parkman stared at his cousin.

"Well, damn it all, you have a book to write . . ."

"And you have a home. What are you saying?" Parkman repeated.

"Well, again, I've never seen California. And I may never get another chance," Shaw finally revealed his intentions.

"For God's sake, Quincy! California!"

"The fact is, Frank"—now that the stopper was out, the surge of words came freely—"the fact is, I miss those children. Crazy, isn't it? But I do. What happens is, well, I think of them traveling alone, only women, mostly women—that pretty young girl—and I think of those cold mountains, rivers and the Indians. Well, I think about all that, and sometimes—did you notice that I haven't been sleeping well lately?"

Parkman had noticed that Shaw snored fairly steadily through the night. But he didn't say anything. He just stared at him.

"Well damn it all, I have nothing to do at home! And it won't be forever. There are ships go out from California, you know. They go around the cape, and up the east coast, and stop at Baltimore, New York, Boston. . . ."

And months and months and months, Parkman

thought. But he said nothing because he had very little to do with any of it now.

Parkman stood on the rear deck of the steamer and waved at them. They had sold his horse and his equipment, and kept the rest. Delorier would take the mules back to Fort Laramie and sell them there, or perhaps they would give them to him, he had left it up to Shaw.

They waved back. Delorier jumped up and down. "Adieu, *mon bourgeois*! Adieu, adieu! When you go another time to the Rocky Mountains, I will go with you. Yes, I will go!"

"You write that book, Frank!" Shaw called. "You hear? I want to read it when I come back!"

If you come back, Parkman thought. One of the less pleasant tasks he faced in Boston was explaining Shaw's decision to Shaw's father. Job again, eh Quincy? "And I only am escaped alone to tell thee." Alone. In person and in a book.

Chatillon said nothing. He just grinned and waved that injured arm a little stiffly. And the image of that man was a picture fixed, unchanging, in Parkman's memory, as clear as a portrait.

The boat moved out and in a few minutes it was in the main channel, slipping strongly downstream. Turning a bend, the boat was carried out of sight of the landing.

Parkman lit his pipe and started back to civilization. He went down to the saloon where the well-dressed, stogie-smoking St. Louis gamblers had set up a table for the innocents and were dealing the cards.